Nic Nelson

and the
Diamonds
of Denmark

by

Derrik Richard

Nic Nelson and the Diamonds of Denmark
Derrik Richard

PHANTASUS
INCORPORATED

Published by Phantasus, Inc., Edwardsville, IL

Editor: Lisbeth Tanz, lis@lisbethtanz.com
Cover Illustrator: Dr. Tracy Hopkins
Interior Illustrator: Don Dillion
Cover and Interior design: Davis Creative, www.Davis Creative.com

Library of Congress Control Number: 2014906716

Library of Congress Cataloging-in-Publication Data

Richard, Derrik
    Nic Nelson and the Diamonds of Denmark

    ISBN: 978-0-9916202-0-3

    Library of Congress subject headings:
    1. Juvenile Fiction/Action & Adventure/General

May 1, 2014

Printed in the United States of America

Acknowledgments & Dedications

Mom: For all your sacrifice, love, dedication, and inspiration

Noah: Nephew and Buddy

Joy Eisenreich: In loving memory of her friendship and guidance

Nicolas Weiss and *Philip Gray:* What can I say? Without you, there would be no book. Hope you enjoy it.

Dr. Jenkins and *Dr. Seckler:* Thanks for your friendship, dedication to teaching, and putting up with my practical jokes.

The Marshi Family: For *Tina,* who gave me the "British" perspective; for *Raafi,* who was the inspiration for Cindy Lin; for *Yousef,* who gave me constructive criticism (even when not asked for); for *Ethan, William,* and *Asha,* who gave me moral support against their dad's not-asked-for constructive criticism. You guys are like a second family to me. Thanks.

Dr. Tracy Hopkins: "Wow," on the exterior artwork.

Don Dillon: "Wow," on the interior artwork.

Tom Rami: For your mentoring and patience

Eric Carlson: For your friendship and advice

Tenor Kapp: For making me laugh and providing new material for future stories; your friendship means the world to me.

The Weiss Family: For valuable support and encouragement

Rick & Marian Embry: For taking me under your wings and teaching me about working with kids

Troy DeRosset: For assisting me with miscellaneous stuff with the book

Tim Ranz and *Scott Deuser:* For the joy of watching you grow from crazy kids to responsible young adults

The Gray family: For support and encouragement

The Ranz family: For your friendship

Ryan Munie and *Jacob Plocher:* If there had been no Nic and Phillip beforehand, I dare say that the main characters might have been named after you two. Thanks for the ongoing adventures.

Zach Plocher: For all the fun with tennis

Mike and Paula Munie/ Dennis and Donna Plocher: Thanks for your trust and friendship.

Jason Reid: For showing me my true calling in life

Lisbeth Tanz of The Hired Pen: Thanks for the fantastic editing job.

Tim Galbeati: For all the fun times

Kevin Paur: For your long time friendship and one-on-one basketball games

Kevin Bell: If our fourth grade teacher could see us now, she wouldn't believe it…LOL.

Mike Firsching: For soccer glory

Devon and Connor "MacCleod" Wilson: Miss you guys a lot.

Fred Fabi: For all of our adventures

Nancy Rinderer: For your friendship and support

Cody Callahan: For being a good target in paintball

Brenton Kastelein: For being a really good target in paintball

Mohammad Saleh: For your friendship, support, and loyalty

Josh Thuenemann: For all of the fun times together and watching you grow up to become a teacher

Dr. Pinkerton: For all of the laughs when we get together

Dave, Vaneta, and Zeke Gregory: Your friendship is priceless.

Dylan Madron: For all of the movies we've watched

The Holland Family: For your friendship; miss you guys a lot.

Dr. Chris Nielsen: For your friendship

Austen Ries: For all of the baseball and hockey games we've watched

Schuyler Lauderback: The hardest working person I've ever met

Officer "JJ" Johnson: One of the funniest people I've ever met

Dr. John Blattner: For all of our talks; I really enjoy them.

Tristan Maslar: Thanks for being my partner in lasertag and I really enjoy our talks about history.

Mat Conway: Keep up the good work teaching future generations.

Dr. F. A. Craig: A true gentleman. I really enjoy our talks.

This is also for all of the other individuals that I may have inadvertently left out who have had a positive impact in my life.

—Derrik

Contents

CHAPTER ONE

The Gang

A s Nic Nelson was about to place a quarter into the arcade game, he felt a hard shove in his back. Almost losing his balance, he would have hit his head on the screen if he hadn't caught himself. Spinning around, he found himself face-to-face with six boys who looked to be about his age of ten. Judging by their initial "welcome," they weren't there to chat.

He recognized the boy standing in front of him as Johnny Parks. Unlike Nic, who was lanky and dark haired, Johnny was heavier, taller, and blonde. Nic was struck with how green Johnny's eyes were. It was a shame they were above a thin-lipped mouth that seemed to be in a permanent sneer.

"Gee, I'm sorry for bumping into you," Johnny said. "It's Mick, right?"

"Nic," he growled.

"Oh, Nic, Mick, it doesn't matter. All I know is you're the new geek in town," said Johnny as the boys moved in closer, surrounding Nic.

"You see, *Geek*, this is my turf; and these are my boys, Jimmy, Joey, Jerry, Jeff, and Mark. We're the *J Gang*. If you want to play any video games here, you have to pay me first and get my permission."

Nic knew he was outnumbered. He gulped and then remembered something his dad once said: *"Nic, you have to stand up for yourself, and do what's right. You can't count on anyone else doing it for you."*

Nic stood a little taller as he stared Johnny down. "I guess I'd be in a bad mood, too, if my breath smelled as bad as yours."

Just then, Jimmy and Joey grabbed Nic's arms. Nic watched helplessly as Johnny began winding back his right fist. Suddenly a deep voice rang out, "Six on one doesn't seem very fair to me, Johnny."

Nic tore his eyes away from the looming fist and glanced toward the voice. He didn't recognize the muscular man approaching, or his sidekick, a freckle-faced, blonde haired boy about Nic's age. Jimmy and Joey let go of Nic's arms as Johnny spun around to size up his new opponents. After a few tense seconds, with a wave of his hand and a last menacing look at Nic, Johnny and his *J Gang* disappeared into the crowd.

Certain Johnny and his gang were gone, Nic turned to thank his rescuer. Before he could speak, the man raised his hand to shake Nic's and smiled, "I figured you could take them all on by yourself, so I was really saving Johnny from getting hurt. By the way, I'm Jason Hornsby; and this here is my young friend, Kevin Becker."

"Hi, and thanks for…whatever," Nic stammered. "It's nice to meet you. My name is Nic Nelson."

"Great to meet you, Nic," Jason said, while bringing his hand down on Nic's shoulder as a welcome. Nic winced slightly — clearly, Jason didn't understand how strong he was. Jason continued talking, "So did I hear right that you're new to the area?"

"Yeah, me and my mom moved to New Bonn only a couple of months ago," replied Nic as he rubbed his shoulder.

"Hey, I thought you looked familiar. You're the kid that's been sitting all by himself in the cafeteria!" said Kevin.

"Yeah, that's me," Nic answered.

"Well, that's going to change. Can't get to know people if you don't meet them, right?" Kevin asked.

"Right," replied Nic.

After a few awkward seconds of silence, Nic piped up, "I was just about to play this video game. Would you guys like to join me?"

"Sure," Kevin and Jason said at the same time. But when Nic turned around, he saw that the quarters he had so carefully stacked on the video game were gone. His heart sank. Where did they go? Then it hit him. Johnny and his gang must have swiped them. "Oh man," he said in frustration. He glanced at Kevin who, seeing Nic upset, asked,

"Nic, what's wrong? You look bummed. What's going on?"

"My money -- it's gone," replied Nic. "I had laid it out to play this video game; and now, it's gone."

"Let me guess," interrupted Jason. "You had it until Johnny and his gang appeared. Sorry you had to learn this lesson the hard way, but never have anything of value out when Johnny's around. Tell ya what," offered Jason as he reached into his pockets. "Why don't you let this round be on me, and you can get the next one some other time." He pulled out a crisp twenty-dollar bill. "This should do it," he stated as he walked to the coin machine.

Nic looked dumbfounded as he began to mutter, "But I..."

Kevin elbowed him gently and whispered, "It's cool. I sucker him all the time for video games by pretending to forget to bring my money."

That afternoon was one of the happiest Nic could remember in a long time. Going from one video game to the next, he learned that Jason was a first year college student at nearby Midwestern University where Nic's mom worked. Jason had an older brother, a dentist, which made Jason feel like he had to do well at something so he could prove himself to his parents. And while he wished he didn't live at home, he still did to save money. Jason had known Kevin since he was a baby and was something like a big brother to him. Kevin was the youngest in his family, surviving the pain of having three older sisters who, according to Kevin, got along as well as cats and dogs.

After what seemed like only minutes, Nic realized it was time to go home. As he thanked his new friends for all the fun, Kevin said, "I'll look out for you at lunch and introduce you to my group of friends in the cafeteria on Monday!"

"Cool!" replied Nic as he turned to leave.

Still smiling about the good luck he'd experienced in the arcade, Nic made his way toward the bike rack. He shook his head as he remembered how Johnny and his *J Gang* had surrounded him. He wondered why it was called the *J Gang* if one member's name didn't start with the letter J.

Nic groaned aloud as he walked up to the bike rack. The back tire had been slashed. "Johnny," he stated flatly. Breathing a heavy sigh, he pulled his bike out and began the long walk home. "This is going to take forever," he mumbled. After only a few minutes, sweat began streaming down his face, and his arms began to ache from pushing his bike. Why couldn't this have happened on a cool and cloudy day?

As he stopped to wipe the sweat from his face with his shirt, Nic heard a loud thunder-like rumble behind him. He turned to see a shiny red car with the letters *GTO* written in the grill, which hid what must have been a huge engine, given the noise. Nic didn't move as the car came closer. He figured the way things were going it was probably Johnny's brother, if he had one, coming to slash his other tire or worse. Nic gripped his bike as the car came to a stop next to him. As the door opened, he steeled himself for the worst, only to heave a sigh of relief as he recognized the people getting out of the car. It was Jason and Kevin.

"Hey, big guy, what's up?" asked Jason, while eyeing Nic's flat tire.

"My tire's flat," replied Nic.

"Well, I figured it had to be something major. Most people ride their bikes, except for Kevin. I don't think he knows how to ride a bike if it doesn't have training wheels attached to it," laughed Jason.

"Ha, ha," laughed Kevin. "I'll bet Nic here could beat you home with two flat tires versus that old bucket of bolts you call a car."

"Old bucket of…I'll have you know that my car -- a 1970 *GTO* -- is very well known by muscle-car connoisseurs. It is extremely fast, tough, and beautiful. Three things you can't say about yourself," Jason retorted, as he playfully punched Kevin's arm.

"Con-a-what?" Kevin asked.

"Connoisseur…it means an expert," explained Jason.

"It doesn't matter what it means. Your car was built in the cave man days. It doesn't even have a CD player in it. And you have to roll up the windows! Where are the buttons to do that?" Kevin asked.

"It's good exercise for you," replied Jason. "Besides, you're just jealous of my good looks and muscles."

"Muscles? What muscles? I could take you on anytime," Kevin said smiling as if he knew what Jason's next move would be.

"Is that so?" Jason asked as he lunged for Kevin.

In an instant, Nic found himself watching a wrestling match between Jason and Kevin. Man, thought Nic, these guys really do act like brothers. After a minute or so, Nic figured he'd better save what was left of Kevin in this mismatch. He asked loudly, "Excuse me, Jason, but weren't you saying something to me?"

Jason stopped and looked at Nic as if he had suddenly appeared out of nowhere. Holding Kevin upside down, he nodded his head and responded with a quiet, "Oh, yeah." He dropped Kevin gently to the ground, head first. "As I was saying, would you like a ride home?"

"That'd be great," Nic exclaimed. "I just live about two more miles down the road at 1815 Waterloo Street."

"That's not far from where I live," remarked Kevin, as he got up scratching his head and brushing himself off.

Jason carefully lifted Nic's bike and placed it into the trunk, while Kevin opened the huge, heavy passenger door. Pushing the front seat forward, both boys scampered into the back seat.

Jason slid in behind the wheel. He looked at them over his shoulder and asked, "So no one is brave enough to sit up front with me?"

Kevin replied, "I know how you drive; and I would like to live to see my 11th birthday, thank you."

"I grew up watching Speed Racer reruns, so I know how to drive. Plus, you've never let that stop you before, Kevin."

"Well, today I don't feel like committing suicide," said Kevin.

"Suit yourself," smiled Jason, while he starting his car. As it roared to life, Nic felt the car vibrating slightly. Jason asked, "Do ya feel that, Nic? That's power, baby. Real power!"

"Yeah, right," whispered Kevin in Nic's ear. "What it really means is that this old piece of junk is two speed bumps away from falling apart."

"Okay, boys, I'm not going anywhere until you buckle up," Jason ordered.

Nic went to pull the seat belt across his chest, but stared dumbly at the back of the seat instead. "Where's the seatbelt?" he asked.

"Oh, these cars are lucky to have them. They're only lap belts, but they do the job," said Jason.

Nic looked down and clicked his belt into place. He'd never worn a seatbelt like this before. It felt weird.

"Now, what were you saying, Kevin?" Jason asked as he stepped on the accelerator.

"Nothinnngggggg," yelped Kevin, as the car took off with a loud 'Vvvrrooooooomm'!

Wow, thought Nic, pinned to the back seat. This must be like what astronauts go through when they launch into outer space.

Suddenly, Jason yelled, "Hold on!"

In the next instant, Nic found himself almost lying down staring at Kevin's shoes, as Jason swerved sharply to the left. A moment later, the side of his face was glued to the window with Kevin's head almost in his lap, as the car swerved to the right. After what seemed like an eternity on an amusement park ride gone wrong, Jason finally stopped his car.

"Sorry about that, guys; but here we are," said Jason, pulling Nic's bike from the trunk. Nic moaned slightly as he and Kevin staggered out of the car. Passing the window, Nic saw his reflection. His dark hair was messy, and his clothes were twisted, looking like he had just survived being stuck in the middle of a tornado. Kevin looked to be in worse shape than he was.

Jason rolled Nic's bike to him. "Here ya go, Stud. Again, sorry about the driving; but I couldn't help it," Jason said, smiling slyly. "Stupid cat ran out in front of the car, and those darn potholes on this street are such a danger. They really need to be fixed. You guys are soooo lucky that I'm such an awesome driver who can maneuver around them."

His thought, as Nic shook Jason's hand to thank him for the ride home, was if that was good driving by Jason, then he definitely didn't want to see his bad driving.

As Jason backed out of the driveway, Kevin shouted from his window, "Look forward to seeing you at school on Monday."

Next time, I'm going to have to ask Jason what the letters *GTO* stand for, thought Nic, pushing his bike toward the garage.

The screen door slammed as he entered the kitchen. "Nic?" his mom called from the family room.

"Yeah, Mom, it's me."

Grabbing a glass from the dishwasher, he busied himself filling it with water. His mom, now in the kitchen, folded her arms and leaned against the counter. Uh-oh, he thought. I'm probably going to be in big trouble for getting a ride with strangers. He quickly came up with reasons for her not to be mad: Jason and Kevin had been so nice to him; he had desperately longed for friends since first moving here…

Prepared for the worst, Nic was stunned when his mom quietly said, "So, I see you've made some new friends today. What happened to 'I don't like it here, and I won't ever like anybody here?'"

Nic smiled and answered, "Yeah, I guess so," while not admitting that she was right *again*. She smiled and tousled his hair saying, "I told you just to have faith and things would work out."

Nic was excited to return to school on Monday, although not because of his teacher, Mr. Smithton. He was nice enough, but had the unusual habit of calling everybody in his class by nicknames instead of their first names. Nic's nickname was Chief. He was sure he wasn't related to any Native American Indians, even though he thought it would have been cool. Other classmates had nicknames like Flash, Dudley Do-Right, and Whiz.

Mr. Smithton didn't explain why he gave a particular nickname to a student, but Nic figured he'd manage just fine with Chief.

The morning seemed to drag as Nic waited for lunchtime. Standing in line for his food, he nervously scanned the lunchroom for his new friend, Kevin. But Kevin was nowhere to be seen. All around him kids laughed and talked about their weekend fun. As Nic approached the lunch lady to pay, his heart began to sink; and a lump formed in his throat. What if Kevin had forgotten his promise? What if Kevin had just been pretending to be his friend?

There was still no sign of Kevin as Nic stepped away from the lunch line. He began walking toward a familiar spot in the corner where he would be by himself again.

"Have faith, indeed," Nic muttered. Who was he kidding? No one wanted to be friends with him. Maybe Johnny had been right after all, and he really was a geek.

Lost in thought, Nic realized someone was tapping him on the shoulder. He turned around to find Kevin looking at him with a big, goofy smile.

"What's up, buddy?"

Nic was so relieved he couldn't speak.

"We're back there," Kevin said pointing to the center of the cafeteria. "Follow me."

Nic happily followed, amazed at how the center of the lunchroom sounded like a beehive from all the chatter.

Kevin spoke loudly over the noise, "Sorry about not being here sooner; but my teacher, Mrs. Payne, was in her usual mood. She let us out late, because someone threw a spitball at the blackboard."

"Do you know who did it?"

"Not a clue," Kevin said, while delivering a smile every ten-year-old boy knows means guilty as charged. They stopped at a table.

"This," stated Kevin opening his arms wide, "is my group of friends. Guys, this is Nic. He's the one I was telling you about."

Nic slowly scanned the table as Kevin made the introductions. The first two kids Nic knew from his homeroom: Herbert Howell III, who wore thick glasses and looked almost as wide as he was tall; and Cindy Lin, a thin girl with shiny, black hair and high pale cheekbones. Then there was Dante Brown, an African-American boy built a lot like Kevin, but with brown eyes and short, dark, curly hair. Last was Philip Browning, the tallest and most athletic of the group, who was as thin as a pencil.

After settling down with his new group of friends, Nic felt as if he had known them all of his life. Dante Brown seemed like a do-the-right-thing type of guy. He did Boy Scouts once a week and volunteered at Shady Valley, the local retirement center, entertaining senior citizens. Cindy Lin seemed very opinionated to Nic and not afraid to ask or answer any questions. Herbert Howell III loved to talk and eat at the same time. Philip Browning loved all kinds of sports, especially in-line hockey. He was captain of his team, the Blue Devils, in the town league for ten- to eleven-year-olds.

As lunchtime was ending, Kevin blurted out, "Nic, the YMCA is having a lock-in next Friday night. Why don't you come and join us in the fun?"

Nic thought about it for a few seconds and replied, "Sure. I'll have to ask my mom first."

CHAPTER TWO

Dodge Ball

Nic paced nervously back and forth in front of his living room windows. He stopped just long enough to look at each passing car. He was on the lookout for Jason's red car. Jason had offered to take him to the lock-in along with Kevin and the other boys. Nic was so excited he couldn't sit still since coming home from school. He had never heard of a lock-in before, let alone being part of one. He still couldn't believe he had been able to talk his mom into letting him go. He smiled to himself as he recalled their conversation a few days ago at dinner.

Putting down her fork with a loud clink, his mom asked anxiously, "A lock-in? What's a lock-in? Did you get into trouble? What was damaged?"

"Mom, Mom!" protested Nic.

"We just moved into a new town, and you're already getting thrown into jail!"

"Mom!" Nic shouted in frustration. "I'm not in any trouble. It's a sleep-over event at the local YMCA, just for fourth and fifth grade boys."

"Well, why didn't you just say that to begin with?" she asked, with a hint of exasperation in her voice. "What're you going to be doing all night? Who's supervising this event? Does it cost anything?"

"I dunno."

"You're just a wealth of information, now aren't you?"

"I dunno."

"Tell you what, Nicolas; after work tomorrow, I'll call and check into it. If it passes the mom-o-meter test, then you can go. Deal?"

"Deal!" shouted Nic with joy. After excusing himself, he dashed back up to his room to call Kevin with the good news.

At least she hadn't said, 'I'll think about it', thought Nic. He knew, as every kid in the world knows, if a parent says, 'I'll think about it', it really means no. Nic imagined it was probably a phrase passed along from parent to parent to frustrate kids in their quest to have fun.

The happy "bing bong" of the doorbell brought Nic back to reality. He rushed to the big, oak front door. He was beaten there by his 90-pound black lab, Wellington, who barked a warning to whoever was outside. Restraining Wellington as best he could, Nic opened the door to see Jason, Dante, Kevin, and Herbert standing on the porch.

"Come on in, guys."

"Nice digs," said Dante, stepping into the hallway.

"Thanks," Nic huffed, as he continued to hold back Wellington, who was intent on licking everyone to death. As the crew shuffled in, Nic's mom magically appeared and, as mothers do best, began what Nic referred to as the "Question Inquisition."

"So who do we have here, Nicolas?" his mom asked.

"Mom, this is Jason Hornsby. He's the one going to the nearby college to become a veterinarian."

"Nice to meet you, Jason."

"The pleasure's all mine, Mrs. Nelson. Nic has told me that you teach Medieval Literature at the university. I must say you don't look old enough to be an English professor," said Jason.

"Ha! Flattery will only get you so far, Jason, but keep trying," she said smiling.

Nic rolled his eyes at this last exchange. He noticed Kevin silently acting as if he were about to throw up. Nic somehow held back from laughing. He introduced the rest of his friends to his mom with the normal pleasantries.

When the introductions were finished, his mom began the Question Inquisition. "Now, Jason, let me get this right. The lock-in is going to be held at the local YMCA?"

"Yes, Ma'am."

"It's being sponsored by the local churches in town and is going to be supervised by the different ministers, as well as adult volunteers like you?"

"That's right, Ma'am."

Smiling, Nic's mom continued, "Are you crazy? Trapped in a gym full of who knows how many kids for 24 hours? I can barely survive when Nicolas has one or two friends over for the night. The next morning, I usually wake up in a cold sweat sporting a few more gray hairs and wrinkles."

"Yeah, right Mom," Nic retorted.

"No, I don't think I'm crazy," replied Jason, "Although my parents would probably disagree with me. Besides, the local police pay the adult leaders handsomely for our efforts when we have the lock-ins. It's the only night they can get some rest."

"Well, I do appreciate your willingness to take Nicolas to this lock-in and to bring him home afterwards."

"No problem. Nic seems like a good kid. Of course, the key word is 'seems.' I've been known to be wrong before," Jason said as he glanced over at Kevin. "Don't worry. I'll have him back by 9 A.M. tomorrow."

"Okay, Nicolas, you guys better get going. Don't forget to grab your sleeping bag, and let me kiss you goodbye."

"Mommmmm, you're embarrassing me," whispered Nic as his mom kissed him on the forehead.

"Just call it a mother's prerogative, and be glad I don't say out loud those horrible words…I love you."

Nic smiled slightly while running out to join his friends. As he climbed into the back seat, Kevin said in a high-pitched voice, "Don't forget to let me kiss you, dear."

Everybody laughed, including Nic, who blushed.

"Don't worry, man. Kevin's just playing with you," said Dante.

"I know," replied Nic.

Kevin turned to Jason as they drove away from Nic's house and said, "Any thicker back there and we all would have suffocated."

"You're just jealous of my refined skills with women."

"Yeah, you have such refined skills that you don't even have a girlfriend. Maybe it's the car. I mean, it is the 21st century; and they make pretty good cars now," chuckled Kevin.

"How would you like to be the youngest astronaut in space?" Jason asked with a menacing tone in his voice.

"I can supply the takeoff power for you," he continued, while waving his fist in front of Kevin's face. Kevin rolled his eyes.

"Are they always this goofy around each other?" asked Nic.

"Oh, yeah. This is mild compared to a normal day for them," replied Dante.

Looking around the car, Nic noticed someone was missing. "Where's Philip? Isn't he coming, too?"

"He'll be arriving separately," volunteered Herbert.

Nic was grateful the drive to the YMCA didn't involve dodging potholes. Upon arriving in one piece, they each took out their sleeping bags from Jason's trunk. As they walked toward the front door, they heard a muffled noise coming from the YMCA. It sounded a lot like ocean waves. Opening the door, the group was hit full force with the noise from a sea of fourth and fifth grade boys. All manners of chaos were taking place. The leaders were attempting to take down the names of everyone who entered as whiffle balls and kickballs whizzed past their heads.

"I'm going to check out the refreshments before things get started," said Herbert. He made a beeline to a table full of jelly donuts and cans of soda. At the same time, Jason strolled away to a check-in table for adult leaders.

"What are we going to be doing all night?" asked Nic, as they put their sleeping bags in a corner.

Kevin and Dante shouted, "Dodgeball!"

They gave each other high fives in excitement.

"This is going to be awesome," yelled Dante.

"We just have to win this year," said Kevin.

"What are you guys talking about?" asked Nic.

"Each year, the leaders separate everyone into two groups, east and west, depending on which side of town you live in. Then, after about two to three hours of warming up with dodgeball, the head leader, who is neutral, will declare a final all-out game to determine the year's winner of the Bragging Rights Dodgeball Championship game," explained Kevin.

"Does the winning team get any prizes?" asked Nic.

"No, but you get to brag the rest of the year," replied Dante. "We're going to be on the east team, since we all live on the east side of town. The west team has won the last five years in a row. We almost had them last year."

Kevin nodded and said, "Yeah, I remember. But we just have to win this time. I don't think I can take another year of Johnny's bragging."

"Look who I just found!" announced Herbert. Kevin, Dante, and Nic all turned around. Walking next to Herbert, whose hands were loaded up with donuts, was Philip.

"Hi, guys. Sorry I'm late, but hockey practice ran long. My mom had to drop off my two brothers, Justin and Jonathan, at home first. They can be so annoying sometimes," whined Philip.

"Hey, I'll trade you my three sisters any day for your two brothers," remarked Kevin, who proceeded to entertain everybody by going into a playful routine, pretending to be his sisters. Fluffing up his hair and blinking his eyes rapidly, he muttered in a high-pitched voice, "Do I look good in this dress? Does it make me look fat?"

Everyone laughed. Nic didn't have any sisters, but he could relate, as his mom would pull the same routine on him whenever they were going out somewhere.

Laughing hard made Nic remember he had to make a pit stop at the nearest restroom. He excused himself and waded through what seemed to be a million kids. He managed to reach the boys' restroom, which was located down a dimly lit hallway. He was pleasantly surprised to find it relatively clean and graffiti free. This was a nice change of pace, as he was accustomed to all the graffiti on school restroom stalls and at gas stations when he had been on trips with his parents.

While he was washing his hands, the door opened. Nic peered into the mirror to see who was coming in. It was Johnny, with one of his gang members, Joey. Joey was the same build as Johnny, with dark hair and brown eyes.

"Well, well, well, look who we have here, Joey." smirked Johnny. "It's the new geek in town without any of his friends to protect him. I think you're in the wrong restroom, Geek. The girls' bathroom is down the hall."

Nic just stared at Johnny and Joey without saying a word. He could feel his heart beating faster and his palms sweating.

"What's the matter, Geek? Cat got your tongue?

I think it's time we gave him an official welcome to our town, Joey. What do you say?"

Joey slowly smiled and nodded his head in agreement.

Before Nic could protest, they grabbed his arms.

"I think this will do just fine for what we have in store for you," snarled Johnny kicking open the nearest bathroom stall door. Nic strained to stay outside the stall, but two against one was more than he could manage. Once inside, he was forced to stand in front of the toilet. Still struggling, Nic felt hands forcing his face down toward the toilet seat. He felt helpless seeing the toilet bowl get closer and closer to his face.

In that awkward position, Nic's feet slipped on the wet floor; and he fell with his face just missing the toilet seat by inches. Johnny and Joey were caught off guard by this sudden turn of events. They fell forward smashing against the wall behind the toilet. Hearing their yelps, Nic realized now would be his best chance for escape. Jumping to his feet, Nic swiftly backed out of the stall. Johnny and Joey tried to lunge at Nic, but ended up getting into each other's way.

To slow them down, Nic flung the stall door shut just as Johnny and Joey were about to reach him. It hit them both with a solid thud, followed by two high-pitched yelps and another thud as the boys, again, hit the stall wall. Nic didn't stay to see what happened next. He pulled open the door and began sprinting down the hallway toward the gym.

As the door closed, Johnny yelled, "This isn't over, Geek!"

Nic slowed to a walk as he entered the gym. He needed a moment to calm down. He was just in time to see the adult leaders putting away the tables and chairs to clear up space for dodgeball.

As Nic approached his buddies, Dante asked, "Where have you been? Dodgeball is about to get started."

Nic casually replied, "I had a little trouble with rats in the restroom, but it was nothing I couldn't handle."

Dante gave him a funny look, but said nothing.

Nic then noticed a tall, thin man with glasses, who appeared to be in his late fifties, approach the center of the gym.

"Okay, boys, I need your undivided attention, please," he bellowed with a deep voice. The room quickly became quiet. "For those of you who don't know me, my name is Mr. Lee. For those of you who do know me, I feel sorry for you."

A low rumble of laughter ran through the crowd.

"I'm glad that everyone could make it tonight. I feel it's going to be a real fun time for everyone, as long as you follow certain rules. One, you will respect all of the leaders and young adults here as if they were your parents. Two, you get two warnings; and on the third warning, your parents will be called to come and pick you up. Three, you will respect the property and follow the rules of the YMCA, which has been kind enough to let us host this event again at their facility. Fourth and final rule, you will have fun! Now that we've taken care of the main rules, let's move onto the fun."

A loud chorus of cheers and screams erupted from the boys.

"All right, I'm not quite finished," stated Mr. Lee, as he waited for the room to quiet again. "This year, as in years past, we're going to get things started by playing dodgeball from now until midnight to warm everyone up; that's about three hours. Then we'll have the dodgeball championship game. After the championship game, you are free to use the gym for different activities and events. Does anyone have a problem with this setup?"

Nic looked around and noticed that no one was about to disagree.

"Good. Dodgeball rules are as follows. My decision is final. If I say you are out, then you are out. No ifs, ands, or buts. You are only out if someone either catches your thrown ball or if you are hit anywhere below the neck. If you're hit above the neck, then you are not out. If you have a dodgeball in your hands and someone throws a ball at you, you may deflect it without penalty. When you throw your dodgeball, you may not cross the centerline of the gym or else you are out. You must release a ball that is in your possession within 15 seconds of receiving it or you will be called out. Finally, for the three leaders that will be on each team, they must throw either underhanded or with two arms to get anyone out, unless they are the last remaining players. Any questions?"

Silence followed.

"Good! Since that's settled, we'll go ahead and break everyone into two groups with kids living on the east side of town going to the east side of the gym and the west side kids going to the west side."

What followed could only be described as a massive stampede. Kids from all over the gym went bumping and scurrying in various directions to reach their destinations. Leaders scrambled about trying to assist kids to the side where they belonged. Nic managed to reach the east side of the gym after what seemed like an eternity of struggle.

"I sure know what a pinball feels like now," he joked.

Once everyone was on their respective sides, Mr. Lee put the dodgeballs in the middle of the gym.

"Okay, on the count of three, the games will begin. One…two…three!" shouted Mr. Lee.

Total mayhem broke loose. A wall of kids descended upon the balls with the force of a hurricane. Nic decided to hang back as part of his initial strategy. Since this was only a warm-up period before the main battle, why risk getting bruised too much early on? After all, he wanted to keep his nose and teeth right where they were.

Occasionally getting in a good throw, Nic looked around to see how much fun everyone else was having. Kevin and Dante were high fiving each other after hits, even as balls whizzed by their heads. Philip and Herbert seemed to be holding their own, too. Jason was laughing and playfully teasing those he hit to get out. Over the next three hours, everything was lighthearted and fun, with an occasional bruise here and there. No one could brag much, because everyone was hit at least once and had to sit out.

At the stroke of midnight, all playing stopped; and Mr. Lee approached the middle of the gym. "This is it, boys, the final game of the night. This will determine which side will win the coveted title of town Dodgeball Champions."

A murmur of excitement swept through the gym. Even Nic was caught up in the fever of competition.

"All right now, everybody line up against the wall on your side of the gym. On the count of three, we'll begin."

Nic turned to look at Kevin and Dante. He could see a focused determination in their eyes. They silently nodded to each other as if saying they were ready for battle.

"One…two…three!" shouted Mr. Lee.

An avalanche of kids made a mad scramble toward the center of the gym. Nic hung back, deciding to stick with his strategy of scavenging for loose dodgeballs and picking his spots for attacking.

He figured the kids up front would be out of the game quickly because of the intense crossfire.

He learned this strategy from reading books. He loved to read, especially history, which was his favorite subject in school. He found it fascinating to learn about how different generals fought and won battles. A lot of boys his age thought he was crazy to read history books all of the time. What they didn't seem to understand was that learning strategies from famous generals could help in games like laser tag or dodgeball.

Nic's favorite period was the Napoleonic era in the 1800s. This was when the Emperor Napoleon had ruled over all of Europe. He was finally defeated by the Russians and the British, led by the Duke of Wellington. Nic admired the Duke of Wellington for his coolness under fire and never giving up. In fact, that's why he named his dog Wellington.

Just as Nic had predicted, a large wave of kids was taken out on both sides within the first few minutes of play. He realized the remaining players were going to take a lot longer to get rid of. Looking around, he could see Jason, Kevin, Dante, Philip, and Herbert were still in it. As he was looking back to face the opposing players, a ball whistled by his head, followed by a strong breeze. It had been literally millimeters from his ear.

"Watch out, Nic!" screamed Kevin as he came over to scoop up the loose ball. "This is not the time to be daydreaming."

"You sure were lucky," chimed in Dante, as Kevin moved forward to take someone out. "You have to be on the lookout for Mr. Mahoney at all times. He was the leader who threw the ball that nearly hit you. He can throw underhand real hard, 'cause he's the star pitcher in the local men's fast-pitch softball league. Next time you might not be so lucky, and you'll be flat on your back; so keep your head up."

"You won't have to tell me twice," replied Nic. He stared at Mr. Mahoney, sizing him up. Mr. Mahoney was a short, stocky man in his late forties with arms as big as bowling balls and legs as thick as tree trunks.

Twenty minutes went by as both sides saw their numbers dwindle. Nic hastily wiped away the sweat rolling down his forehead. His arms were starting to ache from throwing the balls; and his legs were getting tired from having to run, duck, and dive away from incoming balls.

Nick heard an "Ow," and he looked over to see Herbert lying on the ground.

"Out," yelled Mr. Lee as Herbert struggled to get back up.

"All right," shouted Johnny from across the gym. "It's about time somebody hit you, fatso! I would've sooner, but I didn't want you to eat all of the snacks while I was still playing."

Herbert briefly looked at Nic before running off to the side and out of the gym. Nic's fingers tightened on the ball he'd just picked up as he searched for Johnny in the crowd. Nic's anger swelled when he found him. Johnny, seeing Nic staring at him, pointed and screamed, "You're next, Geek!"

Another ball swished by Nic's head, landing with a familiar BOOM as it hit the wall behind him. He didn't need to look to know that Mr. Mahoney had almost hit him again. As if on cue, Mr. Mahoney yelled, "That's twice you've been lucky, kid!"

As Nic fired off another shot, cleanly hitting his target, he thought, great, just great. It's bad enough Johnny will be gunning for me; but now I really have to pay attention to Mr. Mahoney, too. If I somehow survive those two tonight, I'll definitely be the world's luckiest kid.

Another fifteen minutes went by, and each team lost more members. The number continued to dwindle until only six people were left in the game on the east team. Kevin, Dante, Jason, and Philip were still around. So was Carlos Hernandez, a foreign exchange student from Spain, who was in Nic's class.

The west team still had Mr. Mahoney, Johnny, and the rest of the *J Gang*. With dodgeballs whizzing by, Nic concentrated on getting Johnny out as a way to pay him back for his cruel remark about Herbert. Kids were screaming from both teams on the sidelines, encouraging the remaining players to do their best to win.

Nic decided to try a risky maneuver to get Johnny, but knew he would need someone else's help.

Moving over to Kevin, he whispered, "I think I have a plan that would get Johnny out, but I'll need your help."

Kevin replied, "I'm game. What do you need me to do?"

"Next time you get a dodgeball, wait for my signal to throw it at Johnny; but miss him on purpose so he'll pick it up."

"You want me to miss Johnny on purpose just to let him have a free dodgeball?" asked Kevin.

"Yup, that's right," Nic responded confidently.

After a few tense seconds, Kevin replied, "I guess so, but I sure hope you know what you're doing."

Almost immediately, Kevin had another ball. It was from another close encounter with Mr. Mahoney. Catching Kevin's glance, Nic nodded to go-ahead. Kevin threw his dodgeball close enough to Johnny, causing him to duck. The ball harmlessly hit the wall behind him. Johnny scrambled to get the ball, making the fatal mistake of turning his back on Nic in order to get it. That was what Nic had waited for. Carefully aiming, he threw his ball hard at Johnny. He frowned as his dodgeball veered to the right. Then the impossible happened. Just as it was a few feet away from hitting the wall, Joey ran in front of it on his way to pick up another ball. To Nic's amazement, his dodgeball hit Joey on his leg at such an angle that it bounced off toward Johnny. It hit Johnny on his left shin as he turned around.

"Out and out," yelled Mr. Lee.

Johnny screamed, "No!" His cheeks were red with rage. He threw his dodgeball down as hard as he could and walked angrily to the side as he glared at Nic with narrowed eyes.

"Pretty impressive, young Jedi," Jason remarked with a smile. "Two for the price of one. I bet you meant to do that."

Nic smiled back with obvious glee.

Kevin screamed, "All right!" He then headed toward Nic to give him a high five. However, before he could reach Nic someone yelled, "Watch out!"

Kevin was clipped by a hard thrown ball aimed at his knees.

Mr. Mahoney yelled out, "Gotcha!"

Kevin got up and meekly smiled at Nic. He then muttered, "Gosh darn it, I made the very mistake I was telling you not to make. I took my eyes off of Mr. Mahoney." Slowly jogging off, Kevin added, "Don't worry about me, Nic, just win."

"I'll do my best," replied Nic. He was not as happy as he was just moments ago. However, even though Kevin was gone, Nic still figured his team had a chance of winning with Jason on its side.

Sweat was now pouring down his face from the intense running and throwing. It was getting harder to see clearly. His eyes were beginning to sting from the salty sweat flowing into them. His lungs were screaming for air from all of the running back and forth on his side of the gym. His arms were heavy and getting harder to move.

Another few minutes passed by as Philip, Dante, and Carlos were knocked out of the game; but so, too, were Jimmy and Mark. It now boiled down to Jason and Nic for the east team against Mr. Mahoney and a skinny boy with flaming red hair named Jerry for the west team.

The game stopped for a few moments as a wave of anticipation swept through the gym. Nic's hands were trembling as he wiped the sweat away from his eyes.

Jason scooted closer and whispered, "Hang tough, Nic. We'll get through this. Keep your head up, and don't lose your cool. Just remember the five Cs."

Confused, Nic repeated, "The five Cs?" He was thinking this wasn't the best time to be playing word games while Mr. Mahoney was eyeing them like a lion watches its prey.

"Yeah, the five Cs; they stand for Cool, Calm, Collected, Confident, and in Control," replied Jason as he sized up Mr. Mahoney. "If you remember the five Cs, you can handle any situation you encounter."

"Oh," muttered Nic. He felt more like the two Ss -- Scared Stiff.

Another tense minute went by. It appeared that both sides had reached a standoff. Neither side could get the upper hand. All the while, Nic kept thinking of ways he could get Jerry out so Jason could concentrate on Mr. Mahoney.

"Of course," muttered Nic. "Why hadn't I thought of it before?"

Grabbing two dodgeballs, Nic placed one by his feet and held the other in his hands. He surveyed the situation. Timing was going to be everything in what he had planned. He couldn't afford to tell Jason what he was up to; it might give away his gamble.

Nic waited until Jerry attempted to throw at Jason. He totally missed. As Jerry looked for another ball, Nic yelled, "Hey, Jerry, prepare to get out!"

Nic threw a high blooper his way.

"Looks like you're the one that's about to get out. This is too easy," said Jerry as he readied himself to catch the high floater. While Jerry was distracted, Nic nailed him with a low ball that hit him in the right leg.

Smiling, Nic felt a wave of excitement sweep over him, because another one of his plans had worked. A loud roar of approval went up from the east side. Two on one was good odds, thought Nic, especially the way Jason had been throwing all night. At this point, Nic felt the best way he could help Jason was to retrieve dodgeballs for him to throw at Mr. Mahoney. With that in mind, Nic scrambled around to stockpile dodgeballs for Jason.

"Nic," said Jason, "I appreciate what you're doing, but I think you could help me out better if you would attempt to throw at Mr. Mahoney."

"I can't," protested Nic. "He's too good for me to get out."

"No, he isn't. You can do it," Jason shouted over the now deafening roar of the sideline crowd. "No one is unbeatable. If you believe in yourself, you can accomplish anything you set your mind to!"

Sounds like Jason's been talking to my mom or something, thought Nic. He bent down to grab another dodgeball.

It was then Nic heard Jason shout, "No, Nic, watch out!"

Looking up, Nic could make out the blur of a ball quickly flying toward his face. He couldn't move. There was no time to react. He thought he saw all ten years of his life flash before his eyes. Just as he thought he was going to that Big Playground in the sky, Jason's hand passed in front of his face. He had instinctively reached out to protect

Nic from being hit in the face, even though Nic would not have been out according to the rules.

"Out," cried Mr. Lee with a hint of regret in his voice. Everyone in the gym knew the sacrifice Jason had just made.

The east side team was stunned into silence. They absorbed the impact of what had happened, certain they knew now how the game would end. The west side kids roared with approval. Now they were certain the game would definitely end with another west victory.

A lump formed in Nic's throat as he looked into Jason's eyes. He wanted to say I'm sorry, but couldn't make any sound.

Jason placed his hand on Nic's shoulder and said quietly, "It's up to you, stud. You can do it. I know it, and you know it." He pointed to the west side and said, "Now all you have to do is show them you can do it."

The crowd roared and yelled at a fevered pitch. Jason smiled, winked, and gave Nic's shoulder a gentle squeeze. He started to walk away, and then turned around to say, "Remember the five Cs." With that, he was gone.

Nic never felt so alone before in his life. He scanned up and down the side of the gym where all eyes were glued on him. He could hear Johnny yelling, "Get the geek! Get the geek!" Johnny was still furious about being tricked so easily before.

Nic realized that, in a few years, nobody would remember or care about a game of dodgeball played at some all-night event for a made-up title; but at this moment, it was the single most important event in the universe for him and his teammates. He was carrying the weight of dozens of kids on his shoulders.

Reaching deep down inside, Nic summoned up his courage to make a last stand. Eyeing Mr. Mahoney, he tried to come up with a game plan. He has to have a weakness, thought Nic. Just like Jason had said earlier, no one is unbeatable.

Minutes ticked by as Nic continued the game of cat and mouse with his very dangerous opponent. He needed a plan, but his mind was almost numb from exhaustion. His body was tiring from all of his movement. His legs felt like lead weights, and his muscles were screaming for mercy. His lungs were burning, and sweat kept stinging his eyes. Nic knew he couldn't keep this up much longer. He could sense a feeling of hopelessness creep into his mind. No, he thought, he didn't want to give up; but he felt like he was moving in slow motion.

Struggling to get up after another close call, Nic saw the blur of a dodgeball coming straight at him. He had nowhere to go. With nothing left to do but go down fighting, he braced himself for the hit. He put out his hands in what he was sure would be an unsuccessful attempt to catch the ball. BAM! He didn't see the ball as it came crashing into his hands. It was thrown so hard that he fell backwards onto the floor.

As his eyes focused again, Nic saw his teammates jumping up and down in slow motion. He couldn't hear them. He saw Jason pointing up with his right hand. Nic struggled to understand what he was trying to say. Following where Jason was pointing, Nic saw the ball coming back down on him. It was still in play! Somehow overcoming the exhaustion and pain, Nic sat up, caught the ball, and hugged it tightly to his chest.

Nic's ears caught up with his body, and the roar of the crowd flooded his brain. He slowly got up to take in what had just happened.

Nic was surrounded by a surge of kids jumping up and down and hollering all kinds of things.

"Way to go!"

"Awesome!"

"That was so cool!"

"You da man!"

He was being mobbed on all sides.

Jason soon lifted him up on his shoulders and said, "I knew you could do it!"

Nic could see Kevin, Dante, and Philip high-fiving each other in the background. In the commotion, he saw Johnny arguing with Mr. Lee. He learned later that Johnny thought Nic should have been out since he was on the floor when he caught the ball.

A large, sweaty hand landed on Nic's shoulder. He turned to see Mr. Mahoney smiling and congratulating him on a job well done. Nic mumbled a quiet, "Thank you," as Mr. Mahoney made his way back to his team.

Nic heard Carlos Hernandez crying out, "Viva, la Nic!" Soon, everyone on Nic's team joined in the loud chant that echoed throughout the gym.

As the excitement began to wind down, Mr. Lee congratulated everyone on participating and asked the leaders to pass out basketballs, soccer balls, and whiffle balls for everyone to use.

Nic was still reeling from his surprise win. He was both tired from exertion yet full of energy as he enjoyed his newfound popularity. Even some of the kids from the west team were congratulating him on his accomplishment.

Kevin, Dante, and Philip, using whiffle ball bats as microphones, pretended to be doing mock interviews with him and each other, calling it *The Miracle in New Bonn*.

Despite the fun and excitement, something was nagging at Nic. Something wasn't quite right. What was wrong? What was missing?

"Of course..." muttered Nic. "Herbert...

Kevin, have you seen Herbert around?"

"Now that you mention it, no; but I'm sure he's somewhere close by."

"Yeah, he's probably eating some snacks in the kitchen," chimed in Dante.

"I don't know, guys. He seemed pretty hurt when Johnny made fun of him for being fat," said Nic. He was becoming worried.

"I'm sure he's fine, Nic; but if you want, we'll all split up and go look for him," said Philip.

"That'd be great, guys."

With that, the boys darted off into different directions.

Jogging past the restrooms, Nic followed the hallway to the right, stopping at the top of a flight of stairs. He almost turned around, but something inside urged him to keep going.

As Nic crept down the stairs, he began to hear a faint sniffling sound coming from underneath the stairwell. He froze for a moment, unsure of what to do next. Deciding it was better to find out what was making the noise, he walked down the rest of the way and poked his head around the corner. In the dim light, he could make out the shape of a person huddled there.

"Hello?" he whispered cautiously.

"Who's there?" the person demanded.

Before Nic could answer, an excited voice stammered, "Nic…Nic Nelson?"

"Yes," Nic answered.

The figure stood up and walked out of the shadows. It was Herbert. Even in the low light, Nic could see tear tracks on Herbert's cheeks. His eyes were still glistening with wetness.

"Did we win?"

"Yes, we did. It was a real team effort," Nic answered. After a few awkward seconds of silence, he asked, "Are you all right? We've been looking all over for you. We've been really worried."

"I'm fine. It's nothing," Herbert replied while looking down.

Hearing this, Nic eyed him for a few seconds like his mom would do to him when she knew otherwise. "Really, Herbert, what's up? I'm your friend. You can trust me," said Nic in a soft, reassuring voice.

"I…I…Johnny's right. I'm just a fat slob who's good for nothing! I only ended up hurting our side tonight, and nobody really likes me. People are just friendly to me because they feel sorry for me," answered Herbert, his voice cracking and eyes filling with tears.

"That's not true!" stated Nic as he desperately tried thinking of something to say to help his friend.

"Yes, it is!" sniffed Herbert.

"No, it isn't; and I'll tell you why," said Nic.

Herbert looked up with a questioning look on his face.

"Herbert, I know that we haven't known each other for very long, but I really enjoy being around you. You seem like a loyal kind of guy," said Nic quickly.

"I'm fat. What about that?" he retorted.

"Fat, schmat. Who cares? Some of the most famous people in the world were fat. That didn't stop them from doing great things. Napoleon was a famous general who nearly conquered all of Europe.

He was fat. Babe Ruth, probably the greatest baseball home run hitter of all time wasn't exactly skinny. I could go on and on; but I guess what I'm trying to say is that it isn't what's on the outside that counts but what's on the inside that really makes a person great or not."

"Really?" Herbert was perking up. "You really mean those things, and you're not just saying them to make me feel better?"

"You bet I do!" Nic responded. With that, he received the biggest bear hug of his life. Nic made a mental note to himself to wear body armor the next time he had to cheer his friend up.

Back in the gym, the gang was happy to see Herbert; and they all let him know how important he was to them.

The rest of the night was a blur to Nic. He went from one activity to the next. One moment he was playing whiffle ball, the next he was shooting baskets. He finally began to feel accepted by his new classmates.

Around 5:00 A.M., most of the kids had fallen asleep. They were happily snuggled into their sleeping bags scattered around the gym. Nic was still too excited to be sleepy, although he did finally sit down to rest his aching body.

Jason sat down next to him with a low sigh of relief. Looking wearily at Nic, he said, "Wow, am I beat. It feels so good to sit down. I've forgotten how much energy you little buggers have."

Nic chuckled, "It must be from all of the free snacks we've eaten."

Jason and Nic continued their small talk and laughed silently at Kevin and Philip as they rolled around in their sleeping bags, talking in their sleep.

They could even hear Johnny loudly snoring from halfway across the gym.

Jason remarked, "I'd sure hate to be at a sleepover with him next to me."

Nic laughed in response.

"Nic, I've been meaning to ask you something, but I haven't had the chance," said Jason.

"What is it?"

"You've never told me why you and your mom moved to New Bonn. Did your mom get a better job offer or something?" Jason asked.

"Not exactly," responded Nic, looking at the ground.

After a few awkward seconds of silence, Jason said, "I'm sorry for asking. It's none of my business."

"No, it's not that. It just isn't easy for me to talk about," responded Nic. He cleared his throat.

"My dad was killed by a hit-and-run driver last February. He was trying to save a young kid who had run out into the middle of the street to get his basketball," Nic explained quietly.

"I'm sorry," Jason said softly.

"After I finished fourth grade, my mom decided we should move someplace else. She said it would be good for us. So, we moved here."

"I'm sure it wasn't easy, Nic, to leave all of your old friends behind. Hopefully, your new ones will be just as good to you," said Jason.

Nic smiled and attempted to change the subject. "Jason I have a question for you."

"Ask away."

"Why does Johnny seem to hate me so much? I know he treats a lot of people bad, but he seems to go out of his way to make things tough on me," said Nic.

Jason looked ahead for a few seconds. He then placed his right arm around Nic's shoulders and said, "I was hoping you wouldn't notice it, but... I guess it's kind of obvious. I'm not really sure if it's my place to be telling you about this, but here goes. From what I understand, when the university hired your mom, they offered her a position on the Appropriations Committee, which she accepted. This committee is very important, because it's responsible for controlling the university's finances -- what departments receive how much money, what research projects are funded, and the like."

Looking at Jason intently, Nic interrupted, "My mom told me about that. So what does this have to do with Johnny?"

"Well, Johnny's dad, Mr. Parks, works at the university with your mom. He really had his eyes set on the same position. Rumor has it that it was about to be offered to him until your mom's application changed things. In public, he acted fine about the university's decision; but I've heard that in private, he was enraged and blames your mom for his disappointment."

After a bit of reflection Nic responded, "That would explain why Johnny hates me so much. He somehow blames me for his dad's unhappiness."

Jason nodded.

Climbing into his sleeping bag, Nic knew that as long as he was living in New Bonn, he would always be at odds with Johnny and his gang. He didn't want to be enemies with Johnny, but if that was the way it was going to be, then he wasn't going to back down. He was really starting to like it here with his new friends. He smiled, thinking again about the fun he'd had that night until sleep finally claimed him, too.

CHAPTER THREE

The Chamberlains
and the Diamonds

On a sunny, October Saturday, Nic rolled out of bed wondering just how interesting the day was going to be. He was going with Kevin, Dante, Herbert, Philip, and Cindy to the Chamberlain's to rake their leaves and earn some money. The Chamberlains lived across the street from Nic. From what Nic had heard from his mom and had seen for himself, he knew they were different from normal people.

Mr. and Mrs. Chamberlain had originally lived on the East Coast, but had moved to the Midwest about twenty years ago so Mr. Chamberlain could run his father's successful nursery business. Of course, the talk of the town was that Mrs. Chamberlain was the real brains behind the operation. She hadn't wanted to move here. She made it no secret that as soon as Mr. Chamberlain retired, they would move back east where (as she put it) "sophisticated" people lived.

Mrs. Chamberlain was tall and thin. She was in her early fifties, but looked older with her bleached blond hair. She had a long, pointed nose, which frequently carried her reading glasses. Mr. Chamberlain was a short, big-boned man in his late fifties, with thinning white hair, a pudgy nose, and a pair of gray, bushy sideburns. Whereas Mrs. Chamberlain was sharp, penny-pinching and stern, Mr. Chamberlain was forgetful, goofy, and a bit silly. It was a wonder these two ever got married.

Walking out the back door, Nic went over to the garage to get some rakes and a tarpaulin to use for the day. Dante and Philip strolled up just as Nic raised the garage door.

Nic had forgotten how many boxes were still packed from his move.

"Man-O-Man! We're supposed to go through all that to find rakes?" exclaimed Dante.

"It's not that bad," said Nic.

"This reminds me of a scene from one of the Indiana Jones movies where they have to enter some forbidden temple to find an ancient artifact," said Philip.

"Ha, ha. Real funny," protested Nic, even as he silently agreed.

Looking tentatively at one another, the boys stepped into the garage. Sunlight cut through the gloom like knives. Dust, disturbed by their tennis shoes and sudden air movement, danced and swirled around them, making the air stuffy and hard to breathe.

"This feels creepy, like one of those horror films where the monster is hiding in the shadows ready to eat its victims," whispered Dante in a shaky voice.

Philip added, "Or maybe some aliens waiting to take us back to their planet to study us."

"Will you guys cut it out? You're starting to scare me," Nic whispered hoarsely.

Their eyes finally adjusted to the little amount of light, making the search easier. Dante spotted the rakes and tarp and yelled for the others to help him.

Stepping over boxes and old buckets filled with who-knows-what, Nic reached Dante and Philip, who had already grabbed the goods and were heading toward the door.

"C'mon, let's get out of here," said Dante. The boys began to make their way out carefully.

"BOO!" rang out loudly as Nic, Dante, and Philip noticeably jumped at the sound. Looking over their shoulders, they saw a white sheet rising from the top of a stack of boxes.

"Aaaahhhh!" the boys shouted. They made a mad dash toward the entrance. Once safely outside, the three boys collapsed in the grass with the rakes and tarp piled next to them. They gasped for air while they tried to figure out what had just happened.

"I don't know what that was in there, but I ain't ever going back into your garage again, bro," stammered Dante.

"That makes two of us," replied Nic breathlessly.

"Me, three," said Philip, who was looking intently toward the garage. Nic and Dante looked over to see what had captured Philip's attention.

Kevin was coming out of the shadows of the garage with a white sheet draped over his shoulder.

"Ha, ha, ha. You guys should have seen the looks on your faces. You were so scared," laughed Kevin.

Nic, Philip, and Dante all looked at each other and then at Kevin. They all jumped up and ran at him. Kevin stopped laughing and started to run toward Nic's front yard. It was an attempt to flee the scene of his crime; but Nic, Philip, and Dante quickly hauled him to the ground and piled on top of him.

"I give. I give!" Kevin squealed.

In the middle of giving Kevin his punishment, the boys were jarred back to reality by a high-pitched voice.

"Seriously, is that all boys do? Wrestle and fight each other?"

Cindy Lin was staring at them with both hands on her hips and one eyebrow raised disapprovingly. Beside her was Herbert, who was just finishing a donut in one hand, while holding a rake in the other.

"We'd better get going before Mrs. Chamberlain thinks we're not coming at all. Surely you guys have heard how she is about punctuality," lectured Cindy.

Getting up, the boys gathered their equipment and headed over to the Chamberlain's house.

Pushing the doorbell, they heard a loud "Bing Bong" inside the house. They stepped back and waited. A tall, muscular man, formally dressed in a tuxedo, opened the front door. With a crisp English accent, he asked, "How may I be of service?"

For a moment, they stood with their mouths open. None of them had met a real butler before. Nic cleared his throat and said, "We're here to rake Mr. and Mrs. Chamberlain's yard, sir."

"May I inquire as to whom I am addressing?" asked the butler.

"My name is Nic...Nic Nelson," stuttered Nic.

Stepping back inside the house, the butler waved his large hand, inviting the kids into the large, expansive foyer. He then bellowed out in a deep voice, "Lady Chamberlain, a Mr. Nicolas Nelson is here concerning a business transaction."

Nic's hair stood up on the back of his neck. He hadn't realized someone could be so loud without being angry.

Kevin whispered into Nic's ear, "He must be the butler. He makes us sound very important. I bet he could make a soap box derby sound like the Indianapolis 500."

Nic chuckled silently to himself as he took in his surroundings. The entry foyer was a huge room. In front of them, two staircases curved gently toward each other, coming together on the second floor landing. Above them, a large glass chandelier sparkled in the dim light. Nic thought about how cool it would be to slide down the staircase rail. He bumped Kevin slightly as he whispered, "I bet you could pick up a lot of speed going down one of those," he said pointing at the stairs.

They heard Mrs. Chamberlain before they saw her. Quick, but muffled footsteps were coming toward them from over their heads.

"Spencer? Spencer! There you are. Now who did you say was here?" snapped Mrs. Chamberlain as she appeared at the top of the right staircase.

"A Mr. Nicolas Nelson," answered Mr. Spencer.

"Nicolas? Nicolas? Oh yes, now I remember," muttered Mrs. Chamberlain. She came down the steps slowly, carefully placing each foot on the step below. Reaching the bottom, she took a moment to straighten her dress, then approached Nic and his friends. She stared at each of them and finally sniffed disapprovingly.

Placing her hands on her hips, she leaned forward slightly and said, in a somewhat angry tone, "Nicolas, you and your friends are late. I'm a firm believer in punctuality. I will overlook this transgression just this once. After all, I wouldn't want to seem unforgiving to the little people of the world.

"Now then, please follow me to the backyard since you already know what the front yard looks like." With that, she turned on her heel and began almost marching toward the back of the house. They dutifully followed.

Kevin whispered to no one in particular, "I'm sure glad she can forgive us little people. I don't know how I would survive if she hadn't."

Nic, Philip, Herbert, and Dante snickered. Cindy poked Kevin in the ribs.

"Shhhh!"

Nic glanced back and thought he saw Mr. Spencer smile slightly, too. As they filed out the back door, they again found themselves in shock when they saw the size of the job that awaited them. Leaves were everywhere! It looked like some parts of the yard were waist deep with them. They let out a group groan as they realized how much work this job was going to be.

"I want all of this raked up, as well as the front yard, by the end of today. Is that understood? I'm entertaining guests tomorrow from Boston, Massachusetts," Mrs. Chamberlain said in a commanding voice.

"Yes, Ma'am," answered Nic.

Walking away, Mrs. Chamberlain said in passing, "The city doesn't allow the burning of leaves, and I do not want the leaves stacked up in front of the house in bags. It looks so *common*." They looked at each other as both Mrs. Chamberlain and Mr. Spencer returned to the house.

"How are we supposed to get rid of all of these leaves?" Herbert asked.

Looking around, Nic answered, "I guess we'll have to haul them into the woods at the edge of the backyard."

"You mean all of the leaves from the front yard as well?" Philip whined.

"I guess," replied Nic.

"I think it's the only option," added Cindy. "So we better get to work."

The gang split up to tackle different sections of the yard.

After three hours of intense work, everyone agreed it was time for a break. They plopped down in the shadow of the backyard tool shed. Nic noticed that it looked like no one had used it for years. It was rotting out in places, and the windows were covered in dust and spider webs.

"Boy, do my arms ache," grunted Dante, lowering himself to the ground.

"You can say that again," chimed in Kevin. Herbert and Philip were sprawled on their backs in exhaustion.

Cindy said, "At our present rate, I estimate we should be finished in approximately two hours."

"Hey, look! Here comes Mr. Spencer with drinks," said Kevin said with obvious glee. Everyone perked up as the butler approached in his slow, deliberate pace.

"Young masters, permit me to offer refreshments as it is hot, and you've all been working so hard."

"Thanks, Mr. Spencer," everyone said in unison as he passed out the drinks.

"Please, young masters, I would much rather you address me as Captain Spencer, as I prefer it over Mr. Spencer."

"Were you in the military?" Philip asked.

"Yes, I was. I served in Her Majesty's Service for over twenty years," answered Captain Spencer.

"Her Majesty's Service?" Herbert looked confused.

"He means he served in the military for England…more properly known as the United Kingdom," Nic told Herbert.

"Correct, Master Nic. It sounds like you're a man of history and geography."

"I like to dabble in both," Nic answered proudly.

"That's good. As a wise man once said, if you don't learn from history, you'll be doomed to repeat it," said Captain Spencer.

"Without sounding rude, Captain Spencer, why are you working for the Chamberlain's as a butler after having served Her Majesty for so long?" Cindy asked.

"After having finished my duty to Queen and Country, I was looking for employment, as I felt too young to be in retirement. My uncle knew about my desire to continue working. Since he was finishing his service with the Chamberlain family, he recommended me to them. I had always wanted to come to the Colonies---I mean the States---ever since my childhood. As soon as I heard of my acceptance by the Chamberlains, I came over without hesitation. I have served them for twenty years with no regrets."

"Were you in any battles?" Dante asked.

"A few," Captain Spencer replied with a wink and a smile. He busied himself by collecting the now empty glasses.

Kevin asked, "Captain Spencer, what's up with this old shack? It looks like it's been abandoned for years."

"You are quite observant young man, but I believe it is properly referred to as a tool shed. When the Chamberlains first moved into this house, Master Chamberlain had this tool shed built. Master Chamberlain, however, has used it infrequently and has not been inside for many years," replied Captain Spencer.

"It sure would make cool clubhouse," Herbert said.

"Possibly, but we'll never know, now will we? I don't think the Chamberlains would want a bunch of kids tracking back and forth across their backyard to a clubhouse," responded Cindy.

"Well, it was just a thought," Herbert replied meekly.

"I must take leave of you. Good luck in finishing your endeavors," said Captain Spencer. He turned on his heel and walked back to the house.

"Thanks, again, for the drinks," yelled Nic.

When Captain Spencer was out of earshot, Kevin said, "He sure does talk funny. What's with all of the Master Chamberlain or Lady Chamberlain stuff? Who talks like that?"

Everyone shrugged their shoulders and returned to the job at hand. Cindy's estimate of two hours rang true, and they happily put down their rakes. The wooded area that bordered the backyard was full of leaves. The yard looked, as Dante said, "Green and clean."

Kevin added, "All I want right now is some green in my hand, if you know what I mean."

Just as Nic was about to go and tell Mrs. Chamberlain they were finished, he saw her standing on the back patio. She seemed frantic, flapping her arms as if she was trying to do her best imitation of a penguin attempting to fly.

"No! No! No! This just will not do, children!" Mrs. Chamberlain shouted. "You can't have the leaves piled in the woods like that," she said pointing toward them. "It just ruins the view of the backyard. I must insist that you place them elsewhere, or I will not be paying you for your services." She started to head back into the house, satisfied she'd made her position clear.

Kevin's face turned red with anger at this news. He was about to say something back to Mrs. Chamberlain, but Cindy quickly placed her hand over his mouth to stop him.

"Where would you like us to place the leaves, Mrs. Chamberlain?" asked Cindy sweetly. Mrs. Chamberlain stopped and looked at Cindy.

"I don't care. That's why I'm paying you kids to do the job. Next time, I guess I'll have to hire real professionals. I should have known this is what I would get hiring common children," she stated, slamming the door behind her.

"Great! Just great! How are we supposed to get rid of a ton of leaves if we can't bag or burn them and can't place them anywhere within sight of the house?" Kevin blurted, seething with anger.

Philip added, "If I didn't know better, I bet she probably flies around on a broom at night, if you guys get my drift."

Nic, sensing the situation spinning out of control, looked around for a place to hide the huge amount of leaves. Then, it hit him.

"That's it!" he yelled.

"What's it?" Cindy asked.

"We'll place the leaves inside of the tool shed," finished Nic.

"Are you crazy?" screamed Cindy. "I thought Kevin was the only one who came up with crazy ideas."

Slowly smiling, Kevin said, "It's perfect, Nic. Don't you guys see? Just like Captain Spencer told us, no one has used the tool shed in years. Mrs. Chamberlain did say that she didn't care how we get rid of the leaves."

After a few seconds of silence, Philip spoke up, "I hate to admit it, but I think Nic's plan is the only one we have left, unless we want to haul every single leaf to the outside of town."

Energized by Nic's creative solution, the gang split into two groups. One group was responsible for raking the leaves back out of the woods, while the other group was to collect the leaves and put them in the tool shed.

It seemed like a simple enough plan, until they discovered the tool shed door was stuck. Finally, after several few minutes of grunting and pulling, they were able to get the rusty door open. Nic was amazed at how big it was inside the shed. Because the windows were dirty, not much light came in, so it was hard to make out what secrets it held. In fact, there was just enough light to help the gang dump leaves without running into anything.

After what seemed like an eternity of stacking leaves and watching out for the Chamberlains, the job was finished. It had taken everyone pushing against the door to close it firmly.

"I sure hope I'm long gone by the time Mr. Chamberlain opens up this door again," said Nic, too tired to laugh.

Moans and groans were the only response Nic received in his weak attempt at humor. Once they were confident the shed door would stay closed, the gang walked to the back porch door and rang the doorbell.

"Ding dong!"

Captain Spencer opened the door. Seeing them standing there dirty and obviously tired, Captain Spencer wasted no time in calling out, "Lady Chamberlain, Mr. Nicolas Nelson is here to report his progress."

A few seconds passed before Mrs. Chamberlain appeared at the doorway. She looked beyond the kids to survey the yard. Nic saw a look of satisfaction and surprise on her face. As quickly as it came, it disappeared.

"Not quite right, but I guess it'll have to do," she murmured with a dismissive tone. Turning, she said, "Spencer, please see to it that Mr. Chamberlain handles the financial aspect, won't you?" Not really waiting for an answer, she disappeared into the depths of the house.

"Yes, mi-lady," answered Captain Spencer, while bowing slightly. "Mr. Chamberlain, your presence is requested at the back porch door," Captain Spencer said loudly.

While they waited for Mr. Chamberlain, Captain Spencer bent down and whispered into Nic's ear, "Well done, Master Nic. I must say you came up with a most brilliant solution to your conundrum concerning the leaves. The last kid to rake the Chamberlain's yard didn't fare so well."

Nic looked up at Captain Spencer in surprise and worry. "Don't worry, Master Nic. I will not disclose the location of the undesired material. I've been known to keep a secret or two." He smiled.

Just then, Mr. Chamberlain came walking toward the door with a glass of wine in one hand and a cigar in the other. "What's this all about, Spencer?" Mr. Chamberlain asked in a gruff voice.

"Master Chamberlain, this young gentleman, Nicolas Nelson, and his friends were employed by Lady Chamberlain to rake the yard, which they have done to her satisfaction. They would now like to be properly compensated for their services rendered."

"Oh, well then, how much is it, Spencer?" Mr. Chamberlain asked.

Captain Spencer turned to look at Nic. "Master Nic, I believe this would be an appropriate time for you to answer."

"Well, sir, Mr. Chamberlain, sir, we didn't really discuss an exact figure, sir," Nic stammered.

In the background, Mrs. Chamberlain's voice could be heard yelling, "Honey, please stop talking with those children. We really must be getting ready for our dinner with the Johnson's tonight!"

Handing Captain Spencer his drink and cigar, Mr. Chamberlain pulled out a wad of cash from his back pocket. He casually gave Nic a single bill without looking at it. He then said, "I'm sure this will do. I only have my small bills with me when I'm in the house."

Nic turned the money over and did a double take. Mr. Chamberlain had paid them with a crisp $100 bill. Everyone gasped in amazement. Captain Spencer said quietly, so only they would hear, "I would be leaving now, young masters, if I were you, as Mr. Chamberlain did not have on his reading glasses when he gave you your payment."

Not having to be told twice, the gang quickly shuffled off the back porch. They gathered their equipment and headed back to Nic's house for some much needed refreshments.

The gang was crossing the street to Nic's driveway when they saw two men sitting in a small, blue car down the street. The men quickly got out of the car and approached them. Nic saw one of them slip binoculars into his jacket pocket before speaking.

"Hi, kids. Could we have a word with you?"

The gang looked at each other and then at the two men. They mumbled, "Sure," in unison, not knowing what else to say.

The taller of the two men was wearing faded blue jeans and a worn, green jacket. His hair had that greased back look from the 1950s and a five o'clock shadow on his face. His narrow, squinting eyes suggested he was not a person to be messed with. The smaller man was pudgy, with messy black hair; and he was wearing an ugly, out-of-season, Hawaiian shirt.

"Great," said the taller man in response. "My name is Detective Johnson of the local police. This is my partner, Officer Walker."

The smaller man lightly nudged the taller man. In a loud whisper he asked, "Only an officer?"

The taller man flashed him a quick, dirty look, which Nic found to be very similar to the one his mom would give him when he mentions something that he shouldn't.

"Of course, I forgot. Officer Walker was recently promoted to detective, too. Anyway, you're probably wondering why we want to talk to you."

They all nodded.

"Yeah, why do we want to talk to them?" asked Detective Walker.

"Because!" answered Detective Johnson, somewhat angrily. He caught himself, cleared his throat, and continued, "...because we need to ask you kids something that concerns police business."

Nic thought these two men were acting very strangely, unlike any police officers that he had ever met.

"Did you kids see anything strange or out of place in the backyard that you were raking?"

"Well, I did see this neat looking frog that had an extra leg growing out the side of its gut," Herbert answered casually.

"Really? That's so cool," said Dante.

"Where was it?" Philip asked.

"Why didn't you mention it to any of us?" asked Kevin.

"Yuck," said Cindy.

"Ahem! I think we're getting off track, kids. To be more specific, did any of you come across an old suitcase sticking up from the ground anywhere?" asked Detective Johnson with growing frustration. They shook their heads.

"Excuse me, Detective Johnson, but could you please show us some kind of I.D.?" Cindy asked politely, but firmly, while the boys stared at her in disbelief. "After all, anyone can pretend to be a police officer."

"Look here, kid, I've been a police officer for over twenty years and have never been talked to so rudely in my life. I'll determine what I need to show you; and right now, I don't need to show you anything. I'm leaving!" With a wave of his hand, Detective Johnson motioned for Detective Walker to follow him. With two loud bangs from their car doors, they zoomed away.

Nic and his friends were dumbfounded as they looked at each other. Dante finally broke the silence. "Dudes, that was weird."

"They never really told us what they wanted," Phillip responded.

Cindy nonchalantly replied, "Isn't it obvious? They wanted to find a suitcase of some kind, which they evidently think is located in the Chamberlain's backyard."

"I know that! What I'd like to know is what's inside of the suitcase." Philip stated.

Kevin said, "I may not know what that suitcase contains, but I do know one thing for sure; those guys weren't policemen. There's no Detective Johnson or Walker on the local police force."

Nic smiled and added, "I guess you ought to know better than anyone. You've probably been in enough trouble with the local police."

Everyone laughed, including Kevin, who replied, "I can't help it if I like to have fun past curfew."

"Well, enough of this. Let's get to my house for drinks and cookies. We can talk about all of this stuff later," said Nic. He wasn't sure he had the energy to make it back to his kitchen that was only fifty feet away.

Following Nic into the kitchen, the gang made themselves at home with the goodies Nic's mom had put out for them.

"Now this hits the spot," mumbled Herbert between gulps of milk, snack eating, and fighting off Nic's dog, Wellington, who was doing his best to get any scraps that fell to the floor.

"It sure was nice of your mom to do this for us," said Dante.

Before Nic could reply, a voice behind him said, "No problem, kids. I hope you're all enjoying the snacks."

Nic turned around and saw his mom enter the kitchen with their next-door neighbor, Mr. O'Malley, behind her. Mr. O'Malley was older than Nic's mom and a bit chubby. His most interesting feature was a big head of white hair. It always reminded Nic of Albert Einstein's hair.

Everyone nodded with satisfaction.

"Finished with your job?" Nic's mom asked.

Once again, they nodded while continuing to stuff their mouths with food and drink.

"Now that's how it should be for kids. Hard work keeps 'em out of trouble," stated Mr. O'Malley.

Nic almost choked on his snack, holding back a laugh as Kevin rolled his eyes at Mr. O'Malley's statement.

"I'm sure it does, Connor. But kids also need to have time for playing, which is very important in the growing up process," said Nic's mom.

All right, Mom! Score one for us, thought Nic.

"Hogwash, I say, Barbara. Childhood is about a kid learning to become a responsible adult, and a responsible adult is someone who works for a living. So it just makes sense to me that a responsible kid who works will grow up into a responsible adult who works," said Mr. O'Malley.

Boy, this guy must've had an awful childhood, thought Nic, while finishing his milk.

"I don't even want you to try and repeat what you just said, because you lost me after 'hogwash,'" laughed Nic's mom.

"What I mean is…" started Mr. O'Malley, as if on a mission.

"I know what you meant. Anyway, why don't you continue on with telling me about the local history of the town?"

Nic and his friends went on eating, drinking, and laughing, while Nic's mom and Mr. O'Malley continued talking in the background.

The kids largely ignored the adults until they overheard Mr. O'Malley say, "Did I already mention about the diamond heist and how the thief supposedly buried the stolen diamonds right here in town?"

"No, you haven't. It sounds fascinating," replied Nic's mom.

Nic and his friends became quiet as Mr. O'Malley continued, "Well, about twenty years ago, a thief broke into the Chicago Art Museum and stole the famous Diamonds of Denmark. The diamonds were known by this name because, I believe, they had been a present from the royal family of Denmark to their daughter for her wedding in the

19th century. Anyway, after a massive manhunt for the perpetrator, the authorities were able to locate the thief right here in our town and actually ended up apprehending him in the Chamberlain's backyard."

Nic's eyes slowly widened, leaning over to listen more closely.

"When the police caught the thief, he didn't have the diamonds with him. Even after intense interrogation, he refused to tell the whereabouts of the diamonds or even admit he had stolen them. The police searched everywhere in and around town, but they didn't find them. They concluded that the thief most likely had hidden the diamonds elsewhere, or had delivered them to another accomplice along the way.

"The diamonds have never been recovered to this day, and even now they are still the subject of talk among the old timers who insist that the thief hid the diamonds here in town. I think it's ridiculous. I mean, where could you hide a suitcase full of diamonds for twenty years without anyone finding it by now?"

"A suitcase!" Kevin yelled out. Philip turned pale. Dante, Cindy, Nic, and Herbert each choked on their snacks and began coughing. Mr. O'Malley and Nic's mom turned toward the kids in surprise. They didn't know they had an audience.

"Yes, a suitcase, young man. The diamonds were purported to have been hidden in a suitcase when the thief made good on his crime in Chicago," answered Mr. O'Malley, in a somewhat irritated tone. He was not accustomed to being interrupted by a child.

Nic asked, "So the police still aren't sure whether the thief had worked alone or not?"

Mr. O'Malley replied, "Not that I can recall, although I do remember the thief. Oh, what was his name? Michael Marinovich. Yes, that's it, Michael Marinovich! Anyway, Mr. Marinovich did have a younger brother, Roger, who claimed Michael was innocent, because the diamonds weren't found on him when he was caught. But the police had enough evidence with fingerprints and surveillance film to back up their case. I'm sure the authorities kept tabs on Roger Marinovich for a long time, since they strongly suspected that he had been involved somehow."

"Whatever happened to the diamond thief?" asked Cindy.

"I believe he died in prison a few years ago, right before he was scheduled to be released on parole," answered Mr. O'Malley.

"You kids sure seem interested in this story. Any particular reason why?" asked Nic's mom.

A few seconds of silence followed her question, after which, a chorus of mumbling greeted Nic's mom with various vague answers. Finally, Nic said, "No particular reason. It just sounded cool to hear after a long day of hard work."

Looking at the gang, Nic rolled his eyes toward the door and said, "Well, I think everyone's done eating, so I guess I'll be seeing them out the door, right guys?"

"Yeah, right. Gotta go," said Dante.

"Thanks, again, for the refreshments, Mrs. Nelson," said Cindy, while everyone filed on out of the kitchen door into the backyard.

They walked to the edge of Nic's yard in silence before everyone began talking at once. Kevin managed to calm everyone down enough to be heard.

"Okay, we need to stop for a second and think this out."

Nic spoke up, "Kevin's right. We need to figure out what's happening here. All we know for sure is two strange men are looking for a suitcase from the Chamberlain's backyard."

"Yeah, and that suitcase may or may not be hot with stolen goods," volunteered Dante.

"We're not sure the suitcase the strangers are looking for is even related to the one Mr. O'Malley told us about. After all, just like Mr. O'Malley mentioned, the police never found a suitcase here in town even after searching everywhere for it," argued Philip.

"But it's awfully strange two men show up out of the blue asking for a suitcase," Cindy reasoned, "and are evidently willing to lie about who they are to find it."

Herbert piped in, "What can we do about it? We're just kids. No one is going to believe us, especially since we're not even sure about anything ourselves."

"What we need to do is some research into what exactly happened twenty years ago," said Nic. "Then we'll be able to start separating fact from fiction."

"Nic's right, guys," said Kevin. "Cindy, you and Herbert are whizzes on the computer, so why don't you guys scan the Internet for any stories concerning the Diamonds of Denmark and details concerning the heist from the Chicago Art Museum. Dante and I will go to the library and see if we can dig up any old newspaper clippings about the robbery and, possibly, some pictures of the thief and his brother. Nic, I want you and Philip to do some talking with Captain Spencer and some of the other old timers to see what they can tell you about what had happened in town twenty years ago.

"So does anybody have any questions about what to do?"

Everyone shook their heads and, without a word, split up to go their respective ways home.

Staring at the Chamberlain house, Nic wondered about the Diamonds of Denmark and if they really were buried in his neighbors' yard. He shivered as a cool October breeze kicked up. Jamming his hands into his pockets, his right hand closed around a piece of paper. The money! In all the talk about the diamonds, they'd forgotten about the money! With one last glance toward the Chamberlains', Nic sprinted across the yard. Bounding into the kitchen, he yelled, "Mom, do you have change for a hundred?"

CHAPTER FOUR

Easy Ed's

For the next week, the gang busied themselves with collecting information that they hoped would help them make sense of the mysterious strangers. Nic and Philip had agreed to talk with Captain Spencer and some of the long-time residents in town on the following Saturday.

Nic had trouble sleeping all week. He'd wake up suddenly in a cold sweat from the latest nightmare of the two men questioning him repeatedly about the suitcase. When Saturday finally arrived, Philip met Nic in his front yard; and together they walked over to the Chamberlains.

As the boys approached the Chamberlains' front door, Philip wondered out loud, "What are we going to say? I hope he doesn't think we're crazy, because I'm starting to think that we are!"

"Stop worrying, Philip. Nobody is going to think we're crazy," replied Nic, while ringing the doorbell.

"Bong! Bong! Bong!" Nic felt the vibrations from the chimes creep up his legs.

"I don't remember it being that loud last time," whispered Philip.

Slowly, the huge oak door swung open. From the dark depths emerged a familiar figure.

"Captain Spencer, it's me, Nic; and this is Philip. Do you remember us?"

"But of course, Master Nic. The ingenuity with which you solved your dilemma concerning the leaves was quite extraordinary. I may have many years on this body, but my mind is as sharp as it was twenty years ago. So how may I be of service to you and your friend? Do you need to talk to the Chamberlains?"

"No, we want to talk with you. It's funny that you should mention your mind being as good as it was twenty years ago. I'm hoping you can help us with something that happened around that time here in town," said Nic.

Captain Spencer eyed the boys for a second and then said, "Ask away, young masters. I am at your disposal."

Before Nic could say anything, a shrill voice rang out from the background, "Oh Spencer, who is at the door? Is it Pierre for my morning manicure and hairstyle?" asked Mrs. Chamberlain. Before Captain Spencer could answer, Mrs. Chamberlain appeared at the door. "Pierre, I can hardly wait to get started! You must tell me all of the gossip you know about the Hendersons, because I've . . . this isn't Pierre!"

The smile disappeared from her face, replaced with a look of disdain. "Who are these boys? Do they need to speak to me?" Mrs. Chamberlain demanded.

"No, Madame. These are two of the young men who raked your leaves last weekend. They want to converse with me about some past event," replied Captain Spencer as he bowed slightly toward Mrs. Chamberlain. Nic thought he saw a look of shock come over Mrs. Chamberlain's face, as if all visitors who came were for her only and no one else.

Recovering from her surprise, she muttered quietly, "Do make it quick, Spencer." She seemed to melt into the darkness of the house.

"Please continue, Master Nic, with your inquiry," Captain Spencer said in his usual flat voice.

"When you first came to work for the Chamberlains, do you remember a jewel thief caught by the police in the backyard?" Nic asked.

Pausing for a few moments to collect his thoughts, Captain Spencer answered, "Yes, I do recall a jewel thief being apprehended by the local authorities in the backyard about twenty years ago. It was quite a commotion with the media and police swarming all over the place for weeks afterwards. In fact, I was the one who had noticed the gentleman in question sneaking around the backyard at about five in the morning. I immediately phoned the authorities. Little did I expect that I would be helping to apprehend the infamous jewel thief of the Diamonds of Denmark. I truly detest the thought of someone stealing something so historical in value and denying the public its right to admire it."

"So you're familiar with the diamonds and their history?" asked Philip.

"I must plead ignorance on that question. I do love art and history, but I'm afraid that jewels and diamonds are areas in which I lack adequate knowledge. So I'm afraid I really don't know much about the Diamonds of Denmark's history, Master Philip," Captain Spencer replied apologetically.

"Is it true that the diamonds were never recovered?" asked Nic.

"As far as I can recall, I do not think the diamonds were recovered at that time or since. May I ask why the sudden interest in an event which occurred so long ago?"

The boys glanced at each other before Nic answered, "We had heard about it from Mr. O'Malley and just wanted to see if he had been telling us a real story and not some made up one."

"I assure you, young masters, that the events did unfold concerning the thief and his capture. In fact, if you wait for a few moments I will show you a picture of the thief being led off from his point of capture in the backyard," responded Captain Spencer. He went back inside while Nic and Philip nudged at each other in anticipation.

A few minutes later, Captain Spencer returned with a number of old photographs. Sitting on the front steps between Nic and Philip, Captain Spencer explained what he was showing them.

"Here are the pictures I was referring to, young masters." Going slowly through the pile, he paused as he pulled one out for a closer look. "This is the picture of the thief in the backyard while he was being escorted away by the authorities shortly after his capture."

Nic and Philip peered over Captain Spencer's huge arms to get a good look.

Nic asked, "Where were you when you took this picture? It looks like you can see the entire backyard!"

"I was located on the second floor in the hallway, looking out the large window."

Philip remarked, "Wow, look at all of the cops in the backyard. It must've been crazy."

"It was a bit of a nightmare for the Chamberlains to handle," replied Captain Spencer. "They had not been here for very long when this happened. They almost decided to move because of the media circus and curiosity seekers. It persisted for weeks. It finally quieted down, and they decided to stay," he added.

Nic asked if he could get a closer look at the photo. Captain Spencer nodded as he handed it to Nic. As Nic bent down to get a closer look at the thief's face, he bumped heads with Philip, who was attempting the same thing.

"Ouch!" they both cried out as they rubbed their heads.

"Captain Spencer, would you mind if we borrowed this picture for awhile?" Nic asked.

"Not at all, young masters. I do hope it will assist you in your endeavors, whatever they may be. With that," Captain Spencer stood up, saying, "I'm afraid I must take my leave, young masters." He gave a cheerful wave and retreated into the house.

Philip said, "I like Captain Spencer. He seems like a cool guy."

"Yeah, he does. Hopefully, this picture will give us some clues," said Nic.

"Clues? You sound like a Scooby Doo cartoon," laughed Philip.

Smiling, Nic replied, "Well, Shaggy, we'd better get our bikes and ride down to Easy Ed's where all of the old timers hang out."

Within minutes, the boys were making their way to the local barbershop known as Easy Ed's. Even Nic, a newcomer in town, knew Easy Ed's slogan: *If It Wasn't Easy, You Weren't at Ed's.*

As the boys rode, Nic's mind was busy with too many thoughts. Will these guys think we're crazy for asking about the diamonds? Will they be any help to us at all?

After dropping their bikes in front of Ed's shop, Philip and Nic ventured inside. Their noses were greeted with a mixture of smells from hair gel to shaving cream. For a moment, Nic savored the familiar smell while remembering how he used to watch his dad shave each morning. Shaking off his momentary sadness, Nic focused on their task. He could see two old men sitting on one side of the barbershop, while another was getting his hair trimmed by a smiling, middle-aged man with thinning brown hair. Nic assumed that was Easy Ed.

"Morning, kids. What will it be? A buzz or maybe a bowl cut?" Easy Ed asked.

Before Nic or Philip could answer, one of the men sitting on the side said, "All boys should have a buzz. Too many of them are looking like girls with the long hair. Just the other day I…"

"Quiet, Albert. Nobody cares about your opinion on haircuts," said the man sitting next to him.

"Look here, Marvin, I think it's important for boys to look like boys and girls to look like girls. With my poor eyesight, I want to be able to tell the difference," snapped Albert.

"Now behave you two. I don't want you guys scaring away new customers," laughed Easy Ed.

"Actually, sir, we're not here for a haircut. We were wondering if any of you could remember anything about a jewel thief who was captured here in town about twenty years ago," said Nic, somewhat hesitantly.

Both Albert and Marvin stopped their squabbling to look at the young upstarts. Easy Ed abruptly stopped cutting.

"What would two good looking boys want to know about that?" Easy Ed asked.

"Ahh…we're doing a school project about New Bonn's history," said Nic.

"Yeah, that's right; and part of our assignment is to ask townspeople about events they experienced firsthand," added Philip, to Nic's relief.

For a few seconds, no one said a word. Then, all at once, the shop erupted in a noisy free-for-all, as each man tried to speak over the others. Nic turned to Philip and shouted, "I can't understand anybody!"

"What?" shouted back Philip.

Exasperated, Nic held up his hands and shouted, "Please, one at a time!"

The men quieted.

"I'll speak first, if you don't mind," said Albert, giving Marvin the evil eye. Easy Ed nodded and went back to trimming the hair of the elderly man in his chair. As far as Nic could tell, the man sitting in front of Easy Ed was the only person who hadn't said anything.

Seeing the puzzled look on Nic's face, Easy Ed offered, "Don't be alarmed, son. Buford here is completely deaf."

"As I was attempting to say…" Albert stated impatiently, "What you kids are referring to is known as the Diamonds of Monte Carlo Caper, which took place up north somewhere from some fancy, schmancy museum." Albert gave a smug smile, enjoying having an audience.

"As always, you've got it wrong, Albert. They were known as the Diamonds of Denmark, and they were stolen from Los Angeles," replied Marvin in a confident tone.

"I don't know about that, Marvin. I seem to remember the diamonds having been stolen from New York," added Easy Ed.

Nic was beginning to wonder if coming here had been such a good idea after all.

"Anyway, the important point is that the jewel thief was captured here in town, in the park by the waterfall," said Albert.

"He was not caught by the waterfall, you nincompoop. He was caught while hiding out behind Big Joe's Bar-B-Q Rib Shack, when it was located next to the bank," corrected Marvin.

"I thought he had been caught while running behind City Hall in broad daylight," mumbled Easy Ed.

Realizing they were asking questions of men who didn't have a clue, Nic looked at his watch and said, "Gee, look at the time, Philip. Sorry, but my friend and I have to get going. We really appreciate all of your... er ...help in this matter."

Albert stood up and said, "What's the rush youngins? I haven't told you yet where I think the diamonds are hidden."

"You don't know where the diamonds are hidden. You're lucky if you can find your underwear and teeth in the morning," laughed Marvin.

Nic quickly motioned to Philip to hurry out of the barbershop. As they climbed onto their bikes, they heard Albert yell out the closing door, while Easy Ed and Marvin laughed loudly. "The thief hid the diamonds next to a tree."

"Is that what happens when you get old? You sit around and crab at each other?" asked Philip, not really expecting an answer from Nic.

"That was a waste of time. The only thing I know for sure is that none of those guys knows what they're talking about," added Nic.

"I hope the rest of the gang has been having more success with their parts," said Philip, as they approached his street.

"Well, I don't know, but I guess we'll find out on Monday during lunch when Kevin wants to talk about it," said Nic.

"Well, here's where I turn off for home. Catch you later, Nic," said Philip.

"Yeah, catch ya later, Philip," mumbled Nic, who was already lost in thought.

CHAPTER FIVE

Kevin's House

Monday arrived cool and sunny — a perfect fall morning. Nic was having a hard time sitting still. He impatiently counted the minutes until the lunch bell. When it rang, he was the first one out the door. As he walked into the cafeteria, he was relieved and excited. He was relieved because Johnny had been ignoring him. Nic didn't care why; he was enjoying the truce. He was excited because today he would learn what his friends had found out in their Diamonds of Denmark investigations.

Strolling up to the lunch table, Nic could hear an ongoing debate between Kevin and the others. "It'll be fun, I tell ya," said Kevin.

"You're crazy. What happens if we get caught?" asked Dante.

"What's going on?" asked Nic, sitting down between Philip and Cindy.

"Kevin and Jason want us to help them pull a prank on one of Jason's professors. They need help putting a plastic skeleton on Jason's teacher's front porch this Friday," replied Philip.

"On Halloween?" Nic asked. Philip nodded.

"Sounds intriguing and fun," Cindy said.

"Seems too dangerous to me," muttered Herbert between spoonfuls of Jell-O.

"It'll be fun! Think how exciting it will be sneaking up to someone's house at night while he's home and hanging a skeleton right under his nose. That would be the ultimate diss," boasted Kevin.

"More like the ultimate form of suicide. I don't know about you guys, but I don't really feel like going to jail and not being released until I'm old...like, say, twenty-five," responded Dante.

"No one is going to go to jail if we're caught. Besides, I have the perfect plan," said Kevin, smiling and rubbing his hands together like some mad scientist. At this, everyone looked at each other and rolled their eyes.

After several more minutes of heated discussion, Kevin was able to convince everyone, including Dante, to go along with his and Jason's harebrained scheme. Kevin's plan for the evening was simple. He figured everyone could show up around 7:00 P.M. to go trick-or-treating for a couple of hours. They would meet Jason at Kevin's house afterwards to pull off the skeleton prank. Once that was done, all the boys (sorry Cindy) would spend the night. Everyone nodded approvingly at Kevin's plan.

Cindy teased, "I can't imagine anything worse than spending the night with you guys! I'm totally fine going home and sleeping in my own bed!"

They also decided to wait until that night to discuss what they found out about the Diamonds of Denmark, because they'd used the entire lunch period talking about Halloween.

"I must be crazy," mumbled Dante, as the gang left the lunchroom to go back to their classrooms.

"Hey, Nic," Kevin said, while the others walked ahead. "Want to come over at 5:00 Friday for dinner? You can meet my parents and stuff."

"I'll have to ask my mom, but I don't know why that won't be okay," Nic answered.

"Cool," smiled Kevin as he walked into his class.

Nic smiled, thinking, I really like it here.

The week passed quickly, and suddenly it was Friday night. Getting out of the car at Kevin's house, Nic's mom kissed him on the forehead and said, "Now, I don't think I have to tell you to behave, do I?"

"No, Mom. In fact, I'll even pretend to have some manners, too," joked Nic.

She smiled and added, "Have fun, and don't do anything that I wouldn't do!"

He watched as she drove away. If she only knew what kind of night this was going to be. Nic chuckled.

Nic walked up the driveway holding his sleeping bag in one hand and his backpack stuffed with his costume and clothes in the other. He was nervous. He hadn't met Kevin's parents before. They had always been away when he had been over the few times since he met Kevin. He stopped to take a deep breath and calm his nerves. This would be easier if the gang was here, too, he thought. As his pulse returned to normal, Nic surveyed Kevin's house. It was an old Victorian-styled house like Nic's, but bigger, because it had a third story where Kevin's room was supposed to be.

Just as he was feeling back to normal, a sudden blast of cold wind startled Nic. The Halloween decorations hanging between the large columns on the wraparound porch swung wildly. Shivering slightly, Nic trotted the rest of the way to the front door.

Chaotic voices and scrambling feet greeted Nic as he rang the doorbell. Without thinking, he took a step backward, not certain what was going to greet him. When the door opened, he found himself face-to-face with four sets of eyes staring at him. He immediately recognized Kevin, who was on the ground, peeking in between his three sisters' knees. Kevin's sisters blinked in surprise at Nic, as they assessed this new visitor. Their excitement gave way to looks of disappointment and frustration, and they hastily retreated to the kitchen.

"Ha!" bragged Kevin. "I told you guys it was for me." Gesturing for Nic to come in, Kevin continued, "Don't mind them. They're all expecting their boyfriends to pick them up to go to the movies and do mushy stuff."

"Yuck," whispered Nic, stepping into the main foyer.

Kevin took the lead as he grabbed Nic's sleeping bag and guided him upstairs. At the top of the second flight of stairs, the boys stopped in front of a door with various stickers attached to it. While waiting for Kevin to open up the door, Nic took the opportunity to read as many of the stickers as possible.

A few of them contained sayings like: *No Girls Allowed; Don't Go Away Mad, Just Go Away*; and *I'm not Driving Too Fast, I'm Flying Too Low.*

Nic didn't get a chance to finish reading the rest, as Kevin gestured to him to follow while issuing a warning, "Watch out for my trap."

"Trap?" Nic questioned. "What do you need a trap for?"

"You don't have three sisters who bug and spy on you," replied Kevin.

Nic thought to himself that it was probably the other way around. Besides, if the signs didn't scare them off, nothing probably would.

Nic hesitated before following Kevin into the room. Kevin stepped aside so Nic could pass, while keeping his hand on something behind the door. Walking in, Nic saw a long string going from the back of the door to the ceiling. Connected to the string on the ceiling was a large, black, plastic spider.

"Pretty clever, huh?" bragged Kevin. "I have it rigged so if anyone opens the door, it falls down on top of their head and scares them off."

Nic smiled at Kevin's resourcefulness. He stepped into the room and turned all the way around to see all of it. It was huge! Posters of various cars, sports, and superheroes covered the walls from the ceiling to the floor. In fact, there were so many posters, Nic wasn't sure he could even see the actual wall. In one corner of the room was a bunk bed. Next to the bed was a desk piled high with all kinds of toy figures and comic books.

"Cool room!"

Kevin put Nic's sleeping bag and backpack by the bed, "Thanks, I like it. At least I don't have to share it with anybody. That's what the bunk bed was for. Mom and Dad were planning to have another kid, but I think I scared that idea out of them."

Kevin continued, "I'm excited about tonight. I think it's going to be a blast!

"Yeah, I've been kind of looking forward to it, too!" replied Nic.

"C'mon, let me show you the rest of my room before dinner," Kevin said as he nudged Nic to follow. "I like to think of my room as a perfect example of chaotic order. It looks messy and unorganized, but in reality, everything is in perfect order. For example, my clothes over there along the floor are spread out unevenly, right?"

Nic nodded in agreement.

"But, you see, I have them positioned so in the morning I can grab my socks and underwear first, then my jeans and shirt, then finish with my shoes last. It's so well planned, I scare myself," remarked Kevin.

Nic didn't know what to say, so he just nodded again. Kevin wouldn't be the only person he'd scare, thought Nic. My mom would faint if she saw his room. She would declare it a disaster zone ready to be condemned.

They stopped in front of an ordinary looking bookcase. "This is the favorite part of my room," said Kevin.

"A bookcase?"

"No silly. What's behind it," replied Kevin with his usual devious smile.

Nic watched as Kevin pushed the bookcase to one side revealing a small door. Sliding the door open, he said, "Follow me."

Both boys had to bend down slightly to squeeze through the doorway. They emerged into a square room about eight feet wide and eight feet long. All kinds of gadgets and equipment were hanging on the walls. The space also held a small desk with a computer on it and two chairs. Overhead, two light bulbs hung from the ceiling. Nic noted the bulbs were doing a great job of lighting up the place.

"Wow!" said Nic. "This is so cool!"

"Thanks. I thought you might like it. Me and my dad are the only ones who know about this room. We aren't sure why it's here, but I don't care. To me, it's like having the Bat Cave to operate from," explained Kevin.

"Do any of the other guys know about it?"

"Yeah, well, except for Herbert. I'm afraid to tell him 'cause I think he might tell somebody by accident," replied Kevin. "I'm hooked up on the Internet and have all my computer games installed back here. It's also nice for the fact that if I just want to get away from everybody, I can come in here for some privacy," said Kevin.

They heard a muffled woman's voice yelling, "Boys! Boys!"

"Oh, man, that's my mom. She's probably telling us it's time for dinner. Quick, we've got to get out," said Kevin, pushing Nic toward the sliding door.

"Boys!" The cry came again, except it sounded much closer this time. They quickly scrambled out, managing to slide the door closed. But they couldn't budge the bookcase.

"What the...what's the matter with this?" Kevin whispered in frustration. They continued to pull on the bookcase, but it refused to move.

They froze when they heard the doorknob turn on the bedroom door. Consumed by the stubborn bookcase, Kevin had completely forgotten about the trap. They heard the door open and a footstep on the landing.

"Kevin, are you…AHHHHH!" The sound of frantic movements followed and then, "KEVIN BECKER!"

Momentarily forgetting the bookcase, the boys put their hands over their mouths to quiet their laughter.

The footsteps on the stairs reminded them of the bookcase dilemma. Nic grabbed a book off one of the bookcase shelves and said, "Follow my lead. Just keep standing in front of the sliding door with me."

Kevin, not knowing what else to do, did just as Nic ordered.

A woman's head popped up from the stairwell just as Kevin and Nic had taken up their positions. Nic suddenly belted out, "To be or not to be? That is the question."

Kevin looked at him as if he was crazy.

Kevin's mom stood on the top step and leaned on the banister, eyeing the boys with a mixture of anger and confusion. Kevin clearly took after her. She shared the same golden blonde hair and bright blue eyes as Kevin.

"Kevin Becker, that was NOT nice. You know how your sisters and I feel about spiders." She shivered at the memory. "I've been yelling for you to come down for dinner."

"Sorry, Mom, we couldn't hear you."

"It's my fault, Mrs. Becker. I was reading Kevin some Shakespeare," volunteered Nic, while standing next to Kevin in front of the door.

"You must be, Nicolas. I'm so glad we've finally met," she said warmly. "So, Nicolas, you were reading Shakespeare to Kevin. I must say, I'm impressed. Kevin needs more friends like you. All he ever reads are comic books about Soupman and Birdman," said Mrs. Becker.

"Mom, it's Superman and Batman," replied Kevin as Nic chuckled.

"Sorry, dear, you know I can never keep up with what you're doing." She tilted her head as she looked at the bookcase. "That's funny. I don't remember that bookcase being there before. Shouldn't it be over some?"

"Uh, Mom, I think you've been slaving over a hot stove for too long. Besides, I think dad just called you," Kevin answered quickly.

"You did? I declare, your father can't survive one minute without me directing him. Why just the other day…" said Mrs. Becker.

"Mom, you'd better get going. We'll be down in just a minute," said Kevin.

Mrs. Becker smiled and began walking down the steps. She stopped to say, "Don't forget to wash up." Then she quietly closed the door behind her.

Wiping his forehead, Kevin said, "Whew, that was close. Quick thinking, Nic, but Shakespeare?"

"It was the first thing that came to mind. Besides, it worked, didn't it?" Nic replied.

"I guess so. C'mon, let's get this bookcase back to where it belongs and hope it never does that again," said Kevin. A brief investigation revealed the bookcase had been stuck on a snag in the carpet. With the bookcase back in place, the boys washed up and headed downstairs for dinner.

Nic followed Kevin into the dining room where everyone was already seated. The dining room had a long wooden table for eight in its center with a small chandelier hanging over it. Kevin's three sisters sat on one side of the table. His parents sat at opposite ends of the table. Kevin and Nic sat across from Kevin's sisters.

"Well, Son, aren't you going to introduce us to your new friend? He seems to be all you talk about lately, since you guys won that contest at the YMCA awhile back," said Mr. Becker, an athletic looking man with thinning blonde hair and blue eyes.

Nic hated this part whenever he met someone's family. He always felt he was on display, like some animal at the zoo.

"Uh, yeah…sure, Dad. Everyone, this is Nic Nelson. Nic, this is my dad; and you've already met my mom."

Pointing across the table, he added, "Those are my sisters who treated you so rudely at the door," snickered Kevin, while they returned his glare with ones of their own.

"Kevin! Stop teasing your sisters! You have a guest in the house and will act in a dignified manner," said Mrs. Becker sharply.

"Yes, Mom," replied Kevin, meekly turning back toward his sisters and sticking his tongue out at them.

Seeing that, Nic had to stifle a chuckle with his napkin.

"As I was saying, those are my sisters: Suzanne, Shannon, and Stacy."

"Nice to meet you all, and I really appreciate you allowing me to have dinner and spend the night, Mr. and Mrs. Becker," said Nic politely.

"It's our pleasure, young man," answered Mrs. Becker. "So, I understand that your mother works at the university. What does she do?"

"She teaches medieval literature," replied Nic, placing a dinner roll on his plate, then passing the bowl along to Kevin.

"Well, that explains the Shakespeare," said Mrs. Becker.

"What does your father do?" asked Mr. Becker. At this, Kevin looked at his dad in shock while Mrs. Becker gave him 'The Look.'

Nic struggled a second for the right way to reply and finally said, "He died last year in an accident."

Mr. Becker stopped with his fork in midair. Looking at Nic intently he said, "I'm sorry to hear that. I didn't know."

"That's okay," replied Nic, suddenly remembering something he tried to forget. An awkward silence followed until Kevin, always the clown, threw a green bean at one of his sisters. He was banished from the table for a few minutes while Mrs. Becker apologized for her caveman son.

Over the next hour, Nic found out a lot about Kevin and his family. Mr. Becker worked for the local bank as vice president. Mrs. Becker was a stay-at-home mom who did a lot of charitable work in the community. Kevin's oldest sister, Suzanne, was 18 and a senior in high school. The next oldest was Shannon, who was 17 and a junior. The youngest was Stacy, who was 16 and a sophomore. All of the kids had their parents' blonde hair color; but while each had blue eyes, the sisters' varied from light to very dark. Nic noted that Kevin had the coolest eye color, a deep ocean blue.

Kevin's family on his father's side had originally come from Germany and been one of the earliest settlers to the region. Nic found this fascinating, as he had always been interested in his family history and was quite proud of his own British background.

The rest of the dinner went along well enough for Nic. Kevin almost got in trouble again when he threw tiny paper napkin spit-wads across the table at his sisters when his parents weren't looking. Kevin's sisters would retaliate by kicking Kevin underneath the table, occasionally kicking Nic by accident. Each sister left when her boyfriend arrived soon after dinner ended. Briefly helping to clear the table of dishes, Kevin and Nic finally excused themselves to put on their Halloween costumes so they would be ready when the rest of the gang arrived.

Nic had decided to dress up as an army soldier. He had on green camouflage pants and jacket with a plastic army helmet and a toy M16 machine gun.

Kevin was going as a pirate with the complete works. He had on a fluffy, white shirt with a red bandanna over his head and even had a black eye patch. He wore long, baggy pants and black army boots, which Nic wished he had on instead of his tennis shoes.

"You look awesome," praised Nic.

"Thanks. It was my idea. My mom wanted me to wear a teddy bear costume, but there was no way that was going to happen. Can you imagine? A teddy bear? Me?" said Kevin, as he swung his plastic pirate sword.

"I don't know what it is about moms, but they always want to dress you up in geek stuff," added Nic playfully aiming and firing his gun at one of Kevin's action figures.

At the sound of the doorbell, they rushed down the stairs to greet their friends. By the time Nic and Kevin had arrived in the main foyer, everyone from the gang was standing there along with Philip's mom.

"Thanks for bringing them over, Pam," said Mrs. Becker.

"No problem, Charlotte. I was unofficially elected since I'm the only one with a van who could haul all of the kids over here," laughed Mrs. Browning. "Now, does everyone have his or her things out of the van?" she asked.

A chorus of "Yes" followed. "Okay, then, I'm leaving. Don't forget, Cindy, your dad will be picking you up at 10:30 tonight," added Mrs. Browning as she kissed Philip on the forehead.

"Yes, Mrs. Browning. Thanks for the ride," replied Cindy. At this, everyone else thanked Philip's mom, too.

"C'mon, guys. Let's go upstairs and plan out our night!" said Kevin excitedly.

"I thought we were going to talk about..." began Herbert before Cindy strategically stepped on his right foot. "Ow!" yelped Herbert. as he realized he wasn't supposed to say what he was about to say.

"Sorry," replied Cindy sarcastically.

At that, everyone followed Kevin up the stairs with their sleeping bags. "Too bad you couldn't stay over, Cindy," muttered Dante.

"Yeah, why can't you stay?" asked Herbert.

"My father wants me to get a good night's rest at home for my piano recital tomorrow morning," answered Cindy.

"Bummer," said Philip.

"I didn't know you could play the piano. That sounds neat," added Nic.

"I can also play the violin and flute," added Cindy. The boys looked at Cindy with a newfound respect.

"Gee, I can't even play one instrument," said Dante, clearly impressed.

Once in Kevin's room, everyone sat on the floor in the center of the room. Nic took a second to check out everyone's costumes before they started talking. Dante was decked out as a ninja wearing all black clothes with a plastic Samurai sword attached to his waist. Philip was wearing his hockey jersey and pants with a hockey helmet on. Herbert had on a Jedi Star Wars costume with a light saber. Finally, Cindy was wearing an all-white angel costume complete with wings and a halo attached to her head.

"Nice costume," said Dante toward Kevin.

"Thanks. Hey, Philip, that's real original. You only wear that like about 30 times a year," said Kevin.

"Ha, ha. It was the best I could come up with at the last minute. You should see my youngest brother Jonathan. He got stuck being dressed up as a teddy bear by my mom," laughed Philip.

Kevin laughed uneasily.

"That's a real nice costume, Cindy," remarked Herbert.

"Thanks, but I didn't really want to dress up like this. My parents wouldn't let me go as anything else," said Cindy.

"Well, I guess we'd better talk about what everyone has learned about the Diamonds of Denmark now instead of later, since Cindy has to leave," said Kevin. Cindy and Herbert volunteered to share their information first.

Cindy began handing out sheets of paper as Herbert explained. "Cindy and I went to several different websites and downloaded the best information. We thought it would be easier to explain if you each had a copy. Everyone should be able to follow along as I read the main information. The Diamonds of Denmark go back to 1866. They were given as a wedding present from King Christian IX and Queen Louise of Denmark to their daughter and Czar Prince Alexander III of Russia."

"What's a Czar?" asked Dante.

"Maybe it's Zorro's twin brother," joked Kevin.

"A Czar was what the Russian leader was called until early in the 20th century when they were overthrown by the Russian people who were tired of fighting WWI," said Nic.

"You know, Nic, sometimes you really scare me," added Kevin.

"We ought to call you Mr. History from now on," said Philip.

Herbert cleared his throat to regain their attention. "The diamonds were part of a two-piece set: a necklace and a crown, which their daughter, Princess Marie, wore at her wedding.

"How romantic it must have been for her. The gorgeous white dress and veil she must have been wearing. Flowers spread out where she walked down the aisle with her father about to give her away to a handsome prince," said Cindy with a dreamy look on her face.

The boys all rolled their eyes as Kevin remarked, "I feel sorry for the poor prince. He must have done something real bad for his parents to make him have to get married."

"Oh, don't be silly. He loved her," replied Cindy.

"No guy is crazy enough to be tortured like that," added Nic.

Cindy just looked at the others and threw up her hands saying, "Boys!"

"Just like Nic said earlier, when the Czars were overthrown years later, the diamonds disappeared until twenty years ago, when the Russian government allowed them to go on display in the United States as a goodwill gesture. When the exhibit reached Chicago, they were on display in the art museum. Then, the day before the diamonds were to be transferred to New York, someone stole them. The thief was captured here, in the Midwest, in our very own New Bonn, after four days of an intense nationwide manhunt.

"The thief, Michael Marinovich, had a long record of clashes with the law. When he was captured, the diamonds weren't on him; and even after extensive searches around town and in Chicago, they were never found. Mr. Marinovich died a few years ago from heart problems. He never told the police where the diamonds were hidden. In fact, he was still insisting he was an innocent bystander to a government conspiracy," finished Herbert.

"That's what they all say," said Dante.

"Good work, Herbert. Now move over and let me and Dante blow your minds. Well, not really. In fact, we found out pretty much the same stuff from the old issues of the New Bonn Gazette as you and Cindy, with a few additional twists," said Kevin.

"Yeah, remember when Mr. O'Malley mentioned about the thief having a brother? It's true, and it seems he wasn't shy talking to the newspapers about his brother, Michael. His name was Roger Marinovich, just like Mr. O'Malley had said it was," said Dante.

"He claimed that his brother was innocent and should be released immediately. He even stayed in town for a few days after his brother was captured trying to plead his brother's case," added Kevin.

"It sure sounds like he really believed in his brother's innocence," said Philip.

"Or, he was just staying around to get the diamonds, but realized it was too dangerous for him to do that. The papers mentioned how the police and the FBI believed he knew where the diamonds were, so I'm sure they probably had him under constant surveillance," said Kevin.

"Now hang onto your hats, 'cause we made a copy of a picture of Roger Marinovich at a press conference and guess who he looks like?" asked Dante, as he passed out copies of the picture. Everyone gasped.

Kevin said, "That's right…Detective Johnson!"

"That's scary," said Philip.

"Look in the background. There's another man off to the side. He looks familiar too," added Cindy, pointing at the picture.

"You're right, Cindy. That's Detective Walker," said Nic.

"That's wild," said Dante.

"Well, I guess that just leaves me and Philip left to add to the story. Unfortunately, we didn't find out as much as what you guys did," said Nic.

"We did learn not to go to Easy Ed's barbershop for answers to anything unless you want to be attacked by a bunch of old geezers," chuckled Philip.

"Seriously, all we found out was Mr. Marinovich was captured by the police in the Chamberlains' backyard without the diamonds," said Nic as he reached into his jacket pocket. "This is a picture taken by Captain Spencer in the early morning when the police were taking Michael Marinovich away from the backyard."

"Not much here to look at except for a bunch of trees and people everywhere," said Kevin.

"That's what bothers me. We're not seeing something, but I'm not sure what," mumbled Nic.

"Well, did Captain Spencer say when he needs his picture back?" asked Cindy. Nic shook his head.

"Then keep it for a while, and maybe you'll figure it out," said Cindy. Nic nodded stuffing the picture back into his jacket pocket.

"Has anyone seen the detectives since the day we raked the Chamberlains' backyard?" asked Kevin.

Nobody had.

"Are we going to tell the police what we know?" asked Herbert.

There were a few seconds of silence before Cindy said, "Tell them what? We still don't have any hard proof that Detective Johnson really is Roger Marinovich. It sure looks like him in the newspaper photo, but that was taken twenty years ago. Even if he is Roger Marinovich, he hasn't broken any laws yet except for maybe impersonating an officer, and it would be his word against a bunch of kids. Now who do you think the police are going to believe?"

"Cindy's right. We'll just have to lay low for now and keep our eyes open. If something starts to happen, then we can always try the police," remarked Kevin.

"Shouldn't we at least tell the Chamberlains?" asked Herbert.

Everyone looked at Herbert as if he was crazy.

"Now how do you suppose Mrs. Chamberlain would react?" asked Kevin in exasperation.

Herbert just shrugged his shoulders.

"It's safe to say we won't be telling the Chamberlains anything. At least not yet, *right*?" Kevin more stated than asked, standing almost nose-to-nose with Herbert.

Wide-eyed, Herbert slowly nodded. Kevin slapped Herbert on the back and stated, "Good!"

Mrs. Becker's voice suddenly rang out from the bottom of the stairs leading to Kevin's room, "Kids, shouldn't you be leaving now?"

Kevin quickly shouted back, "We're coming, Mom!" Standing up he added, "Well guys, I guess we're through for now about this diamond mystery. Just remember, keep your eyes open."

They rushed down the stairs and onto the waiting Halloween streets.

CHAPTER SIX

The Prank

Once on the sidewalk and out of earshot of his mom, Kevin rubbed his hands together and smiled his best evil grin. "Now, where to start," he mused.

They decided to go left and wind through the streets nearby. By the time they were finished, they would have covered quite a bit of New Bonn.

Nic could hardly wait. This was the first time he would be going with a group of kids, and he was excited!

Dante told Nic that the first block was known as the Street of Sweets, because the people on that block gave out more candy than any other street or neighborhood. Even kids from other towns would come to this street for trick-or-treating. Kevin added he thought they gave out so much candy in order to bribe the kids, because no house on that street was ever TP'd. Nic was shocked at the number of kids walking the Street of Sweets. He was even more shocked at the amount of candy he collected in just a few minutes…more than he'd gotten during a whole night's worth of trick-or-treating before. They each collected so much that the gang had to go back to Kevin's house to drop off their bags and pick up new ones.

Eventually, they made their way over to Nic's part of town. The first stop would be the O'Malley's house.

Nic dutifully rang the doorbell, and it let out a loud Ding Dong! The gang stepped back, waiting anxiously. Within a few seconds, Mr. O'Malley opened the door. He did not look happy as he stood there rubbing his eyes.

"Now really, what's the meaning of constantly ringing the doorbell? I was having a perfectly good snooze," bellowed Mr. O'Malley.

"Trick-or-treat?" said Nic meekly.

Just then, Mrs. O'Malley appeared and said, "Now calm down, Connor. Don't you remember what tonight is? It's Halloween, and kids are going to be coming to our house all night looking for candy."

"They shouldn't be. I worked hard all of my life, and I don't see why I should give out something free to kids who need to be working and earning their own money to buy their own candy," snapped Mr. O'Malley, storming back into the house.

"Don't mind him, kids, he's just grouchy from staying up late last night playing bingo," soothed Mrs. O'Malley as she handed out candy.

Nic thought how Mr. O'Malley probably was the only person who never was a kid. He had been born as an old man.

"I love your costumes, children. Oh, that angel costume is so cute, dear; and Nic, you must tell your mom that you two must come over soon for dinner," said Mrs. O'Malley.

"I will, and thanks for the candy, Mrs. O'Malley!"

The next stop was Nic's house. When Nic's mom opened the door, everyone yelled, "Trick-or-Treat, smell my feet or give me something good to eat!"

She just laughed and invited them inside. "I was wondering when you guys would be making your way over to here," she said as she placed a bowl of candy down for everyone.

"I didn't know you had this much candy in the house. Where was it hidden?" asked Nic.

"Ah, Nicolas, there are some secrets that must be kept. If I had told you earlier, there wouldn't have been any left for Halloween," she chuckled.

Nic smiled and thought to himself that she was probably right. With a quick round of thanks, the gang went back out into the night air. Nic led the way as they walked toward the Chamberlains' house.

Before reaching the door, Philip piped up, "Are you sure we should even try the Chamberlains'?"

"We might as well now. We're here, aren't we?" Cindy answered peevishly. With nervous glances all around, Nic stepped up to ring the doorbell. Bing Bong!

Philip leaned over to whisper, "That doorbell sounds different every time we come here. I bet this house is haunted!"

"Don't be silly. They probably had it worked on," replied Nic, feeling less brave than he sounded.

They were blinded for a moment as someone turned on the bright outside lights. The front door swung open to reveal Captain Spencer holding a silver tray. He looked slightly amused at the costumed visitors. The gang mustered a weak "Trick-or-treat…" then held their breaths as they waited for his reaction.

"Hello, young masters. Quite a clever costume you have on there, Master Kevin. Your costume does bring back some memories for me, Master Nicolas. Very appropriate costume for you, Lady Cindy. Masters Philip, Dante, and Herbert, I am impressed," stated Captain Spencer.

"Really?" asked Herbert.

"Really," replied Captain Spencer. "You children are the first to come to the house tonight or, for that matter, in a number of years," remarked Captain Spencer.

"Maybe if you keep the porch lights on, kids will know that someone is home to give treats," said Nic, trying to cheer up Captain Spencer.

"Oh, no. I would not be able to do that. Mrs. Chamberlain would insist it is a waste of electricity," replied Captain Spencer.

"Old skinflint," whispered Kevin to Nic.

"I do hope these will do for you," said Captain Spencer, bending down slightly and lowering his silver tray, which was filled with candy.

"I think we'll somehow manage," Dante said with a smile. Everyone chose several pieces, careful to leave a few behind just in case someone else decided to stop by.

"Thanks again, Captain Spencer," said Nic.

"You da man," said Kevin.

"You have been very kind," said Cindy.

"Thanks," said Philip and Herbert in unison.

Bowing slightly as he stepped back, Captain Spencer finished with, "Good luck and Godspeed."

Walking down the driveway, Nic bumped Philip on the arm saying, "See, nothing bad happened, Philip. Now aren't you glad we went to the Chamberlains' house?"

"Sure I am. I don't have a problem with Captain Spencer. It's the other people in the house that I don't care for," replied Philip.

"Hey, guys," muttered Kevin looking at his watch. "We'd better get going back to my house to meet Jason or else he may leave without us."

Walking quickly, they made it back to Kevin's house just in time to see Jason pulling up in the driveway.

"How's the candy business going?" Jason asked, getting out of his car.

"Great," was the universal reply.

Nic added, "This is the most candy I've ever received in my entire life."

"So, I see you've been to the Street of Sweets?"

"Oh, yeah," answered Nic nodding vigorously.

"That was always my favorite hangout on Halloween. In fact, I use to change my costume a couple of times just so I could return and get more candy from that area," mused Jason.

"Why didn't you ever tell me this before? That sounds like a great idea." Kevin said admiringly, while attempting to act hurt at the same time.

"I didn't want to reveal all of my trade secrets to you. Besides, I figured a big troublemaker like you would've already done it by now," laughed Jason as he patted Kevin on the shoulder.

"Enough talk. Everybody get inside and change your clothes. We don't have all night to pull this prank off," added Jason.

When everyone was done changing, they met in the living room where Jason and Kevin's mom were waiting. Everybody was buzzing excitedly in anticipation, except for Dante, who was mumbling, "This is going to be crazy! I've got to be crazy! We're all crazy!"

Mrs. Becker said, "Now do be careful with the kids, Jason."

"Don't worry, I will. In fact, I'll make sure your baby comes back in one piece," laughed Jason. He playfully squeezed Kevin's cheeks. Kevin slapped away his hands.

Nic noticed Mrs. Becker was still staring at Jason with her hands on her hips.

At this, Jason spoke playfully, "C'mon, you know me. I'm almost part of the family."

"That's what worries me," replied Mrs. Becker before smiling.

"Okay, guys, let's load up. I know when I'm not wanted anymore," said Jason.

Once outside, Philip yelled, "I got shotgun!"

"No way! You had it last time," complained Herbert.

"You know the rules. Once outside, whoever calls shotgun first wins; and I called it first," argued Philip.

"No arguing, guys. Herbert, you can have shotgun on the way back, if you survive," Jason said ominously.

"Wha...what's that supposed to mean?" stammered Herbert, as Philip and Dante's eyes widened.

"Don't listen to him, guys. He's just pulling your legs," said Kevin.

"Maybe and maybe not," laughed Jason.

"Cut that out!" said Philip sitting down beside Jason. With everyone inside, Jason roared the car to life, speeding off toward the prank adventure.

"I want everyone to stay in the car when we get to Dr. Jones' house," Jason ordered.

"Yes Sir!" Kevin said matter-of-factly.

Dr. Jones' house was on a corner lot, so Jason parked the car on the side street instead of in front of the house. He turned around to face the gang. "Okay, guys, this is how it's going to work. I'm going to get myself invited into Dr. Jones' house. While I'm distracting him and his wife, you guys are going to take the plastic skeleton I have in the trunk and place it on the front porch. I think I can give you a good twenty minutes to pull it off before I'll excuse myself to leave. I'll then meet you back here at the car. Got it?"

Everyone nodded.

"Which house is your teacher's?" asked Dante.

"The one next to us," pointed Jason. "I purposely parked on the side of his house so he wouldn't spot you guys. You also have a pretty good side view of their front porch, so you'll know when I go inside."

"Jason, are you sure Dr. Jones won't be mad at us for pulling this joke on him?" asked Cindy.

"It's cool. Trust me," replied Jason with a smile.

Jason quietly got out of his car and opened his trunk. With a grunt, he lifted out a large plastic skeleton that was wearing an old tattered jacket along with a hat, blue jeans, and worn out tennis shoes. He laid it gently on the ground next to some bushes in the yard.

Motioning to Nic to roll down his window, Jason whispered, "There ya go. Be careful and good luck!"

He walked up to Dr. Jones' front door and knocked loudly. The gang watched silently as Jason shook someone's hand and walked inside.

Nic waited a few more seconds before opening his door. He more fell out of the car than walked, having gotten his feet tangled with Kevin's. Kevin and Dante landed next to him.

"That was real smooth, guys," quipped Cindy as she stepped over them. Nic ignored her, rubbing his head as he got up.

"What now?" asked Herbert.

"However we're going to do what we're going to do, we'd better do it now before it's too late," said Nic in a hurried voice.

Everyone looked at Kevin. "Don't look at me for answers on this one. I can't think of everything."

Nic decided to take charge. "Herbert, I want you to stay here and be on the lookout for any cars that come this way."

"What should I do if I see one?"

"Whistle or hoot like an owl real loud," answered Nic.

"Cindy, I want you to do the same on the other side of the house," said Nic.

"Okay, but I refuse to act like an owl."

"Philip, Kevin, and Dante, I need you guys to help me carry this skeleton up to the front porch. Is everybody with me?" asked Nic. Everyone nodded. "Okay, let's roll!"

As Herbert and Cindy took their positions, Nic, Kevin, Philip, and Dante picked up the skeleton. Philip and Dante each held an arm; Kevin and Nic each held a leg.

"Man, this skeleton is a lot heavier than I thought it would be," complained Dante as the boys made their way forward on the sidewalk next to Jason's parked car.

"Ow! Watch where you're stepping, Nic," said Kevin.

"Sorry, but it's kind of hard to see where you're going in the dark carrying a skeleton. It's not like I do this all of the time," replied Nic.

Just as they reached the walkway leading up to the front porch, a car came around the corner. Caught in the bright car lights, the boys had nowhere to run. They froze in their tracks, not knowing what else to do. Why didn't Herbert whistle, Nic wondered. The car came to a stop on the other side of the street from the boys. They each glanced over quickly and were dismayed to recognize it as one of the New Bonn police cars.

"Maybe he didn't see us," Dante whispered hopefully.

The car door opened, and a New Bonn police officer emerged.

Philip groaned, "We are so busted."

"Hello, boys. Having a fun night trick-or-treating?" asked the officer as he approached them.

Nic and Kevin answered, "Yes sir," while Philip and Dante were too petrified to say anything. Nic could tell the officer had a puzzled look on his face staring at the skeleton. The ball cap on its head hid the face from view. Scanning the boys, the officer stopped at Kevin's face and smiled.

"So, Mr. Becker, we meet again. How are we doing tonight?" the officer asked.

Kevin smiled back and replied quite cheerily, "Just dandy, Officer Williams. It's nice to see you, too, on such a lovely Halloween night."

Officer Williams chuckled slightly and continued, "Who are your friends, Mr. Becker?"

Using his head as a pointer, Kevin replied, "This is Nic Nelson, Philip Browning, Dante Brown, and Billy Bob Jones."

Nic had to stifle a laugh after hearing Kevin call the skeleton Billy Bob Jones.

Becoming more serious, Officer Williams said, "You boys should know that the curfew is now in effect for kids 16 and under. I'm sure you know this, Mr. Becker, as many times as I've taken you home."

Nic wasn't sure what they were going to do. They couldn't tell the officer about Jason being with them without possibly compromising his joke, but if they didn't say something, they could all be heading to jail in a few minutes.

Kevin responded, "You're right, Officer Williams, about our being past curfew, but we have a very good reason for it."

Officer Williams stepped back and crossed his arms over his chest muttering, "I can hardly wait to hear what it's going to be this time."

"You see, it's like this. My friends here were helping me find Billy Bob, because we had somehow got separated earlier this evening," said Kevin. "We just found him a few minutes ago and were heading back home."

"I assume you won't mind if I ask Billy Bob to corroborate your story then?" asked Officer Williams with a smile.

"Not at all," answered Kevin nervously, while wiping his forehead.

Before Officer Williams could begin asking Billy Bob any questions, Nic spoke up. "Officer Williams, I don't think you're going to get very far with Billy Bob."

"And why do you say that?"

"Well, Billy Bob is on a couple of different kinds of medication right now," said Nic.

"What does that have to do with me asking him some questions?" asked Officer Williams, sounding irritated.

"The medications he's taking sometimes make him woozy and sleepy. That's the reason we think he was separated from our group tonight and why I don't think he's really up to answering any questions. Heck, I don't even think he knows who we are, let alone you," said Nic straight-faced.

Officer Williams started to rub his chin with one hand as he began contemplating Nic's story.

"Why aren't any adults with you to look for him, as well? I assume Billy Bob has parents," challenged Officer Williams.

"Yes, well, you see, we haven't told Billy Bob's parents yet. We didn't want to get them worried until we at least attempted to find him ourselves," replied Nic. "We know it was wrong of us to do it this way, and I promise we won't do it again without telling an adult first."

Officer Williams rubbed his chin again and responded, "Okay, kids, I'll give you a break this time since you're helping a friend in need, but don't let it happen again."

They all nodded in agreement.

"Do you kids need a lift for Billy Bob?"

"No, we'll be fine. We're almost to his house," answered Nic.

Officer Williams nodded while looking down the street. For a moment, Nic was concerned he was going to escort them to Billy Bob's house. A crackle on his car radio caught his attention.

"Officer Williams?" the voice on the radio asked.

He looked back at the boys saying, "All right, take care of Billy Bob, and then get home. I don't want to catch you out later tonight. Understand?"

The boys nodded again.

"Thank you, Officer Williams," Nic said a bit too cheerfully.

Officer Williams jumped into his car, answered the radio call, and pulled away from the curb.

"Awesome story, Nic," admired Kevin.

Dante said, "I thought we were going to get it, for sure."

Philip added, "Boy, that was too close."

"We're not out of the woods yet. We've lost a lot of time and really need to get moving on this prank," Nic said as he began leading everyone toward the front porch.

"The prank! I almost forgot," said Kevin, slapping his forehead.

As they got closer to the front porch, Nic noted a thick row of bushes planted next to the house. On the porch, he spied two rocking chairs facing the street with a tiny table and an overhanging plant in between them. Directly behind the chairs was a large window with the curtains open. Nic had a clear view of the living room, which also meant the people in the living room would have a clear view of the front porch.

Reaching the porch stairs, the boys looked at each other one last time knowing there was no turning back. With a slight nod to Kevin, they started up the stairs.

They took their time walking up the six steps. On the fifth step, a loud "CREAK!" sounded under Nic's right foot. Everyone froze. Nic closed his eyes and sucked in his breath. After a few seconds, he opened his eyes and looked around.

Dante, Kevin, and Philip all had their eyes squeezed shut. It appeared none of them was breathing.

"It's okay, guys. Let's go," whispered Nic.

Once at the top, the boys crouched as low to the floor as possible as they moved toward the rocking chairs. Nic poked his head up to peek inside the living room. Jason was sitting with two older men. They were drinking and talking.

"What's going on in there?" asked Philip nervously.

"Nothing much from what I can tell. It seems they're just talking," answered Nic in a whisper.

"What now? Where are we going to put this skeleton?" asked Dante.

"Let's put it in one of the rocking chairs," said Kevin. They repositioned themselves and sat the skeleton on the rocking chair farthest away from the front door.

After taking a few seconds to admire their handiwork, Philip whispered, "Okay, we're done. Now let's get out of here before we're caught."

"Are you kidding me? We just pulled this off. We are so awesome," bragged Kevin, backing up while still crouched low. Too busy being clever, he didn't look where he was going and tripped over the other rocking chair. He fell backwards with a loud thud.

"Nice move, bonehead," said Dante, as the boys all looked at each other.

Their cover was blown.

Philip cried out, "Let's get out of here!" dashing by Dante, Nic, and Kevin.

"Every man for himself!" yelled Dante, as he, too, made a mad dash for the sidewalk.

"My pants…they're stuck on this stupid rocking chair," said Kevin, pulling on his pant leg.

Nic could hear footsteps walking toward the door inside as he helped Kevin unhook his pants.

"Let's get out of here!" yelled Kevin as he jumped off the porch and hid behind the bushes.

Nic heard the doorknob turning. In a panic, he lost his footing and tripped over the same rocking chair.

THUD! Nic saw stars as his face smacked the front porch floor. He groaned as he struggled to sit up. He figured whoever was at the door was taking in the strange sight of him on the floor. He closed his eyes and whispered a silent prayer, asking to survive the trouble he was about to be in.

A worried voice rang out, "Are you all right, young man?"

Nic looked up to see one of the older men he'd watched earlier standing almost on top of him.

"Yes, sir, I'm fine," replied Nic as politely as possible. He realized one side of his face hurt.

The man stretched out his hand and said, "Let me help you up. These old rocking chairs do have a way of being where they shouldn't." Once on his feet, the man looked Nic over and then took a step back and said, "What brings you here? I thought trick-or-treating was officially over for the night."

Nic was too stunned to answer.

"Of course, let me introduce myself. My name is Dr. Jones," he said while extending his hand. Nic put his hand out and weakly shook Dr. Jones' hand.

"Nice to meet you, sir. My name is Nic Nelson."

Just as Dr. Jones was about to ask another question, his eyes looked over Nic's shoulder. He slowly walked past Nic toward the rocking chair with Billy Bob in it.

Dr. Jones began to laugh, "Well, isn't this funny? This took a lot of courage and daring. I assume you're the responsible party, Nic?"

Jason's voice came from the doorway. "I'm afraid I have to take the brunt of the credit or blame, Dr. J. I thought it would be fun to put a skeleton on your front porch on Halloween as a prank," he continued.

"It figures you would somehow be involved," chuckled Dr. Jones.

"It's also pretty ironic that Jason would be putting up a skeleton on the porch of an anatomy professor's house," laughed the other man, who was now standing next to Jason.

"I thought so, Dr. Stevens," laughed Jason.

"I hate to think how much you must've corrupted this poor kid to have him pull a stunt like this for you, Jason," Dr. Jones chuckled as he patted Nic on the back.

As the rest of the gang appeared out of the darkness, Kevin asked, "Does this mean it's safe to come out?"

"Goodness gracious! You mean to tell me that all of these kids were involved in your little prank, Jason?" asked Dr. Jones.

"Afraid so, Dr. J.," laughed Jason.

"With a role model like you, I'll hate to see what kind of citizens these kids are going to grow up to become," replied Dr. Jones, shaking his head.

"Jason, you've outdone yourself. You're the first student to pull a prank like this," stated Dr. Jones. "Now, how to 'reward' you for this…." he added.

Jason's eyes grew wide, "Uh, Dr. Jones, it was meant as harmless fun."

Dr. Jones couldn't hold in his laughter any longer. "I'm just giving you a hard time, Jason. You got me. I owe you one. Now, this old professor needs to be heading to bed," he added, yawning.

"It was very nice to meet you, Dr. Jones," said Nic. The others nodded and expressed their thanks for his not being mad at them.

"Goodnight, kids!" he responded cheerfully.

Walking toward the car, Dante asked Herbert, "Why didn't you whistle or something before that police car stopped in front of the house?"

"What car?" Herbert asked.

"What car? The one that almost got us hauled to jail," replied Kevin.

"Honestly guys, I never saw a car or anything unless…" said Herbert.

"Unless what?" asked Philip.

"Unless it drove by when I was cleaning my glasses. They were fogged up, so I took them off to clean them," answered Herbert.

Kevin looked like he was going to strangle Herbert. Instead, he laughed and said, "Only you, Herbert. Only you."

On the ride back to Kevin's house, everyone was talking at once explaining his or her version of events to Jason. Jason was getting frustrated with trying to make sense out of what he was hearing. He stopped the car in front of Kevin's house with a short screech of the tires, then shouted, "Quiet!"

The air was thick with the sudden silence.

"Now that I have everybody's undivided attention, why don't we go up to Kevin's room? Then you can each tell me what happened *one at a time*."

Jumping out of the car, Kevin turned to face his friends. Hitting his hand on his forehead, he said, "Do you remember what tonight is?" They looked at him dumbly. "It's HALLOWEEN!" he cried.

"Kevin, that's really not news. We all knew that," Jason responded. "All the excitement tonight must have messed with your brain."

Kevin gave Jason a withering look. "Fine. You don't get any of my candy," he said squinting at Jason.

"Candy!" the others yelled, running toward the front door and leaving a stunned Kevin to bring up the rear. They each made a mad dash for their candy bags before sprinting up the three flights of stairs to Kevin's room. Jason shrugged his shoulders and smiled as Mrs. Becker commented that the kids sounded like a herd of cattle running through the house.

For a few minutes, the only sound in Kevin's room was the ripping of candy wrappers and the munching of sweet treats. Herbert tried to steal a candy bar from Cindy's pile. She gave his hand a loud slap.

Mrs. Becker and Jason appeared with glasses of milk. "I assumed you'd be thirsty after all your candy gorging and pranking," she explained.

With their mouths full, the best any of them could do was say, "Mph phoo," as she was leaving.

Jason rubbed his hands together making himself comfortable on the floor. "All right, all right. Who's going to talk first?" he asked while eyeing Kevin's candy haul. Kevin used his forearm to pull his candy closer to him.

"I'll start!" Dante volunteered.

They each entertained Jason and the others with their stories of what had happened at Dr. Jones' house during the prank.

While Nic was laughing about Herbert claiming he saw Bigfoot in the bushes during the prank attempt, the doorbell rang and soon after Mrs. Becker shouted, "Cindy, it's your dad. It's time to go!"

"Coming," Cindy replied as she got up to leave.

"Thanks for coming over, Cindy," quipped Kevin.

"Wait up, Cindy, I'll go with you. I've got to be leaving anyway," said Jason, snatching some more candy from Kevin's pile.

"Hey!" Kevin protested.

"Snooze you lose, Dude," Jason retorted, following Cindy down the steps.

"Catch you guys later, and thanks for helping me out with my prank," he added as he closed the door.

The boys gathered up the empty candy wrappers and stuffed them into Kevin's trashcan. Kevin brought out a board game to play, but it wasn't long before Dante nodded off…then Philip…then Kevin.

Only Nic was awake — and thinking. *I feel awful lying to Officer Williams. I have to do something.* He sighed and then smiled as he formed an idea.

"Yeah, that's it," he said aloud to no one. Kevin mumbled and rolled over. Nic settled deeper into his sleeping bag and was soon fast asleep.

CHAPTER SEVEN

The Apology

N ic was worn out from the excitement on Halloween, so the rest of the weekend he slept, hung out at home, and did his homework. Before he knew it, it was Monday again. He was still feeling giddy from his action packed weekend, but he knew he had an important piece of business to take care of at the police station. He was going to see Officer Williams after school and tell him the truth.

Nic jumped on his bike and headed for the police station downtown as soon as school ended. He took the long way, so he had time to think about what he was going to say. He put his bike on the station bike rack and locked it securely. Now this seems silly, he thought. Who would steal a bike in front of a police station? He turned to walk into the station and ran into Johnny, who had quietly come up behind him. The *J Gang* hung back menacingly.

"Well, guys, look who we have here. If it ain't the geek," said Johnny as he poked Nic in the chest. "What are you doing here? No, wait, let me guess. A mama's boy like you got teased by some nerd, and you're here to snitch on him," laughed Johnny along with his gang.

Nic looked firmly at Johnny and replied, "Well, at least I didn't just get out of jail for being more stupid than is legally permitted." Johnny and his gang quit laughing and began to surround Nic.

Nic braced himself for the worst, unsure of how he would survive this encounter. Just then, a voice rang out, "We wouldn't be about to have a fight now, would we boys?" Turning toward the voice, Nic was relieved to see Officer Williams.

"No, officer. We were just goofing around," replied Johnny.

"Is that right?" Officer Williams asked Nic.

"Yeah, I guess," he replied.

"Well, then, I suggest everyone continue on their merry way," said Officer Williams, looking directly at Johnny.

Brushing by Nic's shoulder, Johnny whispered, "One day your luck's gonna run out. It's not over yet between you and me." Nic just stared back at Johnny as he led his gang down the sidewalk.

"It's Nic, isn't it?" asked Officer Williams.

"Yes, sir, it is."

"Don't you need to be getting somewhere, son?" Officer Williams asked.

"Well, sir, I actually came to talk to you," said Nic while clearing a lump in his throat.

"Whatever for? Did Billy Bob get lost again?" smiled Officer Williams.

"No. That's what I wanted to talk to you about. You see…Billy Bob doesn't exist. That was the name Kevin gave to the plastic skeleton we put on Dr. Jones' porch as a joke on Halloween," answered Nic.

Officer Williams remained quiet as he listened to Nic intently.

Swallowing hard again, Nic added, "I'm sorry I lied to you about it; and if anyone deserves to be punished, it's me."

A few seconds passed before Officer Williams spoke. "You know, it takes a mighty big man to admit he's done something wrong, and for that I respect you. I wish other kids in this town would be as honest in admitting their faults." He nodded his head in the direction of where Johnny had gone.

"Besides, I've known the Becker family for a long time; and I know how goofy Kevin can be. I knew you boys were up to something, but duty called so I couldn't stay to figure it out." He added, "We're cool, Nic, but in the future just be up front with me and tell the truth, okay?"

Relieved that Officer Williams wasn't mad at him, Nic nodded saying, "Okay!"

When he got back on his bike, he felt like a ton of bricks had just been lifted off his shoulders. Nic thought, this must be what they mean by that old saying — *The truth will set you free.*

CHAPTER EIGHT

Johnny's Challenge

November came and went quickly. No one had seen the mysterious Roger Marinovich or his weird partner again; and much to Nic's delight, Johnny had been lying low since the conversation with Officer Williams.

Nic had not been looking forward to his first Thanksgiving without his dad. He and his mom spent the holiday with her parents, his grandparents. Nic loved them, but felt like they were trying to make up for the loss of his dad during his visit. He appreciated their efforts, but they only made things more awkward. He was happy to return home. There he spent the rest of the Thanksgiving holiday reading books and visiting Kevin to goof around more in his hidden room.

December brought the anticipation of Christmas break, which made the school days seem even slower than usual. On the last day of school, Kevin told Nic about Crazy Man's Hill while waiting for his mom to pick them up after school.

"Is everybody going to be around town for the holidays?" asked Kevin excitedly.

All the boys and Cindy nodded; and Nic asked, "What's up?"

"Nic, you just have to come with the rest of us to Crazy Man's Hill for sledding if it snows by Christmas," said Kevin.

"It's so much fun," added Herbert.

"Yeah, we build ramps and everything," said Dante.

"It's the place to be if you're a kid and there's snow on the ground," Cindy stated.

"Crazy Man's Hill?" asked Nic.

They laughed while Philip explained, "It's called that because it's so big, and you have to be a little crazy to go down it."

"I guess I can try it," remarked Nic hesitantly, not sure if that was really such a wise thing to say.

"Great. It's settled then. We'll all meet at Crazy Man's Hill the day after Christmas," said Kevin.

"What happens if it doesn't snow by then?" asked Nic curiously, as he and Kevin waved goodbye to the others before climbing into the car.

"It will. I just know it," replied Kevin.

Nic scratched his chin and half-expected Kevin to brag he had a remote in his pocket to control the weather, as well.

It didn't take long for Kevin's prediction to come true. A snowstorm rolled through just in time for Christmas Day. Actually, that was an understatement. A blizzard hit New Bonn, leaving behind a record snowfall.

The next day, Nic found himself slowly dragging his sled behind him as he trudged through the blindingly white snow trying not to sink too deeply in any one spot.

He thought about the day before when he and his mom spent Christmas Day with the O'Malley family. There they'd eaten a delicious Christmas meal with turkey and dressing and the whole works. He would never tell his mom that Mrs. O'Malley was a better cook, but facts were facts. He had even been entertained by stories told by Mr. O'Malley about his boyhood. Nic was happy to learn Mr. O'Malley hadn't been born as an old man like he'd thought.

Mr. and Mrs. O'Malley's son, daughter-in-law, and 10-year-old granddaughter were there, too. Their son, Andrew, was a diplomat for the government who told interesting stories about his travels abroad. Nic felt sorry for Mr. and Mrs. O'Malley, because their son rarely visited because of his job.

Nic reached the place he'd been told the gang usually meets on Crazy Man's Hill. He gasped in amazement as he took in the view. Before him was the largest hill he had ever seen. It was covered with what looked to be hundreds of kids running all around with sleds and saucers plowing through the snow. Nic immediately understood why it was called Crazy Man's Hill. Nic wondered how he was supposed to find Kevin and the others. He was overwhelmed with all of the chaos.

Nic heard a familiar yell. Looking up the hill, he found himself in the path of a sled ridden by Herbert and Philip.

"Look out below!" yelled Herbert. Philip had his hands over his eyes. Not caring where he ended up, Nic hugged his sled and dove to one side, as Herbert and Philip swooshed past him. Nic chuckled, watching Herbert and Philip end up buried in a large snow pile.

Getting up, Nic saw Kevin, Dante, and Cindy running down the hill to pull Herbert and Philip out of the snow bank. Running past Nic, Dante said, "Glad you could make it, Nic."

Walking past, Cindy insisted, "Don't just stand there. Help us out with Herbert and Philip."

"Nice to see you, too," mumbled Nic, as he followed the others down the hill.

"Are we dead?" stammered Philip, spitting out snow from his mouth while Dante and Kevin were tugging on him.

"I'm blind!" said Herbert, whose face was covered in snow.

"Don't be silly. You just need to wipe off the snow from your face," stated Cindy, who was attempting to free Herbert by herself, but failing to budge him. Once Philip was free, everyone worked together to pull Herbert out of the snow bank.

"That was so cool," shouted Herbert, who was glad that his blindness had been temporary.

"Next time, Herbert, I'm driving. You almost got us and Nic killed," chuckled Philip.

"Sorry about the close call, Nic. Great reflexes, though," added Herbert.

"C'mon guys, let's get this show on the road. It ain't going to be daylight forever," said Kevin.

As the gang trudged back up the hill, Kevin said, "You haven't missed much, Nic. That was our first go around. By the way, what did you get for Christmas?"

Nic smiled and replied, "Money, some Star Wars figures, and clothes."

"That sounds awesome, except for the clothes part," said Kevin.

"Yeah, I got clothes, too. What is it about parents, especially moms, giving out clothes as presents? I'll take a bike or video game any time over clothes," said Philip.

Dante and Herbert looked at each other and said at the same time, in a disappointed tone, "I got clothes, too."

"Well, for your information, I got clothes mostly; and I'm happy with them. I don't understand why you guys don't like clothes." mused Cindy.

"What can you do with clothes? At least with Star Wars figures, bikes, and baseball or football cards you can play with them or trade them for other things," argued Kevin.

"Who wants to collect grubby old baseball cards? With clothes, you can dress to impress others and give the appearance of being halfway educated and proper. Haven't you guys ever heard of the saying, 'Dress for Success?'" asked Cindy.

"Baseball cards aren't grubby; and for your information, collecting and trading baseball cards is a multimillion-dollar business," retorted Philip.

"That's probably because so many misguided boys like you are ripped off by others," rebuffed Cindy, rolling her eyes.

Sensing things getting out of control, Nic mentioned, "Whose sled is this?"

"It's mine," answered Dante.

"Don't the rest of you guys have sleds?" asked Nic.

"Mine broke last year, and I haven't really thought about asking for a new one from my parents yet," answered Philip.

"My sister, Shannon, ran over mine this morning as she was backing her car out of the garage. I couldn't believe it. I'm still mad. My sled and I have been through a lot together over the years," said an exasperated Kevin.

"I forgot to bring mine with me, and I didn't want to go back home to get it. With all this snow, it would take me forever to go back and forth from my house," said Herbert with a sigh.

Nic waited for a few seconds before looking at Cindy, who shrugged her shoulders admitting, "I don't have a sled."

"Why not?"

"My parents don't feel I should be wasting my time in pursuits that are unladylike, and they consider sledding one of those things," answered Cindy matter-of-factly.

Nic considered going deeper into this, but thought it wiser to hold off for another day.

"Here's our starting point, Nic," proclaimed Kevin, opening his arms wide.

"It's my turn to go and Dante's," declared Cindy.

"Why don't you guys race me and Nic down the hill?" Kevin challenged.

Cindy and Dante, never ones to turn down an opportunity to try to best Kevin, accepted.

Nic took the driver position in the front of his sled. Cindy had this same position on Dante's sled. Kevin and Dante were behind, ready to push to get each sled going and then jump on.

"Three...two...one...go!" Philip yelled.

With loud grunts from both boys, the sleds slowly began moving. Kevin almost knocked Nic off when he jumped on, but Nic was able to hang on somehow. Taking a second to glance at his competition, Nic saw Cindy staring ahead with a serious expression on her face and Dante screaming encouragement into her ear.

Both sleds were picking up speed. The cold air whistled past Nic's ears, which made hearing anything else almost impossible. He shot a glance in Cindy and Dante's direction and was disappointed to see they were keeping up.

Snow had been blowing up since they started, but it now was making it hard to see ahead. Nic wiped his face with his glove, but it didn't help much.

Nic started squinting to keep the snow out of his eyes. As they passed the midpoint of this hill, he gasped at what both sleds were racing toward. Directly in front of them was a large pile up of kids and sleds. It was like a massive sled traffic jam. Nic knew that he and Cindy would have to stop *now*, or they might end up hurting themselves or one of the others ahead of them.

From the corner of his eye, Nic saw that Cindy must have come to the same conclusion. She had already begun applying the brakes to slow the sled. Not wanting to waste any more time, Nic began to apply his brakes, too. But the sled wasn't slowing down. He pulled harder. Still nothing.

Now the people in front of him were a lot closer. Trying to stay calm, Nic scanned for options. He noticed a small ramp of snow to the right of the traffic jam. Without really thinking, he steered the sled in the ramp's direction. It was a risky move.

"Why did Cindy and Dante stop their sled?" yelled Kevin in Nic's ear.

"You don't want to know!" Nic shouted over his shoulder.

Feeling the sled shift, Kevin peered around Nic. Realizing what was about to happen, his eyes grew as wide as silver dollars, and his voice came out high pitched as he yelled "Nooooooo!"

Nic skillfully steered the sled onto the ramp, jumping over the crowd that had been in front of them seconds before.

For a split second, they were flying. All too quickly, gravity caught them, and they came down with a hard THUD. The rough landing knocked Kevin off. Nic was able to stay on and safely stop the sled.

Nic inhaled deeply and pushed the air out of his mouth. Watching his breath, it looked like smoke in the cold air, rising toward the clouds. Standing up, he checked how he felt, making sure he wasn't too bruised --- or worse. Satisfied he was okay, he looked back at the kids he'd avoided by using the ramp. To his surprise, they were now clapping.

"That was awesome!" and "Nerves of steel!" were some of the remarks he heard. Nic didn't know if the kids really knew why he had to jump over them, but he wasn't going to spoil the moment.

By now, Kevin was on his feet and running towards Nic. Wiping snow from his eyes and out of his hair, he commented, "That was awesome, Nic. Crazy, but awesome."

Nic smiled before replying, "I didn't really have any choice."

Kevin looked puzzled, "What do you mean?"

"My sled's brakes didn't work, so we couldn't stop. I had to do something else. It was lucky that ramp was there. I'm glad everyone is okay," Nic added.

Nic was feeling happy about the whole thing when Dante and Cindy walked up. After a new round of "That was amazing!" and "I can't believe you did that!" comments, Dante said, "That was great, Nic, just like in a movie!" Then he pointed at Nic's sled — or what used to be Nic's sled. "Sorry about your sled, though, Dude."

Nic had been so caught up in the moment that he hadn't even looked at his sled's condition. He couldn't believe his eyes. His sled was a bunch of broken boards and bent metal. It had just seen its last run down a snowy hill.

"Aaah, man, this is terrible," said Nic with frustration. He'd always had this sled. He and his dad used it together every winter, until this one. Nic felt that familiar lump forming in his throat. He bent down over his sled so his friends couldn't see how upset he really was.

"We should get this out of the way," he said quietly, picking up pieces to carry to the trash.

"Let me help you," Cindy volunteered. She looked over at Nic and whispered, "I'm sorry." All Nic could do was nod his head.

He grabbed a small piece of wood and slipped it into his pocket. One less thing I have that I shared with my dad, he thought sadly.

Nic's thoughts were cut short when the sneering voice of Johnny pierced his ears.

"That was a pretty lucky stunt, geek. I'm almost impressed," said Johnny as he and his gang approached. "I'd challenge you and your wimpy friends to a fight, but I have something better in mind. Plus, I don't want to get your blood on my new, expensive winter coat," he smirked while his gang laughed loudly.

Nic put down the pieces of his sled and stood up to face Johnny. He didn't know what Johnny was getting at, but he knew the sadness he had been feeling was giving way to anger and frustration.

"Let's find out just how lucky you are. I challenge you to a race down the hill starting from Suicide Drop. If I win, you'll have to pay me fifty bucks and if you win...Yeah, right," laughed Johnny coldly.

Kevin and the others began pleading with Nic not to do the challenge.

"Suicide Drop's too dangerous, Nic. Only the best sledders attempt it," cautioned Dante.

"I've heard all kinds of bad stuff about Suicide Drop from my sisters' boyfriends," added Kevin.

"Don't let Johnny bait you, Nic," pleaded Cindy.

"It's not worth it," said Philip.

Herbert ended their pleas with "I wouldn't do it."

Johnny folded his arms and shook his head. Turning to go, Johnny taunted, "C'mon, guys, I knew he was just a momma's boy. Not having a dad around has turned him into a wimp."

Nic's face, once red from the cold, was now red with anger; and his hands were clenched fists. He took a step toward Johnny and blurted out, "You're on, Johnny! If I win, you'll owe me fifty dollars!"

Johnny stopped walking, then spun on his heel to face Nic. For a split second, no one spoke.

For a brief moment, a flicker of doubt and fear showed in Johnny's face before he retorted, "So you do want to race? Are you sure? I wouldn't want you to hurt yourself and go home crying to mommy."

"Johnny, you're the only one that's going to be running home crying," said Nic, not feeling quite as brave as his voice sounded.

Pounding his fist into his hand, Johnny shouted, "Let's go then!" .

Both gangs started the long walk up to Suicide Drop.

While his friends were still trying to convince him not to do it, all Nic could think about was how he was going to make Johnny pay for teasing him about his dad. He knew Johnny had deliberately used the fact that he didn't have a dad to bait him, but he didn't care. Johnny had been getting on his nerves all year, and Nic's patience had finally run out. Whatever happens…*happens,* thought Nic, even though he would have to pay Johnny with all of his Christmas money if he lost.

When they finally reached Suicide Drop, Nic understood why it had that name. He had never seen such a steep drop before. It looked more like a ski run than a sledding route. He had to squint into the distance to see where the ground leveled off.

"What have I gotten myself into this time?" mumbled Nic.

"So, Geek, you still up for a race?" sneered Johnny.

Nic looked over the edge again. Then, with more bravado than he was really feeling, answered, "You bet." Inside, he was wishing he could back down.

"Then let's get this race started," said Johnny with a bit less enthusiasm than he'd had just a moment ago. He positioned his snow saucer at the edge of the drop.

Only then did Nic remember that his sled was broken.

"My sled's broken. I'll need to borrow someone else's," declared Nic.

Johnny glared him. "Just use your geek friend's sled."

Nic looked at Dante's sled and realized he had a way out of the race. "I don't want to risk breaking Dante's sled. Besides, everyone here knows that a snow saucer is faster than a snow sled any day of the week. I wouldn't stand a chance against that."

Relief washed over Johnny's face as he responded, "I knew you were too chicken to race me. Sorry to disappoint everybody, but it looks like there's not going to be a race."

A voice from the back of the *J Gang* changed everything. To everyone's surprise, Mark, from Johnny's gang, stepped forward and said, "I didn't walk all of the way up here for nothing. I want to see a race."

Looking at Nic with begrudging admiration for taking on Johnny, Mark continued, "You can use my snow saucer, Nic. If you break it, you can buy me a new one."

He handed his snow saucer to a stunned Nic. Nic hadn't expected this show of respect from a member of Johnny's gang, but it was a nice change of pace.

Johnny's smile disappeared, replaced by the meanest look Nic or his friends had ever seen. Johnny glared at Mark for his disloyalty and started to say something, but then stopped.

Instead, Johnny growled through gritted teeth, "Okay, let's get this race over with before you come up with another excuse to back out."

Nic's heart was pounding. He couldn't believe what had just happened. All the nervousness was gone; it was replaced with excitement and determination. He eagerly took his starting position by Mark's saucer at the drop's edge.

Dante came up to Nic and softly patted him on the back, while whispering, "Good luck, Nic. The best advice I have for you is to hold on to the saucer's straps really tight and be on guard for a slight bump about midway down. I don't think Johnny knows about it, and I only know about it from overhearing other people talk about it. It doesn't seem like a big deal now, but as fast as you'll be going, if you're not careful, you'll get knocked off of your saucer when you hit it."

Nic looked back at Dante and said, "Thanks for the advice. If I don't survive, tell everybody it's been nice knowing them."

Nic took one last look at his friends. Kevin and Dante both flashed him a thumbs-up sign. Philip pumped his right arm up and down while circling it above his head. Herbert had both hands covering his eyes, while Cindy looked worried.

I hope I don't break too many bones, thought Nic to himself, as he felt a bead of sweat roll down his cheek. Looking down below him, Nic could see a crowd of people at the bottom of the hill looking up at them and pointing. They're probably thinking how crazy we are, mused Nic; and he thought they were right.

"On your mark…Get set…Go!" shouted Jerry, as both groups began cheering.

Nic pushed off, jumping onto Mark's snow saucer. He sank a bit into the snow, but it didn't matter. His forward motion increased as he felt the saucer begin to tip over the edge. Nic held his breath, taking in the view before him. It looked worse-- much worse-- than when he was still standing on the edge. No going back now, he thought.

His hands tightened around the straps, and he braced for the drop. Whooooooosh! Every muscle in his body screamed as he struggled to stay on the saucer and remain upright. He had never gone so fast in his life!

By now, he was gripping the saucer's straps so tight that he was sure he had no circulation left in his fingers. Between the speed and the cold air, seeing was almost impossible. His eyes watered, and his nose was starting to run.

The saucer turned slightly to Nic's left, giving him a good view of Johnny's progress. Johnny wasn't looking as cocky or in control as he had before they started the race.

Johnny's face was as pale as the snow. He had only one eye open and seemed to be having trouble staying on his saucer.

Nic's saucer spun back again so he could see what was ahead. He wasn't sure, but he thought he was probably near the halfway point. He tightened his grip even further on the saucer's straps and tried to relax his body to absorb the blow of the bump Dante had warned him about. Tense seconds went by as he waited. Maybe Dante had heard wrong. Maybe there was no bump in the middle of the hill, thought Nic, as Johnny's saucer was slowly creeping ahead of his.

Johnny hadn't missed the fact he was now in the lead at a little over halfway down and had turned his head back toward Nic.

"Hey, Geek, look who's winning. I guess you're just going to have to kiss my…aaaah!" shouted Johnny, as his saucer connected with the bump, sending them both into the air.

A second later, Nic also found himself flying high into the air. Nic stayed with the momentum, as Dante instructed. He landed with a hard thud. The impact almost threw him off the saucer, but he managed to maintain his upright position. The only problem was he was now facing backwards. While not great for seeing where he was going, it did give him a front row seat to what was happening to Johnny.

As Dante predicted, Johnny had not been prepared for the bump. He landed hard and on an angle, which caused him to roll off to one side. Johnny cried out in pain as he grabbed his wrist. The saucer's impact was so great that it cracked in half.

Wow, that has to be unusual, thought Nic. He'd never seen a snow saucer break like that before.

With Johnny down, now all Nic had to do was finish the race. Still facing backwards, he had to crane his neck to see what was coming up. The bottom of the hill was coming up fast. He saw a large snow embankment in front of him.

Oh, no, thought Nic, if I don't slow down and do it fast, I'm going to end up hitting that really hard. Nic furiously fought for control over his saucer to slow it down and turn it around. He wasn't used to riding on snow saucers, and so he wasn't sure of what to do. I sure hope I can live through this, thought Nic, as he tensed up and got ready to smash into the snow bank.

Instead of hitting it, though, he found himself airborne. To his horror, he realized the snow bank was sloped; and he had hit it just right. The rush of wind across his face temporarily blinded him as he felt the saucer spinning in the air. Thud! Back on the ground, Nic and his saucer were sliding through the parking lot that led to the street.

The parking lot was like an ice rink, and Nic still couldn't slow down. Is this ever going to end? His mind screamed as he saw his next obstacle — a parked semi-truck with a long trailer. Nic was headed for the middle of the trailer. He tried to free his fingers from the saucer's straps, but they were wrapped too tightly. He was stuck. Not wanting to be bug splatter on the side of the semi-truck's trailer, Nic did the only thing he could think of. He leaned backwards on his saucer and became as flat as possible.

Not brave enough to look, Nic closed his eyes tight and felt his chest just brush the trailer's underside as he zipped below it. A second later, he opened his eyes and sat up. More trouble ahead — another snow bank.

Not again. I definitely don't want to jump this one and end up in the middle of the street with heavy car traffic, thought Nic.

Nic struggled desperately with the saucer. Within a few feet of the embankment, he was finally able to roll off. He wanted to yell for joy, but didn't have time as he slammed into the snow bank face first. Everything went black.

Nic didn't know how long he had been out; but as he came to, he heard mumblings like, "…hit it hard…crazy. Is he dead?"

Opening his eyes, Nic saw a crowd of kids surrounding him.

"Out of the way! More important people coming through," shouted Kevin, leading the others to where Nic was lying down against the snow bank.

"Oh, Nic, are you all right?" asked Cindy.

Nic sat up, then took a deep breath and slowly rose to his feet with Kevin's help. He responded with a meek smile while rubbing his head.

"Other than for a terrible headache, I guess so. I think I've had enough of snow sledding for one day."

"That was the most awesome race I've ever seen in all of my life! You were incredible, Nic!" exclaimed Dante.

"Great job, Nic," added Herbert, slapping Nic on the back. Nic cringed in pain from his bruises. "Sorry, I guess I'm just too pumped up about what you did," apologized Herbert.

"That looked just like what those extreme sports guys do for a living. Too bad nobody taped the race. We could've sent it into one of those TV shows and won some money," said Philip.

"Too bad nobody talked him out of it. He could have been seriously injured or killed. Must I always be the practical one of this group?" Cindy asked, to no one in particular.

Cindy turned her attention to the saucer. It was more than half buried into the snow bank. With Dante and Herbert's help, she was able to wiggle it free.

"Doesn't look like it's broken anywhere," said Dante.

"In fact, it looks in better shape than you do, Nic," Phillip chuckled.

Nic hadn't even had a chance to gauge how he was since the crash as everything had occurred so fast.

"Do I look that bad?" asked Nic. Everyone nodded.

"You look like one of those horror movie victims," added Kevin.

Nic wiped his forehead with his hand and was surprised to see blood on his fingers, mixed in with sweat and snow.

"Wow! I must've really done a number on myself," stated Nic.

"Not bad, Nic. How's my saucer?" asked Mark, as he approached Nic and his friends.

"Seems fine, Mark. Thanks for letting me use it," replied Nic.

Mark casually scanned his saucer, as if he really didn't care what it looked like, and said, "Looks okay."

Nic looked at him and asked sympathetically, "What happened to Johnny? He looked like he hurt himself bad when he fell off his saucer."

Mark looked at Nic, surprised that he would care about what happened to Johnny.

"I don't know. It looks like he broke his wrist, but nobody knows for sure. Johnny claims you pushed him off his saucer halfway down the hill. He says he isn't going to pay you anything for cheating. He would've told you himself, but he took off with the others to head home to go see a doctor about his arm. Gotta go myself. Good race, though."

As Mark walked away, Nic grumbled loudly, "I didn't cheat. I never touched Johnny on the hill. He fell off of his saucer all by himself."

"We know, Nic. We could see everything from where we were," said Dante.

"Johnny just plain screwed up," said Philip.

Nic, eager to change the subject commented, "Mark seems okay. He doesn't act like the rest of Johnny's gang."

"I've never understood why he continues to hang out with Johnny. We get along all right at family gatherings," said Kevin.

Nic stopped and looked at Kevin curiously. "Family gatherings?"

Kevin smiled slightly and answered, "He's my cousin."

"Hey, Nic, Cindy and I brought all the pieces left from your sled over," said Herbert.

Nic looked sadly at the remains of his sled. "Thanks guys." He stooped to pick up the pieces and groaned as his head began to throb.

"We'll get them, for you, Nic," Cindy offered.

Kevin helped Nic up again.

"Thanks, Cindy, Herbert. That means a lot," Nic said, wincing as his voice echoed uncomfortably in his head. Taking one last look at the hill, the gang began their walk home just as dusk began to cast its long shadows over the snow-covered town.

CHAPTER NINE

The Break–In

One by one, the gang separated along the way until only Nic was left walking by himself. As he got closer to his house, Nic worried about how he was going to explain everything to his mom. He knew from experience (and he had plenty) that she was going to be very upset with him...first, for breaking his sled, and next, for getting all cut up and bruised because of a race.

To make matters worse, he wouldn't be getting the fifty dollars Johnny owed him for beating him down the hill. All of his efforts had been for nothing. But at least he knew he had beaten Johnny fair and square, even if Johnny was too much of a wimp to admit it.

It was dark by the time Nic got home. His mom had turned on the porch light and the strings of Christmas lights decorating the front of the house. The cheerful colored lights reflected off the white snow, making it glisten like multi-colored jewels.

Nic opened the garage door and put the pieces of his sled inside. At this point, his body was aching as much as his head. He closed the garage door and made his way to the back door.

It creaked as he opened it. Stepping into the mostly dark kitchen, he mused that when you want to sneak into some place, anything you do becomes loud and noisy. He was just about to flip on the light when his mom appeared out of nowhere.

"It's about time, young man. I've been worried sick. Just where have you been?" she demanded, walking toward him.

Nic nervously mumbled, "Just went sledding like I said I was." He moved around her. He wanted to get upstairs to wash and change before she could really see how banged up he was.

He made it to the other side of the kitchen, but stopped when she said angrily, "Nicolas Timothy Nelson! Don't you dare walk away from me when I'm speaking to you!"

Yikes! She used my middle name. She never calls me by my middle name, unless she's really mad. I'm really goin' to get it now, thought Nic. He froze and slowly turned around to face her. She flipped on the light and gasped.

Nic watched her expression change from anger to worry back to anger as she rushed over to examine the cuts on his face.

"Nicolas! What happened? How did you get these cuts? Are you hurt?" she asked, spinning him around to check the back of his head.

"Well, Mom…" Nic began.

Before he could continue, she fired off more questions, "When did this happen? Where did this happen? Was anyone else hurt?"

"I'm trying to tell you, but you keep talking," said Nic in as innocent a tone as he could muster.

"Don't you get snippy with me, young man. I'm not in the mood for any of your back talk. Just tell me what happened," she said as she led him to a seat at the kitchen table.

Nic told her about all that had happened while she wiped his cuts clean with antiseptic solution and put his coat and clothes into the laundry. He didn't leave anything out, because he figured she usually found out everything anyway. He could tell by her expression that she was upset when he mentioned the part with Johnny and the race.

"How could you let Johnny bait you like that? Don't you ever let him do that to you again! You could've been seriously hurt. You're grounded for the rest of this week, young man!" she stated, while at the same time a tear escaped from the corner of her left eye.

Nic cried out angrily, "Don't you still care about Dad? Johnny was making fun of me and insulting Dad! I'm not going to let anyone do that to him. At least I still love him, even if you don't anymore!"

With that, he rushed from the kitchen with tears in his eyes. Nic ran up to his room, threw himself on his bed, and buried his face in his pillow.

He didn't hear his mom come into his room, but he raised his head when he felt her hand across his back. She had tears streaming down both of her cheeks.

She smiled sadly and said, "Oh, Nicolas, you're just as impetuous and daring as your father was."

Nic found himself hugging his mom with all of his strength. "I'm sorry, Mom. I didn't mean what I said about you not loving dad anymore," whispered Nic into his mom's ear.

"I know, Dear. It hasn't been easy for either one of us. I miss him very much, and I know you do, too. I'm very proud of the way you've handled everything since his…. I'm very proud of you," Nic's mom said softly.

Nic felt so secure in his mom's arms that he wished the moment would never end. Eventually, she gently pried him loose and said, "I'm sorry for getting so upset with you, Nicolas. You have to understand that we only have each other; and if anything would ever happen to you, I don't know what I'd do. So in the future, be careful. And if Johnny says something about your father again, slug him one for me."

Nic smiled and whispered, "I will," and gave his mom one last hug before letting her go. As she was about to leave his room, Nic said, "Mom, I love you."

She stopped and smiled at him over her shoulder. "I love you too, dear."

Nic felt better after showering. Soon his stomach reminded him he hadn't had anything to eat all day. He walked down the stairs gingerly. It seemed that every muscle ached. He made a ham and cheese sandwich (heavy on the ham). He was about to take a bite, when the front of the local newspaper, **The New Bonn Gazette**, caught his attention.

The headline on the front page was big and bold with the words, "**Hornsby Hardware Store Vandalized**." Jason's dad owns that store, thought Nic, as he put his sandwich down and reached over to begin reading the article.

According to local authorities, Hornsby Hardware Store was vandalized last night. Mr. David Hornsby, the store's owner, said a number of areas in the store had been spray painted with graffiti. The only thing stolen was a metal detector. Police are following all leads in the case. They suspect the vandalism was the work of some local teenagers as part of a gang prank. Mr. Hornsby has offered a $500 reward for any information leading to the capture of the vandals.

Poor Jason! What an awful thing to have happen on Christmas, he thought. Who would go to the trouble of messing up a store and then take only one thing? Nic contemplated this as he bit into his sandwich. Sure, a metal detector would be fun to play around with. You could search for metal stuff like coins in the ground or….

Nic froze. It couldn't be; it just couldn't be that obvious. He had to be wrong about it. Surely he was wrong. Lost in thought, Nic put his sandwich down. After running the possibilities through his head, Nic called Kevin.

"Can you get everyone together at your house tomorrow?" he asked.

"That shouldn't be a problem, but why?" Kevin responded.

"I'll fill you and everyone else in tomorrow," Nic promised.

Still thinking about the burglary, Nic walked back to the kitchen to finish his sandwich. Apparently, Wellington decided an unattended sandwich was fair game. He was licking his lips contentedly when Nic walked in.

"Wellington!"

The next morning, the gang gathered in Kevin's room. Despite his exhaustion from sledding, Nic hadn't slept much the night before. Instead, he had tossed and turned thinking about his vandalism theory of the Hornsby's store. When he arrived at Kevin's, he discovered everyone else was talking about it, too. He walked in on the tail end of a conversation between Philip and Dante.

"That's a crazy idea," said Philip.

"No, it isn't," retorted Dante. Upon seeing Nic enter Kevin's room, Dante said, "Let's ask Nic!"

"Ask me what?" asked Nic.

"Have you heard about Jason's dad's store being broken into on Christmas?" asked Dante.

"Yeah," answered Nic.

"Well, I think Johnny and his gang did it. They're the only ones crazy enough to do something like that," remarked Dante.

"Dante has a good point," said Cindy confidently.

"No way. Even Johnny wouldn't do anything as stupid as that. We're talking big time trouble if he's caught," said Philip.

Nic sat quietly as everyone took a turn at agreeing or disagreeing with Dante's position until finally Kevin looked at Nic and asked, "You've been awfully quiet, Nic. What do you think about Dante's idea?"

"I thought you'd never ask. This is exactly why I wanted to have everybody meet today. I have a hunch on who might have broken into Hornsby's Hardware Store and why," said Nic, then he paused for a moment.

"Don't keep us in suspense, Nic," said Cindy.

Nic eyed the room before saying, "I think the police have it backwards. They think the metal detector was taken as a joke after the vandals broke into the store to mess it up. I say that the people responsible for breaking into the store were after the metal detector and vandalized everything else to make it appear that they weren't."

"No way. Why do you think that?" asked Philip.

"Because of who I suspect," said Nic.

"And that is?" asked Cindy.

"Roger Marinovich," Nic announced.

The room went silent.

"But why would Roger Marinovich need a metal detector? Besides, nobody has seen him since the fall. He's probably given up and moved on," said Cindy.

"The reason he would need the metal detector is so he could look for the Diamonds of Denmark quicker and more efficiently. What would be a better way to look for something buried than with a metal detector? Secondly, he doesn't seem like the type to give up so easily, especially when millions of dollars are at stake. He's been waiting for so long already," replied Nic.

"I must admit, you've made some good points, Nic. Let's say you're right; what do we do now? We can't go to the police. They would just laugh at us and your idea," remarked Kevin.

"We could at least tell Jason about what we think," said Nic.

"I don't know, Nic. He might not believe us," remarked Kevin.

Nic persisted, "What have we got to lose? So the worst that can happen is he thinks we're crazy. You, of all people, should be used to that kind of response from others, Kevin."

Kevin smiled as everyone else laughed. The group agreed to Nic's plan to tell Jason everything they knew (or thought they knew) about Mr. Marinovich and the Diamonds of Denmark.

"You guys are crazy," laughed Jason, as Nic and the others finished explaining their theory.

Kevin glanced over at Nic, shrugged his shoulders and said, "Looks like the worst just happened, Nic."

It was not more than two hours ago that Nic had convinced the gang to tell Jason his idea about the break-in. But Jason wasn't buying it.

"Why do you think it's crazy? Everything we've explained to you makes sense," said Nic in exasperation.

"Look, don't get me wrong. I really appreciate you guys caring about what happens to me and my family, but this all sounds like scenes from a mystery movie. I mean, come on, a diamond heist from decades ago? A surviving brother of the thief masquerading as a cop? Jewels buried in the Chamberlains' backyard? I half expect you guys to tell me next that an alien flying saucer is somehow involved," said Jason stifling a laugh.

Nic frowned and couldn't understand why Jason was laughing them off when they were trying to help him.

Jason stood up and turned toward Nic. "I really do appreciate your help, Nic; and I'm sorry for laughing at your idea. I just don't think it has anything to do with the break-in at my dad's store. I need more facts to go on other than theories and a strange encounter with two suspicious people who asked you weird questions concerning a suitcase."

"Thanks for trying, guys. I'll catch you later on in the week for a movie or something," said Jason as he left Kevin's room.

Nic was still frowning as Kevin came over and put his hand on Nic's shoulder.

"Don't mind, Jason. You gave it your best shot, and it didn't work. We know what really is happening, which makes it even more important for us to keep our guard up."

Philip piped up, "Yeah, Nic, when we do get enough evidence on Mr. Marinovich, then think how silly Jason's going to feel for not believing us."

Nic smiled and said, "You're right. I guess it's up to us from now on. I thought we could get some adult we trust to help us out, but I was wrong."

With that, everybody promised to alert the others if they saw or heard of anything suspicious occurring around town. The meeting ended with everyone saying goodbye and heading home.

As he walked home on snow-covered sidewalks, Nic made a vow to himself that he was going to get Roger Marinovich and prove to Jason that he was right and not crazy. How he was going to get him was another matter.

Oh, well, all I want to do now is go home and eat Christmas dinner leftovers before mom gives them to Wellington again, like last year. He stepped up his pace down the sidewalk, arriving home quickly.

CHAPTER TEN

Mr. Chen's Shop

The snowy New Bonn winter gave way to an early spring. March, true to its nature, had come in like a lion and was going out like a lamb. The excitement stirred by the Hornsby break-in had died down, especially since no new leads had been uncovered since January. There also hadn't been any sightings of Roger Marinovich or his accomplice by Nic and his friends.

Maybe Cindy was right, and they had left town in frustration, thought Nic. He didn't believe this, but it was puzzling that they had just disappeared again. Staring out the window, Nic wished he were anywhere but at school on this sunny March morning.

Mr. Smithton's class was so boring, thought Nic, as he hurried his way toward the cafeteria. He couldn't remember the last time he had been so happy to hear the lunch bell. Who cares about punctuation, thought Nic, feeling weak with hunger.

"The only thing I care about right now is what the cafeteria is serving for lunch," he said to no one in particular.

He met up with Dante, Philip, and Herbert, and they got in line together.

Nic whispered, "I hope they're serving spaghetti today. It's the only food I can recognize as being edible. Everything else looks and tastes like road kill."

Dante and Philip nodded and laughed.

"I disagree, Nic. I think everything here tastes pretty good," Herbert said seriously.

"Only you would, Herbert, only you," chuckled Dante. He continued, "I know what you mean, Nic. Just yesterday, I honestly thought I saw some of my meatloaf move on my plate. I lost my appetite, but now understand why the cafeteria calls it 'meatloaf surprise.'"

All of the boys laughed. Philip then added, "I sure wish they would serve fast food like tacos here."

They all agreed fast food in the cafeteria was a great idea.

Dante lowered his voice to say, "Seriously, guys, I want to warn you about Kevin. I think he's going to try to drag us into another harebrained scheme."

"What makes you say that?" asked Herbert.

"The look on his face and the way he was acting this morning," replied Dante.

"I can hardly wait to hear it. Maybe we're going to help Jason hang another skeleton, but this time in front of the police station," laughed Nic, rolling his eyes.

Sure enough, as the boys approached their usual seats at the lunch table, they saw Kevin smiling at them with his eyes gleaming. Nic thought, oh no, here we go again.

"Whassup," Kevin said as they sat down.

"No!" said Dante emphatically.

"No?" replied Kevin.

"That's right. No," insisted Dante.

"What are you talking about?" asked a perplexed Kevin.

Dante took a second to breathe deep and explained, "I've known you long enough now to know when you're about to get us all involved in some wacky scheme of yours. I'm just giving you my answer ahead of time so you won't bug me about whatever it is you're going to bug me about."

Kevin put his hand on his chest. "I can't believe you would feel that way about me, Dante. Especially after all we've been through. Remember when I saved you from getting in trouble with your parents last year after you had..." Kevin said sounding hurt.

"Okay, okay. I'll listen to what you've got to say, but it doesn't mean I'll do it," interrupted Dante while turning to Nic and whispering, "I hate when he does that."

"That's all I'm asking from you guys. Just hear me out," said Kevin as he excitedly rubbed his hands together.

Last time he rubbed his hands together, we almost ended up in jail, thought Nic, remembering Halloween.

"How would you guys like to enter into the New Bonn paintball tournament?" asked Kevin.

A few moments of silence prevailed before...

"Paintball? Isn't that where you go around and shoot at people with guns filled with paint?" asked Philip.

"Something like that. The guns shoot out little balls of paint which burst open when they hit you or any other hard object," answered Kevin.

"Doesn't it hurt?" asked Dante.

"Not as much as you might think. You can barely feel it from far away; but if you're hit up close, it does sting a little," replied Kevin.

"How do you know?" asked Herbert.

"I've played a couple of times with Jason and his friends," said Kevin.

"When and where is this tournament taking place?" asked Nic.

"It goes down in May and takes place in a wooded field about three miles outside of town, off Highway 70," replied Kevin.

"Who would we be competing against?" asked Nic, who was worried at the prospect of going up against older kids in something he knew very little about.

"We'd be competing against kids in the 10- to 11-year-old bracket," answered Kevin.

"Can girls play, too?" asked Cindy.

"Of course; I wouldn't think of not having you on our team, Cindy," replied Kevin.

"Sounds like a lot of fun, but what are the rules?" asked Herbert.

"Basically, it's don't get hit by the other team while trying to capture a small flag or painted object before your opponents do. Once your team has the flag or object, then you have to try and return it from where you started before time runs out," explained Kevin.

"Does the winning team get anything?" asked Philip.

"A small trophy and mention in the New Bonn Gazette," answered Kevin.

"One last question, and I'm sure I'm speaking for everyone here when I say this. I don't have a paintball gun, and it sounds like neither does anyone else, so how are we going to be able to play in this paintball tournament?" questioned Nic.

Kevin frowned for a second while mumbling and scratching his chin, "That could be a problem."

While waiting for Kevin's response, Nic took a few moments to scan each person's face at the table. It appeared to him that Kevin had made his case and that they all were interested in this tournament. Nic had to admit he was interested in the idea, too. After all, it sounded like playing Army to him, except in this game you knew when you were hit. There was no arguing about who hit who first, which was the main problem with imaginary bullets.

"Let me talk to Jason to make sure, but I think there might be a way for us to get paintball guns. I believe the owner of a sports shop in town sells and loans out paintball guns for use. We could all go over to his shop after school tomorrow and check it out. What do you guys say?" asked Kevin with his characteristic goofy grin.

Nobody spoke. Everyone seemed to be on the edge of telling Kevin "yes," but they needed a little more encouragement.

"C'mon, it'll be loads of fun," pleaded Kevin.

"That's what you told me when we were seven years old, and you convinced me to go digging around in the garbage dumpster behind McDonald's to find Happy Meal toys. I stunk for a week afterwards. That's not including the fact I was grounded for a month when my mom found out," said Philip.

Kevin smiled coyly and replied, "Well, everyone is entitled to one mistake, aren't they?"

"Only one mistake? In your case try several thousand," added Cindy.

"Ha, ha, ha. So, guys, what's it going to be?" asked Kevin anxiously, as he looked around the table.

"Okay, Kevin, I'm in. It sounds like it could be a great time. Besides, I would like a chance to shoot you to get you back for scaring me, Dante, and Philip in my garage last fall when we were going to rake the Chamberlains yard," said Nic with a sly smile of his own.

Kevin smiled as they all agreed to meet after school the next day.

Nic was the last one to meet the others at the bike rack after school the following day.

"C'mon, slowpoke. Let's get this show on the road," yelled Kevin.

"Now, before we leave, I need to mention something that I forgot about yesterday at lunch," said Kevin.

Dante's eyes widened, and he said, "I knew it. I just knew it. There's a catch to all of this, isn't there? I knew it was too good to be true. How much jail time are we looking at?"

Kevin laughed, "What are you talking about? There's no jail time involved. What is it with you? Have you ever ended up in jail because of one of my ideas?" Dante opened his mouth to answer, and Kevin said, "Never mind. Don't answer that."

"What I forgot to tell you is that the owner of the sports shop is a little unusual, so don't freak out. Let me do all of the talking," said Kevin.

Nic glanced over at Dante and could see he was about to start up again, but decided not to say anything. Satisfied that everyone was ready, Kevin rolled away on his bike with the gang following.

Nic was barely paying attention until he had to slam on his brakes to avoid hitting Herbert in front of him. Philip, who was not as quick, bumped into Nic's bike rather hard.

"Sorry, Nic, I was lost in thought."

"It's okay…me, too," replied Nic who was looking ahead to see why they all had stopped.

"I think we need to go that way now!" yelled out Kevin as he pointed to his left.

"You think? I thought you knew where this place was," said Cindy with a hint of irritation.

"I do! I do! It's just that it's been awhile since I was last there with Jason," said Kevin.

"Maybe we should have had Jason take us," said Herbert.

Kevin gave Herbert a glare and said, "We'll be fine. Trust me."

"That's what he said on Halloween before we pulled that joke, and look how much trouble we almost got into," Nic said to Philip as they made a left turn.

This new street looked more like an alleyway to Nic.

"Where did the sun go?" Philip asked.

Nic realized Philip was right. It was gray and misty on this street. There were no obvious lights or even windows visible.

"This is creepy," Philip said in a low voice to Nic.

Right before he suggested they turn around, Kevin stopped in front of a small brick shop with an old metal sign hanging above its door. The sign read: **Chen's Sport's Emporium. If Chen don't got it, then you can't get it.** As the rest of the group came to a stop, a cold breeze kicked up making the sign swing back and forth on noisy, rusty hinges.

"Is this it?" stammered Herbert nervously, while he slowly got off his bike.

"Yep. I know it doesn't look like much, but it's cool," replied Kevin.

"Maybe it's cool for a horror movie set, but I don't know about it as a sports shop. It's even scarier looking than your garage," whispered Philip to Nic, who smirked, "Real funny."

"C'mon, guys, let's go inside," said Kevin as he led the way. Nic tried to sneak a peek through the glass window in front of the shop before following Kevin, but it was too dusty and dark to see anything.

The door hinges protested loudly as Kevin opened the shop's heavy wooden door.

"Sounds like it needs an oil job to me," said Dante softly as everyone followed Kevin inside.

BAM! Everyone jumped at the unexpected noise. Herbert grabbed Nic and Cindy, nearly crushing them as he buried his head on their shoulders while crying out, "What was that?"

"Sorry, I didn't know the door was going to slam shut like that," said Philip, meekly shrugging his shoulders.

"Would...you...mind...letting...us...go...now...Herbert?" asked Cindy between gasps of air.

Herbert quickly let them go and sheepishly said, "Sorry, I guess I was startled." Nic took a deep breath to recover from Herbert's chest lock. Nic stepped away from the wide-eyed Herbert to put additional space between them. He had no desire to be crushed again anytime soon. As Nic's eyes grew accustomed to the low light inside, he marveled at the odd assortment of sports equipment on the shelves and in display cases.

The dim lighting made it difficult to see clearly. He noted two overhead fans slowly spinning on the ceiling. He found it odd that a misty cloud seemed to hover a few inches off the floor. Nic couldn't tell whether it was from dust or a fog that had seeped in from outside. There were five rows of shelves with various sporting equipment lined on them. There was more equipment on shelves lining the sides of the store's walls, as well.

"C'mon, guys, this way," Kevin instructed as he led the gang to the front of the store where a long glass counter awaited them.

"Hello, anybody here?" asked Kevin over the counter. There was no answer.

"Okay, nobody's here. Let's go," said Herbert as he turned around, only to have Cindy stop him.

"Not so fast, Mr. Brave. We just got here," she said.

"I wonder where Mr. Chen could be?" mumbled Kevin.

"Look, on the counter," pointed Philip. A small bell was on the counter with a note beside it that read: ***Please ring this bell three times for service.***

"Funny, I don't remember this being here the last time I was with Jason. I guess I'll try this," said Kevin as he picked up the bell and rang it six or seven times. No one appeared.

"Well, we tried, so now it's time to go," mumbled Herbert as he began to turn around again.

"Hold up. Someone's got to be here or else how could the store be open? Try it again, Kevin," remarked Nic. Kevin rang the bell again six or seven times. There was still no response.

"Maybe Mr. Chen's sleeping in the back," said Dante.

"He could be dead. Maybe someone like a mass murderer came in before us and chopped his head off," added Philip.

Kevin, Nic, and Cindy all looked at Philip as if he was crazy. Nic said, "Philip, you have an overactive imagination." Meanwhile, Herbert was trying to slip past Cindy toward the door, but she stopped him again.

"How many times are you ringing the bell?" asked Nic.

"What does that matter?" asked a flabbergasted Kevin.

"Maybe nothing or maybe everything. The note does say to ring the bell only three times, Kevin," Nic replied.

"So you're telling me that if I ring the counter bell exactly three times then Mr. Chen will suddenly appear to help us out?" Kevin asked Nic.

"Yeah, I guess that's what I'm saying. Nothing else seems to be working," said Nic defensively.

Kevin rolled his eyes before shrugging his shoulders. "That's the most ridiculous idea I've ever heard, but I'll try it," said Kevin as he began to count loudly, "One ring...two rings...and three rings."

An elderly voice rang out from behind Herbert, "How may I assist you children?"

Everyone visibly jumped in surprise. Nic managed to avoid a wild, swinging Herbert as he grabbed Cindy and Philip to hold onto this time.

"Who...are...you?" stuttered Dante.

"I am he whom you seek," said the old man calmly, remaining motionless.

"Hey, guys, this is who I was talking about. This is Mr. Chen," explained Kevin excitedly.

"Okay, Herbert, please let us go...again!" demanded Cindy.

"Sorry," mumbled Herbert, releasing Cindy and Philip, as they both gasped loudly for air.

Mr. Chen was a short, wrinkled, old man with a long, flowing, gray beard and long gray hair pulled back in a ponytail to match. He must be about a hundred years old, thought Nic. His outfit was unusual, green and loose fitting with dragons printed all over it. There was something very mysterious about Mr. Chen, which Nic couldn't quite explain.

"Mr. Chen, I don't know if you remember me, but..." started Kevin.

"You are Kevin, young friend of your mentor, Jason. You and your friends seek those things which may help you in your endeavors," Mr. Chen calmly stated.

Nic didn't know what to make of Mr. Chen, but he definitely wasn't your normal New Bonn citizen.

Kevin was silent for a few moments while composing himself to continue, "Ahh yes, that's right. My friends and I are here to see about renting and possibly purchasing some of your paintball equipment. Could we please have a look at what you have in stock?"

Mr. Chen smiled slightly underneath his gray beard and slowly shuffled behind the long glass counter. He pointed to the top two shelves in the display case. He bent down to remove a few of the items. Each had a tag to identify what it was.

Nic picked up a mask which, according to the tag, was worn to protect the eyes and face from flying paintballs. He tried it on for size and felt like an astronaut as he looked around the store through the lenses. His breathing was loud and noisy. Good thing I'm not claustrophobic, Nic thought, as he took it off.

Setting down the mask, Nic picked up a bag of paintballs. Mr. Chen had opened a bag so they could feel some. Nic took one and looked at it closely. Initially, it felt hard like a marble. But after a minute, it started to feel a little wet, as if it was melting. He instinctively put it down and wiped his hand on his pants.

"They are in harmony with water and seek to rejoin it at first opportunity," Mr. Chen said softly from the other side of the counter,

"Really?" Nic replied. "You mean the paintballs are water soluble?"

"Yes," answered Mr. Chen, who continued to gaze at Nic intently.

"What is your name, young one?" asked Mr. Chen.

"Nelson, Nic Nelson," replied Nic.

"You are someone who feels he needs to prove himself."

Nic was startled by Mr. Chen's statement. He had never thought of himself that way before.

"Don't be alarmed, young one. This is not a bad trait to have, if channeled properly. But beware of allowing this desire to overwhelm and control you. Then you may face terrible consequences," he added.

Before Nic could respond, Mr. Chen whirled around to find the source of a crash behind him. Philip had attempted to grab a hockey stick from a higher shelf. He got the stick, but it came with an avalanche of other items that landed on him as he fell to the floor. Cindy and Dante ran over to help him.

"I'm sorry, Mr. Chen!" apologized Philip whose face was as red as a ripe apple. Philip, Cindy, and Dante picked up the fallen items, placing them carefully on the shelf.

Nic started to say something to Mr. Chen, but found he had disappeared to the other end of the counter. How could he have moved so fast? He hadn't even made a sound, thought Nic, as he walked down to join Kevin and Herbert.

"Are these the only paintball guns you've got as rentals?" asked Kevin, his voice dripping with disappointment.

"These are all you will need," assured Mr. Chen.

As Nic inspected the paintball guns on the counter, he asked, "What's wrong, Kevin?" .

"Mr. Chen only has Predator V paintball guns available for rental," replied Kevin.

"So, what's wrong with that?" asked Cindy.

"They're old school. They're not as good as the newer guns that everyone else has. We won't stand a chance against any of the others," sighed Kevin.

"The elephant is bigger, the cheetah is faster, and the bear is stronger, but who is the master of all these creatures?" asked Mr. Chen. Nobody answered.

"The answer is Man. It is because of our intelligence that we may rule over all of the creatures on Earth. It is not because of our strength or speed or size," finished Mr. Chen.

"What's that got to do with paintball guns?" asked a perplexed Kevin.

"I think he means that it doesn't matter what kind of paintball guns we end up using, because we'll have to win by out-thinking our opponents, not by out-gunning them," said Nic.

"Correctly put, young one," slowly nodded Mr. Chen.

"How much for rental, Mr. Chen?" asked Nic.

"What you see before you will cost five dollars for all day use, including face masks and filled CO_2 tanks. Paintballs are extra," replied Mr. Chen.

"Excuse us for one moment while we discuss this," said Kevin to Mr. Chen.

"Huddle!" cried Kevin as he motioned for everyone to follow him to a corner of the store. With everybody hunched over in a circle, Kevin asked, "Okay, so what will it be? Do we rent our paintball gear here or do we buy it from someplace else?"

"How much does a paintball gun cost to buy?" asked Dante.

"Well, it depends on what brand and type of paintball gun you're wanting. A good brand of a semi-automatic paintball gun is going to cost a lot more than five dollars. That's not including a face mask, CO_2

tank and hopper, which holds the paintballs while you're firing," answered Kevin.

"Sounds too expensive," gulped Philip.

"I don't have much in my savings account. I wish I did though," remarked Herbert.

"I'll probably have to save up my allowance for the next six months before I'll be able to buy a paintball gun," declared Dante.

"My parents won't allow me to buy something that expensive unless it's going to further my education, and I don't think this applies," added a disappointed Cindy.

"Hate to admit it, Kevin, but I'm in the same boat as everyone else. I don't think my mom is going to let me buy an expensive paintball gun for an activity that I have yet to try and not really sure whether I'll like or not," said Nic.

There was a short silence before Kevin said, "I guess the answer is obvious. We'll rent our paintball supplies from Mr. Chen for the time being until we decide whether or not to get our own equipment down the road. Does everyone agree?"

Everybody nodded before following Kevin back to Mr. Chen.

"Mr. Chen, we've made up our minds. We'll rent the paintball equipment from you," declared Kevin.

Mr. Chen smiled and nodded his head in acknowledgment.

"We'll let you know when we'll need it," finished Kevin. The gang began to file out of the shop.

"Thanks, again," said Nic, taking one last look at Mr. Chen, who remained motionless at the counter.

"May good fortune smile upon you, Nic Nelson," whispered Mr. Chen.

Gathering around their bikes outside of the shop, Kevin said, "Using those older paintball guns will definitely put us at a disadvantage; but if that's the only way everybody is going to be able to play, then so be it."

"We'll be fine, Kevin. We just have to remember Jason's saying about the five Cs," remarked Nic. Kevin rolled his eyes as the rest of the gang gave Nic puzzled looks.

"He never told you guys about the five Cs?" asked Nic.

Philip, Dante, Cindy, and Herbert all shook their heads.

"The five Cs stand for Cool, Calm, Collected, Confident, and in Control. That's how you should be when facing any tough situation. It worked for me in dodgeball last fall," explained Nic.

Kevin, a little irritated that Nic interrupted him continued, "Anyway, moving right along, is there anybody here who doesn't think his or her parents will let them enter the paintball tournament?"

"I should be good to go," said Dante.

"Me too," added Philip.

"I'll probably be able to play as well," said Herbert.

"I may have to beg and plead for awhile, but I think my parents will let me go. I just have to think of a way that makes paintball educational," replied Cindy.

"Tell them you'll learn survival tips that may come in handy down the road," laughed Kevin. "No, I've got something better. Mention how you'll be observing people react under pressure."

Cindy looked at Kevin sharply and asked, "Does that include you when you mess up?"

Kevin quickly stopped laughing and stared at Cindy for a few seconds before turning to Nic, "That just leaves you, Nic."

Hesitating, Nic finally said, "Sure, I'll be able to play," even though he wasn't sure how his mom would react.

"Okay, that settles everything. I'll let you guys know in a few days when the practice session is for teams entering the paintball tournament," said Kevin as he hopped on his bike and began to take off.

"Practice session? What practice session?" yelled Dante. They all chased after Kevin to hear his answer.

"Oh, I thought I had mentioned it before," replied Kevin, stopping to let everyone catch up.

"No, you hadn't," replied Dante angrily.

Kevin shrugged his shoulders before continuing, "All of the teams entering the tournament get one practice session before the tournament begins. It's all part of the entry fee for participating."

"Entry fee?" repeated Philip.

"Didn't I mention that?" asked Kevin.

"No!" barked Dante and Philip in unison.

"Well, each team of six people has to pay an entry fee of $50 dollars in order to play in the tournament. The fee charge includes a practice session, CO_2 fills and T-shirts for entering," stated Kevin.

"T-shirts? That's cool; but Kevin, are there any other things you've failed to mention about the paintball tournament?" asked Nic. He didn't want to hear about any more surprises. By the way everyone else was looking at Kevin, Nic knew they were feeling the same way, too.

Kevin shook his head and replied, "Nope. That should do it."

"If it isn't, I vote we should have Jason give Kevin a roughhousing to straighten him out," said Dante.

Everyone yelled and clapped in agreement. Kevin mumbled, "Real funny. I can hardly stop laughing, guys."

With the conversation over, they rode as a group down the alley toward Main Street. They were stunned when they made the turn. It was bright and sunny on Main. Nic stopped to look back toward Mr. Chen's building. It was gray and dark.

"Weird, huh?" Dante commented. Nic hadn't realized Dante was there and visibly jumped.

"Yeah," he muttered.

As he headed home, Nic kept thinking about how his mom was going to react to the news. He figured he couldn't just say, "Hey, Mom, what's up? By the way, I'm going to be in a paintball tournament, and I'll need some money. Oh yeah, I almost forgot to mention that I might come home with some bruises and be covered in dirt; but I'll have fun."

No, Nic knew he would need to handle it with a more delicate touch. Maybe he could say, "Hey, Mom, you're the greatest. Remember how you're always telling me to try new activities to expand my horizons and how I don't know if I'll like something unless I try it? Well, I want to try paintball out to see if I'll like it."

Hmmmm, that sounds better, thought Nic, as he rode his bike up his driveway.

When he walked in the house, Nic was attacked by a very happy Wellington. Nic did his best to fight off Wellington's slobbery licks and avoid "the tail of steel." Nic had gotten more than one bruise from Wellington's strong, happy tail. Sometimes he thought it would be so much easier if Wellington were a cat instead. His mom watched all of this with an amused look on her face. She was sitting at the kitchen table reading the paper and eating some soup.

"Where have you been? Dinner's been ready for a while."

"I was out riding bikes with Kevin and the gang," answered Nic while he washed his hands. He then put some soup in a bowl and sat down across from his mom.

She looked down at the paper before saying, "I don't mind your doing that, Nicolas, but make sure it doesn't interfere with your homework getting done."

"I won't."

Minutes went by as Nic struggled to think of a good way to begin the paintball conversation.

"You're awfully quiet, Nicolas. Any particular reason?" she asked. Nic just shrugged and continued eating his soup.

Smart move, thought Nic. That would have been a good opportunity to get the ball rolling, but now he had blown it.

"There are some interesting activities coming up for kids in the New Bonn area according to the paper. One event appears like it would be pretty fun for a boy your age. I'm surprised you haven't asked me about entering it," she said, glancing up from the paper.

Nic stopped eating with the spoon poised in mid-air and looked at his mom questioningly. He figured it was probably some poem-writing contest she wanted him to enter. She loved poems almost as much as Shakespeare plays.

Almost too afraid to ask, Nic said, "What's the event?"

"It's called paintball and seems to be geared toward kids. It sounds like something right up your alley. Are you interested?" responded Nic's mom.

Nic's eyes widened in surprise. He dropped his spoon, which landed with a "plunk", spilling soup all over his face and shirt.

"Nicolas, for heaven's sake, be careful!"

Nic walked to the sink, washed off his face, and blotted the soup off his shirt.

"I wouldn't have mentioned it if I knew you were going to get that upset," finished his mom.

Without trying to sounding too interested, Nic asked, "Are you serious about letting me try paintball?"

"Sure, why not?"

Nic thought long and hard for about two microseconds before jumping up and down and answering gleefully, "All right! You bet I want to play paintball. You're the greatest, Mom!" He hugged her so hard and forcefully that she almost fell over backwards in her chair.

As he scurried up the stairs to begin his homework, Nic heard his mother joke, "If I'd known you wanted to play that bad, I would've had something in the bargain for me!"

Nic could hardly believe his luck. He hadn't even had to bring up the subject with his mom. In fact, she had practically begged him to enter.

Opening up his math book to begin his assignment, Nic thought, boy, it doesn't get any better than this…unless I could somehow make tonight's homework disappear..

CHAPTER ELEVEN

The Document

Kevin wasted no time in registering the gang for the paintball tournament.

"I figured I better get it done before somebody changed his mind," Kevin stated while eyeing Philip, Herbert, and Dante. He also told them the practice session for their group would be in early April, three weeks before the tournament.

"That's a long time before the tournament," Cindy observed. "Why is it that far in advance?"

Kevin answered, "There are a lot of teams, and everyone gets time to practice. It was just where we ended up."

The gang was excited, but so was the rest of the school. In fact, the tournament was all everyone was talking about at school. Nic hadn't realized how much of a buzz it was creating until Mr. Smithton brought it up during the last few minutes of class one day.

"I've noticed many of you seem…distracted. How many of you are planning to play in this paintball tournament?" he asked. About half the kids in class raised their hands. "My, that's a lot of you. I imagine it's probably the same amount in the other two fifth grade classes.

"Have any of you played paintball before?" asked Mr. Smithton. Only a couple of hands went up this time. "I see," stated Mr. Smithton.

Nic was relieved at this showing of hands. At least most of the kids hadn't played before, so he and his team might actually have a chance.

"Who does everybody think is going to win?" asked Mr. Smithton casually. The question surprised Nic. He hadn't really thought about it. He had figured it was up for grabs between all of the teams.

At first, no one answered, then a voice behind Nic answered, "I think Johnny's team will probably win."
Nic frowned.

"And why do you say that?" asked Mr. Smithton, scanning the young faces in front of him.

"I've heard they play a lot and have the new Commando 88 paintball guns," replied the boy. Several of Nic's classmates gasped at this news.

"What's a Commando 88?"

Another boy answered, "It's the newest and best semiautomatic paintball gun. I've heard if you have one you can't possibly lose." Another round of gasps erupted.

"Is that so? Does everybody else agree, then, that Johnny's team is too good to beat?" queried Mr. Smithton.

Nic blurted out, "I don't think Johnny's team is too good to beat."

Everyone stared at Nic in surprise. Mr. Smithton continued, "Why do you say that, Nic?"

Nic quietly cleared his throat, aware that everyone was looking at him and waiting for his answer. He answered quietly, "As someone once told me not too long ago, no one is unbeatable."

Mr. Smithton nodded. A faint smile crossed his lips as he said, "Sounds like someone with very good advice."

Another of Nic's classmates added, "But Johnny and his team have the Commando 88s. How can you compete against that?"

"The Commando 88 may be a great paintball gun; but as Mr. Chen made clear to me, if you can out-think your opponent, then it doesn't matter what they have, because you can still win," Nic responded, a little too defiantly.

Half of Nic's class erupted into laughter, while the other half looked at him with puzzled faces.

"Who's Mr. Chen?" asked a girl next to Nic.

Before Nic could answer, someone yelled out, "Mr. Chen's the nutcase who owns the sports store off the alley on Main Street."

Another classmate added, while laughing, "My parents won't let me go near his store, 'cause they're afraid he's crazy."

Nic's face turned beet red with embarrassment and anger as he heard the laughter around him intensify.

"That will be quite enough, class!" yelled Mr. Smithton, just as the bell rang.

Saved by the bell, thought Nic. He wished he could disappear.

A hand on his shoulder stopped his hasty exit.

He was startled to see Mr. Smithton looking down at him saying, "Just a second there, Chief. I'd like to have a word with you."

Great, thought Nic as he sat back down, I'm probably in trouble for causing such a ruckus in class with my goofy ideas.

Mr. Smithton sat in the desk next to Nic's. By now, the last person had left the classroom. Nic could hear the remains of his classmates' laughter filling the hallway.

"My, I forgot how tiny these things are to sit in. Mind you, it has been a few years since I've been in one," quipped Mr. Smithton. Nic smiled weakly. "I respect what you did before class ended, Chief," said Mr. Smithton.

"Like how I made a goof up of myself?" responded Nic.

Mr. Smithton smiled and said, "No, that's not it at all. And, by the way, I don't think you made yourself out to be a goof."

"You seem to be the only one," replied Nic as faint laughter drifted into the room.

"It takes a great deal of courage to go against the crowd. You weren't afraid to speak your mind about how you felt, even if it wasn't the popular feeling among your classmates. I wouldn't be too surprised if more of the kids in class feel the same way you do, but were too afraid to admit it aloud," said Mr. Smithton.

Nic rolled his eyes, "I don't know if I can believe that, Mr. Smithton."

"You might be amazed. Stranger things have been known to happen in life," smiled Mr. Smithton, easing himself out of the tiny desk.

Nic watched Mr. Smithton walk back to his desk before getting up to leave. He felt better and appreciated Mr. Smithton's words of encouragement.

As Nic reached the classroom door, Mr. Smithton said with a wink, "Hey, Chief, the next time you go to Mr. Chen's store, tell him that you know me. He just might give you a discount."

Nic looked at Mr. Smithton with wide eyes, and his jaw dropped in amazement.

"Mr. Chen and I have been fishing buddies for as long as I can remember. He might be a little strange sometimes, but he's definitely not crazy. In fact, he's probably one of the wisest and kindest men I know," said Mr. Smithton with a smile as he began grading papers.

"I will. Thanks, Mr. Smithton!"

Nic's good mood was short lived. Johnny and his J Gang confronted him in the hallway. Great, just when I thought things were getting better, he has to show up, thought Nic.

"Hey, Geek, I heard you say that my team wasn't good enough to win the paintball tournament," Johnny sneered, as he got up into Nic's face.

"You heard wrong, Johnny. What I said was I didn't think your team was unbeatable."

"That sounds to me like you don't think my team can win," growled Johnny.

"No, that isn't it. Really, Johnny, we could argue all day about word use, but you'd be at a disadvantage due to your lack of vocabulary skills," Nic shot back.

Johnny's eyes widened. He wasn't used to being challenged or insulted in front of his gang.

"Whatever, Geek. I'm not surprised that you hang out with Mr. Chen. You're both losers," snapped Johnny.

"I guess you're right, Johnny. But you know, it takes one to know one."

Johnny got even closer to Nic and sneered, "You may be brave on school grounds with teachers around to save you, but wait until we play against each other in paintball. I'm going to mess you up, and there'll be nobody to save you."

Nic just stared back at Johnny without moving. After a few tense moments, Johnny and his gang headed toward the other side of the school building.

With Johnny out of earshot, Nic sucked air in noisily, blowing it out of his mouth, and closing his eyes for a few seconds. Man, Johnny's like a bad cold that just won't go away, he thought, heading home from school.

The sunny day put Nic in a better mood, and he actually enjoyed the bike ride home. He dropped his bike in the front yard and climbed up the front porch steps. He could hear Wellington whining inside.

Nic cautiously opened the front door, hoping to avoid a full-on Wellington attack. Too late! Wellington jumped, body slamming Nic against the doorframe.

"Woof!" Wellington exclaimed.

Nic pushed Wellington down and finally was able to give him a belly rub. Wellington's tail thump, thump, thumped happily on the rug. With belly rubs over, Wellington sighed happily and ran back to the kitchen to finish his dinner.

"Hello, Dear." Nic nearly jumped out of his skin upon hearing his mom's voice from the living room. He looked over and saw her sitting on the floor with papers spread out on every possible surface, including the floor.

"Hi, Mom! What's up? Nic looked at the mess and quipped, "This kinda looks like my room on a good day."

"Very funny, Nicolas. For your information, I'm grading research papers from my classes."

"Oh. Sounds awful. So, what's for supper?" asked Nic.

"I'm afraid you're on your own tonight. This is my focus for the next several hours. I'm sure you're capable of fixing yourself a sandwich," replied his mom.

Nic smiled, "Yeah, I think I'll be able to manage, but if this gets to be a habit with you, young lady, I'm going to have to report you for child abuse."

She shook her head, laughing, "You wouldn't know what child abuse is as spoiled as you are." Pointing in the direction of the kitchen, she ordered, "Now get!"

Nic stepped over a now-sleeping Wellington and opened the refrigerator. As he stared at the food available, he yelled out, "Hey, Mom, I'm going to need some camouflaged clothes for paintball. Do we have any around here I could wear?"

"What about your Halloween costume?" she shot back.

"It was almost too small in October. I won't fit in it now," Nic answered.

"I think your father used to have some. You'll have to go out into the garage and dig around in some of the unpacked boxes. Make sure when you're through you put everything back where you found it!" she answered.

"And close the refrigerator! You'll let all the cold out!" she added.

"How does she know what I'm doing?" Nic mumbled.

"Okay, thanks, Mom!"

He made sure the refrigerator closed loudly, just in case she was still listening. He decided to look for his camo gear right after supper.

Even with the overhead light blazing and his bright flashlight beam piercing the darkness, the garage was still creepy and full of shadows.

"How am I ever going to find anything in this mess?" mumbled Nic as he walked around his mom's car. How is it possible we still have so many unopened boxes, he wondered. He was hoping the box he was looking for had been labeled, but the only markings seemed to be "Office," "Garage," "Stuff," and other unhelpful tags.

Not really knowing where to start, he randomly stopped in front of a stack of boxes and began lifting them down to the floor.

"This is going to take awhile. Glad I didn't have any homework tonight," Nic whispered.

His searching method was simple. Pull boxes down, open a few, realize what he wanted wasn't in any of them, close the boxes, and restack them elsewhere. He lost track of time while searching, but his persistence paid off. He finally found a box full of his dad's things.

Nic paused for a moment before opening the box. When he pulled the tape back to reveal the contents, the faintest smell of his dad's cologne wafted to Nic's nose. The smell brought a rush of emotion. Nic took a deep breath and began digging into the box.

His dad's diploma from Duke University was on top. It had some dust on it, but otherwise looked in pretty good shape. Nic remembered how he and his dad would play against each other in basketball. His dad always had to be Duke University, and Nic would be whoever happened to be good that week. He smiled at the memory as he placed his dad's diploma to the side and continued his search.

Next were his dad's old history journals. Nic thought back to how his dad would encourage him to read them so they could then discuss the articles. He'd forgotten how much he had enjoyed those moments with his dad. Those discussions had sparked Nic's love of history and for reading books.

Stacking the journals to the side, Nic found his dad's old camouflage hunting outfit. It was complete with his hunting cap and boots. He remembered his dad telling him how he would go hunting with Nic's grandfather, but would never shoot at anything because he loved animals too much. Nic had asked him why he went hunting if he wasn't going to hunt, and his dad told him it was so he could spend time with his dad. When he noticed that Nic was looking at him with a puzzled expression, he continued by saying that one day Nic would understand how precious it is to be with those you love,,because you never know when you might see them again. Tears welled up in Nic's eyes at that memory. He wiped them away with his shirtsleeve.

He pulled the clothes out of the box and took a second to size up each piece. He decided they would serve his purpose, although both the pants and jacket were going to be too big on him.

"Maybe mom could work on them, so they're closer to my size," mumbled Nic.

He was about to put the other items back into the box, when he saw a large, fat envelope sealed with tape. It had a label marked, *Nicolas Nelson's baby pictures.*

Mom must've forgotten she had these out here, thought Nic, as he flicked at the loose end of the tape on the back of the envelope. While he was fussing with the envelope, the label on the front came off and fluttered to the ground. Nic looked at the space where the label had been. Something was handwritten there. He strained to read the words, *Important Preliminary Report - For Investigative Committee Eyes Only.*

Shocked, Nic stared at the envelope in his hands. Wow, I bet this must be something really important for it to have those words written on it. I wonder what's inside of it, and why the label was put on it, he mused. Nic tried again to loosen the tape that was holding the envelope closed.

CRASH! That came from the Chamberlains' house! Nic dropped the envelope back into the box and hastily threw the journals and diploma in before closing it.

I wonder if Mom or anybody else heard that, thought Nic. He crept out to the edge of his driveway, keeping in the shadows so he remained hidden.

He peered across the street at the darkened house. With no moon to light their yards, it was hard to make out anything. Unexpectedly, he heard the loud roar of a revved car engine and then the squealing of tires. Nic looked down the street in time to see a small car zooming away. He couldn't tell what the car looked like for sure, but it seemed a lot like the one Roger Marinovich and his partner had been driving last fall.

Nic slowly walked across the street to the Chamberlains' driveway. He noticed one of their garbage cans lying on its side with trash everywhere. That explains what caused the noise, Nic thought.

Before he had a chance to get away, the Chamberlains' front lights lit up, shining on him and the mess around him. Too stunned to move, Nic was suddenly the center of Mrs. Chamberlain's attention, "Who's there? Answer me now or I'll call the police!"

Nic quickly blurted out, "It's me, Nic Nelson, your neighbor, Mrs. Chamberlain."

"What are you doing over here? What's all this racket about?"

Before Nic could answer, Mrs. Chamberlain caught sight of the overturned garbage can and demanded, "Why did you knock over my garbage can, young man?"

Nic shook his head and answered, "I didn't do this. I heard a loud noise and came outside to investigate."

Mrs. Chamberlain gave Nic a fierce look before stating, "I expect you to clean this mess up before morning, young man, or I'll report you to the police for vandalism."

Without waiting for his response, she turned and walked back into her house.

Great, just what I wanted to be doing tonight, thought Nic, as he refilled the Chamberlains' garbage can.

"I'd love to give her a piece of my mind one of these days," mumbled Nic.

He quickly finished. Returning to his garage, he restacked the boxes before grabbing the clothes and shutting the door. He was happy to return to the safety of his house and a full cookie jar.

At least I found some camouflage clothes to wear for the paintball tournament, Nic thought, as he scrambled into bed. Staring up at the ceiling with heavy eyes, Nic pondered the day's events.

If it was Roger Marinovich and his partner tonight, then it must mean they still haven't found the Diamonds of Denmark. They must either be dumb criminals or else the diamonds are hidden extremely well. I sure wish I could figure out where the diamonds are so I could find them. Right before he fell asleep he thought…then I could return them to their rightful owners.

Sitting at the lunch table the next day, Kevin asked, "Do you really think it was the thieves you heard last night?"

"I think so. Who else could it have been?" replied Nic.

"It could've been their cat," offered Herbert.

"Maybe, but that wouldn't explain the car leaving in a hurry," answered Nic.

"Also, knowing Mrs. Chamberlain like we do, I doubt if she would let her cat outside to get dirty in the garbage. I'll bet their cat wouldn't know what a mouse was if you showed it one," chuckled Philip.

"Are you sure it was their car?" asked Cindy.

"No. It was too dark for me to tell for sure, and they left in a real hurry. But my gut instinct tells me it was them," said Nic.

"I wish there was something more we could do to help you, Nic," stated Dante.

"Maybe we could set up traps in the Chamberlains' backyard to catch Roger Marinovich. We could spread them all over so that every inch was covered!" As Kevin hatched his trap idea, he rubbed his hands together in anticipation, chuckling.

Herbert added, "Yeah, and maybe we could install video cameras to catch them on tape."

"Great idea, Herbert," said Kevin as he gave him a high five.

Nic, Philip, Cindy, and Dante all looked at each other and then at Kevin and Herbert.

"You've had some real crazy ideas before, Kevin, but this one takes the cake," exclaimed Cindy shaking her head.

"What do you mean? It's brilliant," Kevin exclaimed.

"For one thing, I don't think the Chamberlains are going to want a group of kids running around in their backyard setting up traps without knowing why; and they wouldn't believe us even if we told them why," said Cindy.

"Okay, but why else?" asked Kevin, not as confident as before.

"What happens if someone we don't want to capture gets caught up in one of your traps? I don't think they'd be too happy, do you?" added Nic.

"I hadn't thought of that. Man, you guys can be real party poopers sometimes," smiled Kevin. They all stood up to return to class.

CHAPTER TWELVE

Paintball Practice

D-Day, thought Nic, or at least practice D-Day. Everyone was quiet in Philip's van as his mom drove the gang to the paintball practice session. Nic's stomach churned uncomfortably. He was nervous.

"This is going to be so awesome!" stated Kevin, trying to sound brave.

Nic just shook his head and returned to his thoughts. At least everyone was able to find camouflage clothes so no one would stand

147

out. But the black face paint seemed silly for Philip and Kevin to have done.

"We're here, kids!" announced Philip's mom.

The air was cool and misty, with morning dew slowly rising from the ground like steam from a hot bowl of soup as the gang got out of the van with their gear.

"Thanks for the lift, Mrs. Browning," said Cindy.

"Have fun everybody; and for goodness sakes, I don't want anybody getting hurt," said Philip's mom.

"We'll be fine, Mom. You're such a worry wart," replied Philip, slamming the van's sliding door shut.

She rolled down the passenger window adding, "Don't forget to call me when you're done, Philip!"

Philip raised his hand to let her know he'd heard her without saying a word.

"What do we do now?" asked Dante.

Kevin pointed toward a large white table under a tree and said, "First off, we need to sign our team in at that table and find out what time we're supposed to play."

"Will we know who our opponents are?" asked Nic as they walked toward the sign-in table.

"Nope, and we won't know until it's our time to play. They're picked at random."

Nic couldn't believe the amount of people standing around. It looked like the whole town of New Bonn was there. No one seemed to know where to go, so the scene was a bit crazy. They found the sign-in table line and waited patiently for their turn.

"We're here to sign-in," said Kevin to the frazzled woman behind the table.

"Team name?" she snapped, without looking up.

Team name? Kevin never mentioned anything about needing a team name, Nic thought. He and the others stared at Kevin.

"Team Kevin," answered Kevin proudly.

"Be ready to go at 11:30 A.M. at Field A." She never once looked at Kevin.

As the gang moved aside, Dante asked in disbelief, "Team Kevin? What kind of a name is that?"

"I think it's a cool one," replied Kevin.

"Says you," quipped Cindy.

"Doesn't sound cool to me either," added Herbert.

"I had to put something down when I entered our team," said Kevin defensively.

"Is it too late to change our team name?" asked Dante.

"I suppose not, since today is just for practice. Do you have a better name for us in mind?" asked Kevin angrily.

Pausing for a few moments, Dante replied, "Yeah, I do. How about Team Dante?"

Cindy scoffed, "That's not much better. I like the sound of Team Cindy and Her Helpers!"

The boys stared at Cindy. Philip replied, "I don't think so, Cindy. That name wouldn't exactly strike fear in anybody; and besides, it sounds like the name of some cooking show."

"Do you have a better one?" she asked. She was now standing with her hands on her hips attempting to stare Philip down.

"Maybe. How about Team Philip and His Destructive Crew?" He was unfazed by Cindy's weak bullying attempt.

"Nah, it doesn't sound quite right. I've got a good one now. The Nasty Bunch could be our name, and we could refer to each other as such. For example, I would be Nasty Kevin, and you would be Nasty Nic and Nasty Philip," stated Kevin boldly while pointing.

"I think not, Nasty Kevin," replied Cindy, "The other teams wouldn't know whether to be scared of us or laugh at us."

Before Kevin could reply to Cindy's criticism, Herbert blurted out, "I know, how about Team Herbert and the Herberteers?"

Everyone stared at Herbert and then at each other as if Herbert's idea wasn't even worth a response.

Finally, Nic spoke up, "I think I might have a name that sounds good for us. I saw it once in one of my dad's old books, and I thought it sounded neat."

"It's Sokoor."

"Soccer?" repeated Herbert.

"No, not quite, Herbert. It's pronounced So- Koor," said Nic.

"Soo- core?" said Herbert.

Nic stifled a laugh and said, "Close, but try saying so-cool, except add the letter 'r' to the end; and you'll have it."

Herbert mumbled it a few times to himself before saying it aloud again, "Sokoor?"

"That's it! Good job, Herbert," said Nic.

"I like it," said Herbert with a smile.

"Me, too. What language is it, and what does it mean?" asked Cindy.

"It's Arabic, and it means eagles," answered Nic.

"I like it, too. It sounds much better than Team Kevin," smirked Dante toward Kevin.

Kevin returned a quick look at Dante before saying, "Now that everybody's happy with our new team name, I suggest we find a nice spot to wait until our time comes up to play."

It took a while to find a good spot, since it seemed everyone else had the same idea. They finally settled in under a shady tree. The coolness of the early morning was gone. Flopping on the ground, Dante said, "It's getting hot! I'm exhausted already, and we haven't even played yet."

"I know what you mean. Lugging all of this equipment around can be quite a workout," added Nic sitting down next to Philip.

"Does anybody know what time it is?" asked Philip.

"The time as of right now is 10:20," answered Kevin looking at his watch.

"I don't know if I can wait until 11:30. I'm too excited!" said Philip.

"You might as well try and relax, since we won't be doing anything for awhile," said Nic as he leaned back on the grass and closed his eyes. He hadn't slept much over the past week. *This feels so good,* he thought.

Nic suddenly felt his body shake; and as he opened his eyes, he saw Herbert's face inches from his own.

"Wake up, Nic, wake up," said Herbert. "It's time for us to go."

"Already? I just laid my head down a second ago," protested Nic groggily.

"You've been sleeping for the last hour," pointed out Cindy.

"Really, Nic, I don't know how you could sleep at a time like this. I'm so full of excitement and energy that I haven't been able to sit still since we got here," said Philip.

"I guess I'm just talented," joked Nic as he wiped his eyes.

"C'mon, guys, let's get going. We have to be at Field A in five minutes or else we'll forfeit our practice time," declared Kevin, leading the gang toward the field.

Nic somehow managed to shake off his sleepiness and catch up to his friends before they got too far ahead.

Following arrows along a small dirt path, they soon came across a sign, which read, *Field A*. Before them was a large area sectioned off by long, thick stretches of rope. As they entered the field, they began to get a sense of what was waiting for them. To the left were three round targets spread out at different distances from a wooden stand. A dirt path in front of them led into a wooded area. To their right was an open field with objects and obstacles scattered about and a tall observation tower. Loud noises and yelling were coming from the woods in front of them.

"Sounds like there are other teams already playing," said Herbert.

"I wonder what we're going to be doing first," mused Dante.

They were startled by an all-too-familiar voice taunting them from behind.

"That should be the least of your worries. What you should be afraid of is how badly we're going to whip you guys! I didn't think you losers were really serious about entering the paintball tournament. Of course, by the time we get through with you today, you'll wish you had never heard of paintball," bragged Johnny, while the other members of his gang hooted with delight.

Nic frowned as he turned to face Johnny. He could feel anger building, but didn't want to give Johnny the satisfaction of seeing he'd gotten to him.

"This is just for practice, Johnny. You know it doesn't mean anything today," said Kevin, who moved next to Nic.

"Maybe not," said Johnny. He continued while pointing at Nic, "But I made a promise to him that I was personally going to take him down if we ever played against each other."

Nic could feel the hairs on the back of his neck standing up as Johnny and his *J Gang* approached.

"See this, geek? This here is a Commando 88 semiautomatic paintball gun, the best one around. It's a hundred times better than those dinosaurs you guys have. Get a good look at this barrel, 'cause you'll be seeing a lot of it aiming at your face like this," growled Johnny, as he pointed his gun at Nic's face.

"What in blue blazes are you doing, son?" bellowed a deep commanding voice.

Johnny lowered his gun and took a step backwards as a large, husky man in fatigues and military beret marched toward them.

"Do you understand the English language, boy? I'll ask you only one more time. What do you think you were doing pointing your paintball gun at that young man's face?" the man demanded.

"I...I...I was just showing him what it looks like up close," stuttered Johnny.

"Yeah, and I'm Miss Universe. Don't ever let me catch you pointing your gun at anyone again outside of an actual game. And never, ever point it at their face. Do you understand?" he yelled.

"Yes," answered Johnny.

"Yes what?" commanded the man.

"Yes, sir," replied Johnny meekly.

I think I'm going to like this guy, thought Nic, struggling to hold back a smile at Johnny's predicament.

The man addressed the two groups. "Now that I've made my grand entrance, I'll introduce myself. My name is Mr. Payne, retired Sergeant Major of the U.S. Marine Corps and proud owner of Wild Wild Wacky Weekend Wrecking Warrior Enterprises, which runs these paintball fields. I'll be taking a few minutes to discuss the finer points about paintball and paintball rules before we proceed with your practice session. Any questions?"

Everyone shrugged or shook their heads.

"I can't hear you!" bellowed Mr. Payne.

"No, sir!" was the collective reply.

"Saddest bunch of kids I've ever laid eyes on. I see we're going to have a lot of work ahead of us. First, I want everyone to say his or her name as I point to you, so we can get to know each other better," said Mr. Payne.

He pointed at Herbert. Poor Herbert, thought Nic. His face was pale when he answered, "HHHHerbert."

Mr. Payne walked closer to Herbert until he towered over him and said, "I don't think I've ever met anybody named HHHHerbert before."

Johnny and his gang started laughing. Mr. Payne strode over to Johnny. Bending so his face was inches from Johnny's, he said with a low growl, "Was I talking to you, son, or any of the rest of your sorry lot?"

Johnny's gang stopped laughing. Johnny looked like he was going to faint.

"I think what we have here is a failure to communicate. Again I ask, was I talking to any of you?" Mr. Payne demanded.

"No, sir!" replied Johnny and the others.

"Good! Then shut your traps until pointed to," said Mr. Payne as he returned to Herbert's side.

"Son, let's try this again. What is your full name?" asked Mr. Payne calmly.

Herbert swallowed hard and then said, "Herbert Cuthbert Howell III, sir."

Cuthbert? What a strange middle name, thought Nic.

"Good, now that wasn't so hard," said Mr. Payne. He moved down the line of kids. Kevin was last.

"Kevin Scott Becker, sir."

Mr. Payne took a long step closer to Kevin so he was standing directly in front of him. He softly said, "So, you're the infamous Kevin Becker I've been told about. Your reputation precedes you."

Nic could see Kevin's confusion. Mr. Payne slowly smiled, while looking like a predator about to pounce on its prey. He said, "Surely my wife has mentioned me in your class?"

For a moment, Kevin stared wide-eyed at Mr. Payne. "Your wife is Mrs. Payne, my fifth grade teacher?" he asked incredulously.

Mr. Payne smiled and said, "Yes, she is."

"But she said her husband was like a…teddy bear," stuttered Kevin while swallowing hard.

Mr. Payne smiled again and whispered into Kevin's ear just loud enough for Nic to hear, "Only when I want to be, which in your case isn't likely to happen in this lifetime or the next."

Nic wanted to laugh so badly, but knew he shouldn't. He didn't want to face the wrath of Mr. Payne.

"Now that we all know who's who, the next step is to instruct you on the paintball rules of play. The first rule is safety first. Until you are told that play is to commence, all paintball guns are to have their safety switches engaged like this and are to be pointed downward with a safety plug inserted into the gun's barrel as such," said Mr. Payne, taking Kevin's paintball gun to use as an example.

"The next rule is that everyone must have his or her face mask on in order for play to start. You are not allowed to take it off for any reason until you have left the field of play and are at a safe distance away.

"The third rule is if you surprise someone at close range, you offer them a chance to surrender or else get shot which, I might add, can really sting up close.

"The fourth and last rule is the most important one. If anyone breaks one rule, they and their team will be eliminated from the paintball tournament and will never be allowed to play here again, as long as I'm running the show. Are we clear on that?"

"Yes, sir!" yelled everyone.

"Good! Now, on to the next part of our discussion. Please follow me," said Mr. Payne.

Nic and the others followed Mr. Payne over to the round targets.

"This next part will consist of everyone getting a chance to shoot at the targets for practice and at me to make sure the velocity on your gun is set within safety limits," explained Mr. Payne.

"Now we're getting to the fun part," whispered Kevin to Nic.

"Line up! Single file!" Mr. Payne ordered.

Johnny was the first person to practice. Nic couldn't believe what he was seeing. Johnny was firing at one target to the next with pinpoint accuracy.

"Well done, Johnny. Your gun is within the safety limits. Next!" yelled Mr. Payne.

Johnny walked back and bumped hard against Nic and whispered, "You are so dead meat."

Nic glared back at him and said softly, "We'll see come game time, Johnny."

Johnny replied with a smirk as he sat down a few yards away and began polishing his gun barrel.

Over the next twenty minutes, all of the kids had their guns checked while firing at the targets. Nic felt he hadn't done too badly, since it was his first time using a paintball gun. Most of his shots had come close to the center of the bulls-eye, with an occasional stray shot missing the target completely. Herbert, on the other hand, didn't do so well. He somehow managed to hit several trees splattering paint on an unsuspecting squirrel.

Kevin whispered to Nic in exasperation, "I'm not sure if having Herbert play with us was very smart. I think he's going to be more dangerous to us than toward anyone else. I mean where do you put him? If he's behind you, you run the risk of getting shot by him; and if he's in front of you, you could still get hit by him."

"Give him a break, Kevin. Other than you, this is everyone else's first time out. I'm sure he'll improve," said Nic.

"I sure hope so or else there could be a lot of angry animals turning on us," chuckled Kevin. Nic couldn't help but smile at that.

Mr. Payne didn't seem to know what to say when Herbert finished. "Son, I think you could use a lot more practice. I'm certain the squirrel would agree. Your gun checks out fine, though," he finally said.

Herbert took his gun and walked dejectedly over to Nic, who patted him on the back and tried to make him feel better.

"Let's move on to the next step," said Mr. Payne as he led the kids over to the obstacle filled area of the field. "This is the type of course your age group will be using during the tournament. There are two more courses like this one on the other fields," informed Mr. Payne.

At first glance, the field looked like a giant messy maze. The field was littered with overturned picnic tables, oil drums, old furniture, and pieces of sheet metal stuck into the ground. In the center of the course stood a single black pole with a small red flag attached to it.

"The type of paintball game you will be playing is referred to as Speedball. It consists of two teams starting opposite of each other from those white circles and running into the center of the course to capture the red flag first. Whichever team acquires the red flag must then take it back to their starting circle in order to win. Any questions so far?" asked Mr. Payne.

"No, sir!" was the collective reply.

"Good. You win the game in one of two ways. The first is whichever team captures the flag and returns it to their circle. The second is by winning an accuracy shootout. That is only needed when there is a tie. This can happen if, after twenty minutes, neither team has captured the flag. The accuracy shootout determines the game winner."

Philip raised his hand. "Do you have a question, son?" asked Mr. Payne.

"Yes, sir. What's an accuracy shootout?" Philip asked.

"An accuracy shootout is where each player on each team shoots at a target. Whichever team scores the best wins the shootout. Understand?" asked Mr. Payne.

"Yes, sir," replied Philip.

Cindy raised her hand, and Mr. Payne pointed to her and asked, "Yes?"

"How does one get out, sir?" asked Cindy.

"Excellent question. A player is considered out of the game when any part of his or her person is hit by a paintball that bursts. If a paintball hits a player without breaking, then the player hit is not out.

If a player's gun is hit by a paintball, the player is not out regardless of whether the paintball bursts or not. If a player is not sure about whether they or another player is out, they can ask for a paint check from a field referee. The referee's decision is final. The referee will also call a player out if it's determined a player is cheating. A player is also out of the game if their gun malfunctions," explained Mr. Payne.

Herbert raised his hand and when called on by Mr. Payne asked, "What do you do when you're out, sir?"

"When a player is determined to be out, he or she needs to put their barrel plug back into the barrel of their gun first. Next, holding their gun straight up into the air, the player needs to march out of the field of play while keeping their mask on until safely out of harm's way," answered Mr. Payne.

"That's about all there is to know about the rules. Any other questions?" asked Mr. Payne.

"No, sir," replied everyone.

"Good. Then let's get this started. What's your team name?" asked Mr. Payne, pointing to Johnny.

Johnny smiled and replied, "Team Bad to the Bone."

Mr. Payne smiled slightly, "Yeah, that's real original."

Mr. Payne looked at Kevin. "What's your team name?"

Before Kevin could speak, Nic said, "Team Sokoor."

Mr. Payne looked surprised. "Nice name. Means eagles in Arabic, doesn't it?"

"Yes, sir, that's what it means."

"I've learned a few Arabic words over the years from friends," said Mr. Payne, as if anticipating Nic's next question.

"Okay, Team Bad to the Bone, load up your hoppers with paintballs and go to that circle. Team Sokoor, load up your hoppers and head to the other circle. When you hear my air horn, you may begin the game," instructed Mr. Payne.

Nic popped open his hopper's lid and proceeded to fill it until it was completely full. He next checked to make sure the hopper was secure in its place on top of his paintball gun. He didn't want to be running around and have his hopper fall off so his gun wouldn't fire anything. That would be exactly what Johnny would want to see happen to him, thought Nic. Nic put his mask on last and made sure it was snug before gripping his paintball gun.

"C'mon, guys, we've got to get mov'n. Let's go!" shouted Kevin as he waved everybody to follow.

Nic, Cindy, Philip, Dante, and, finally, Herbert all reached the white circle where Kevin was waiting for them impatiently.

"Took you guys long enough. Everybody good to go?" asked Kevin. His voice was muffled because of his mask.

Nic and the others nodded their heads and readied themselves for the air horn to start the game. Nic hadn't felt his heart beating this fast since the dodgeball game at the YMCA. It seemed to Nic as if time had stopped while he stood ready to go. The air was pierced with the harsh sound of the air horn. Game on!

The gang followed Kevin to hide behind the nearest object, an overturned picnic table.

"What now?" Dante asked Kevin.

"Why are you asking me?" replied Kevin.

"Oh, I don't know. Maybe because you've only mentioned a thousand times how you've played paintball before with Jason and his friends," said Dante.

"I've played paintball before, but not this version of the game," answered Kevin.

"We're going to die," said Herbert.

"Herbert, stop!" said Cindy.

"What are we going to do?" asked Philip.

"One thing is clear. If we don't start moving, Johnny's team will capture the flag first without a fight," Nic responded.

"Nic's right, guys. Let's all move over there. By staying together, we should be in good shape," directed Kevin, pointing where they should go.

"Why should we all stick together? Shouldn't we spread out?" asked Nic.

Kevin looked exasperated. "C'mon, Nic, haven't you ever heard of the saying, 'Safety in numbers?'"

"Kevin's right, Nic. We should all stay together," said Dante.

"I'm in favor of that," added Herbert.

"Okay, on the count of three, move," commanded Kevin. Nic had a bad feeling about their plan. Kevin shouted, "Three!"

He sprinted off to the next barrier, while Philip shouted, "What happened to one and two?" as he nervously followed.

Dante and Nic were close behind. Nic saw blurs of orange and purple whizzing by his visor and barely missing Philip and Dante. Reaching the safety of their new obstacle, Nic looked back to see that Herbert and Cindy hadn't crossed over yet.

Nic tapped Kevin on his shoulder and said, "Hey, look; Cindy and Herbert are stuck behind. We need to give them some cover fire so they can get over here." Kevin and the others nodded their heads in agreement.

"Move it now, guys!" screamed Kevin as he, Nic, Philip, and Dante stood up to fire toward the other side.

Nic couldn't really see anyone to aim at, so he fired in a wide sweep pattern hoping for a lucky hit. He could see out of the corner of his eyes that Cindy was moving first, with Herbert following. More purple and orange paintballs flew across the air beside Nic's head and at Herbert and Cindy. This looks like a scene out of some war movie with tracer fire erupting everywhere, thought Nic.

"C'mon, Cindy and Herbert!" encouraged Nic to his teammates.

Cindy dove safely behind Nic. Herbert was not as lucky. Just before reaching them, he was pelted by an avalanche of paintballs bursting all along his arms and legs. He stumbled sideways from the impact, which caused him to turn his back toward his opponents. Paintballs burst on Herbert's rear end like an angry swarm of bees. Nic felt helpless. Herbert fell to his knees saying, "Ow!"

Mr. Payne ran up to Herbert and yelled, "Out!" He then helped a limping Herbert off the field.

"Poor Herbert. He looks like he fell into a vat of paint," mumbled Philip.

"I sure hope he's not seriously hurt," offered Cindy.

"What do we do now?" asked Dante.

"Keep moving!" said Kevin, sounding less brave than before.

Everyone else was too nervous and scared to disagree. Even Nic found himself freezing up as his thoughts became overwhelmed with uncertainty as to what to do. Everything is happening too fast to think clearly, thought Nic, as he felt his heart rapidly thumping against his chest.

"Three!" yelled Kevin, taking off toward another obstacle.

"I wish he'd stop doing that," exclaimed a frustrated Philip.

"Well, I guess we'd better get going too," said Dante slowly.

Everyone got ready, and with one quick look, Nic took off in the lead.

Once again, Nic found himself dodging a hail of paintballs. Within steps of his destination next to Kevin, Nic suddenly heard grunts behind him. He looked over his shoulder to see that Philip and Dante had been nailed on the sides of their heads with orange goo running down their necks. Further behind them, he saw Cindy. She'd fallen down and was struggling to get back up.

Without hesitating, Nic turned around and ran between Dante and Philip to help Cindy. He grabbed her left arm and pulled her to her feet. Paintballs were bursting all around them as each hit the ground with a solid plop! Nic tried to give them cover as they ran by, shooting wildly toward Johnny's side of the field. He was happy to see Kevin doing the same thing.

"I dropped my gun, Nic!" yelled Cindy in despair.

"We can't go back for it!" he answered as they made it to where Kevin was hiding.

"Dante and Philip are out of the game, and Cindy dropped her gun," Nic reported to Kevin. They all paused for a moment to catch their breath.

"I think it's safe to say we're in deep doo doo," half-joked Kevin.

"Maybe we should give up," offered Cindy.

"No way, I'm not surrendering to Johnny, even if it means getting hit a hundred times by his team," replied Nic.

"But there are only three of us left with two guns. They still have six people," Cindy pointed out.

"Doesn't matter, I'm not surrendering; and that's final," answered Nic.

Cindy shook her head and declared, "Oh, Nic, you're being too stubborn."

Nic noticed that Kevin had been strangely quiet throughout the discussion and asked him, "What do you think?"

"Shhh!" said Kevin.

"What is it? Do you hear something?" whispered Cindy.

"No, and that's what scares me," Kevin replied.

Then Nic noticed it too. A strange calm had come over the field.

"Maybe Johnny's team has captured the flag and won the game," said Cindy.

"I don't think so, because we would've heard Mr. Payne's air horn going off," said Nic.

"Whatever the case may be, I'm going to pop up and take a look," said Kevin as he readied himself.

"Be careful," said Cindy.

Kevin had barely poked his head over the top of their hiding spot, when his visor was pelted with paintballs.

"Gosh darn it!" said Kevin angrily, as orange and purple paint ran down his mask. "Yuck, this stuff tastes terrible, and I can barely see anything out my mask now," complained Kevin, slowly making his way off the field.

We're really in trouble now, thought Nic, as he and Cindy watched Kevin walk off. Even he had to admit the odds were now heavily stacked against them, with six on two and only one gun.

"We should have asked Kevin to give you his gun," said Nic to Cindy.

"I don't think it's going to matter at this point," replied Cindy.

Nic didn't know what else to say, as it seemed like his confidence was melting away, too. Nic saw movement out of the corner of his eye and yelled, "Move!" He pushed Cindy down; and it was a good thing, because a couple of paintballs splattered where she had been just moments before. Nic returned fire.

"They're moving to the sides of our position. We're going to have to fall back!" screamed Nic as he attempted to help Cindy back up.

"Shouldn't they already have captured the flag if they're this close to us?" asked Cindy as she recovered.

Nic didn't answer, but knew Cindy was right. What was Johnny's team doing this far over? He was about to move backwards when Nic heard a sarcastic voice from behind declare, "Surrender or die!"

Nic turned around to see who it was even though he already knew. Standing a few feet away, with his paintball gun aimed at Nic's face, was Johnny. "Remember what I said earlier, Geek?" teased Johnny.

Before Nic could respond, Johnny fired at him and Cindy, knocking them back to the ground.

Nic felt sharp pain coming from his stomach where Johnny had nailed him as he rolled to his side. He bit his lip to stop from yelling, as he didn't want to give Johnny the satisfaction of knowing how much it had hurt. He did, however, hear Cindy yelp with pain; and he could see Mr. Payne and the others running toward them.

"Kids, are you okay?" asked Mr. Payne with concern, as he knelt between Nic and Cindy.

"Yeah," said Nic in a confident tone that hid his true discomfort from Johnny.

Cindy sobbed, "I guess."

Kevin, Herbert, Dante, and Philip assisted Nic and Cindy to their feet.

Mr. Payne turned to Johnny and asked, "Why did you shoot at them when you were so close? Didn't you ask if they wanted to surrender first?"

Johnny replied as innocently as he could, "Of course, I did. When I didn't hear a reply and saw him turning around, I thought he was going to fire at me."

Mr. Payne looked doubtfully at Johnny and then at Nic and Cindy before asking, "Is this true?"

"He didn't give us time to say anything," said Cindy between sobs, as Nic kept silent, knowing they were in a no-win situation. If he told the truth, Johnny would just deny it and say they were sore losers; and Nic didn't want to give him any excuses to use against them.

Mr. Payne looked at Nic for a few seconds before realizing he wasn't going to say anything. He then looked at Johnny and stated, "Next time, wait a few seconds to hear their response before firing at someone that you have completely surprised."

"Yes, sir," answered Johnny with a hint of sarcasm.

"That's it for today, kids. Next time, it'll be for all the marbles. Let's move off before the next two groups get here," commanded Mr. Payne while clapping his hands.

Nic and the others dutifully collected their paintball gear and began to leave Field A. When Mr. Payne was out of sight, Johnny bumped up hard against Nic again as he passed on the way off the field with the other *J Gang* members.

"Nice game…not!" crowed Johnny as the other *J Gang* members laughed. Nic, Kevin, and the rest of the friends just glared at Johnny. "You guys were pathetic. You should really think about giving it up before one of you gets seriously hurt." Pointing at Cindy, Johnny continued, "By the way, what were you guys thinking by having *her* on your team?"

"What's that supposed to mean?" asked Nic defensively.

"You know exactly what I mean, Geek. She's a girl. This is a sport for boys," answered Johnny, his words dripping with contempt.

"She's our friend, and that's good enough for us," responded Nic.

He looked at Cindy and sneered, "If I were you, I'd go back to playing with your dolls where it's safe. And to the rest of you losers, so long!"

Nic and the others watched in silence as the *J Gang* disappeared down the trail leading to the front entrance. Nic felt a hand on his shoulder, and he turned to see Cindy's face.

"Thanks for sticking up for me, Nic. You didn't have to."

"Yes, I did. You're my friend, along with Kevin, Philip, Dante, and Herbert. I know you would've done the same for me," replied Nic.

"Oh, Nic, that's the sweetest thing anyone has ever said to me," said Cindy as she hugged Nic. He was caught off guard as he saw Kevin and the other boys roll their eyes at him and each other.

When Cindy finally let go of Nic, Kevin joked, "Just like my dad always says, 'Can't live with them and can't live without them.'"

Cindy looked at Kevin and let out a loud "Hmph!" in response. She marched off toward the entrance to wait for Philip's mom.

CHAPTER THIRTEEN

Captain Spencer to the Rescue

Nic was frustrated and disgusted. Apparently, everyone else felt the same way, as no one was talking in Mrs. Browning's van. Nic had never been so humiliated in his life. This was even worse than when he had milk squirt out of his nose during lunch from laughing at someone's joke in second grade. Johnny and his J Gang had thoroughly outclassed and beaten them today. Johnny and his team were so cocky and arrogant that they hadn't even tried to capture the flag. Even though Nic knew it had just been for practice, the sting of losing so badly was eating at him. The bruises on his stomach only served as painful reminders of their defeat.

With his frustration and anger building, Nic asked, "Mrs. Browning, could you please drop me off at the next street corner?"

"But, dear, we're still a ways from your house," she replied.

"I know, but I would really like to walk back home from here, if you don't mind."

Mrs. Browning shrugged her shoulders at the unusual request and replied, "Fine, if that's what you want."

Nic's dad told him once that when he was frustrated or mad at something, he would go for a walk by himself to clear his mind. This is as good a time as any to test out Dad's advice, he thought.

Nic climbed out with his gear. He thanked Mrs. Browning and was about to close the van door when Kevin stopped him.

"Wait! I'm coming, too!"

The boys watched as Mrs. Browning drove away with the others. They began walking, but neither wanted to break the silence. They were both lost in thought until Nic abruptly yelled, "We stink!" with such force that he caused two dogs to stop barking at them and a cat to jump up from its peaceful slumber on a nearby porch.

"Gosh, Nic, don't hold back. Tell everyone how you truly feel," joked Kevin.

"How can you joke around after what we just went through? Don't you take anything seriously?" growled Nic.

"You're absolutely right, Nic. We stunk real badly today, and Johnny's team really creamed us. But so what?" replied Kevin defensively.

"So what? What do you mean by so what?" asked Nic.

"Exactly by what it means," answered Kevin.

The boys stopped and glared at each other for a few moments before Nic apologized, "I'm sorry, Kevin. I didn't mean to get mad at you. I'm just upset at the way things turned out today."

"It's okay, Nic. I'm sorry about joking around earlier. I guess I sometimes tend to make light of stuff when I'm mad or frustrated as a way of handling it," replied Kevin solemnly.

The boys began to walk again, when they suddenly heard a loud sounding vrroom nearby.

"That sounds awfully familiar," said Nic.

Kevin smiled and replied, "It should. That's Jason's car. He's probably working on it again. He's always working on that old heap of junk. When I ask him why he doesn't just buy a new car he says, 'I can't, it's my baby.'"

"You mean Jason lives on this street?" asked Nic.

"Yeah, in fact, we're coming up to his house now," said Kevin pointing to their right.

Nic hadn't thought about where Jason might live. His house wasn't anything fancy, but then most houses in New Bonn weren't — except for the Chamberlains', of course. Jason lived in a two-story, red brick house that looked smaller than it was, because of the enormous weeping willow tree that shaded the entire front yard with its branches. Small bushes outlined the sidewalk to the front door. There were four people in the open garage. Three seemed to be analyzing Jason's engine, while a fourth kept revving the motor at Jason's command.

Vrroom! Vrroom! Nic and Kevin walked up the driveway to investigate.

"That's enough! Turn off the car!" shouted Jason from under the car's hood.

"Sounds like the carburetor is mixing too richly," said someone next to Jason.

"I don't think so. Maybe it's a bad spark plug," remarked someone else.

Sounds like a foreign language to me, thought Nic.

Jason popped his head out from underneath the hood and spotted Nic and Kevin. "What happened to you guys? You look like death warmed over," commented Jason, surveying their paint-splattered military fatigues.

"We had our practice session for the paintball tournament today," answered Kevin.

"That's right, I'd completely forgotten all about the practice sessions starting up this weekend. Come to think of it, I'm not really sure when my team's is. Do any of you guys know?" Jason asked his friends, scratching his head.

"No," was the collective reply.

"Oh, well, I guess I'll have to check up on it Monday morning," stated Jason.

"You're playing in it, too?" asked Nic.

"Sure am. Wouldn't miss it for the world. In fact, let me introduce you to most of my team," said Jason. Pointing to his right, Jason said, "This is Rich, to my left is Scott, and just getting out of my car is Tim. Everybody, this is Kevin's new friend, Nic."

"What's up, Kevin? Haven't seen you around for awhile," asked Tim, as he strolled on up to where the boys were standing.

"Not much. You know me, just trying to stay out of trouble," answered Kevin.

"Didn't think that was possible," smiled Tim. Looking at Nic, Tim asked, "Since you're friends with Kevin, I suppose you know my cousin, Philip, as well?"

"Philip's your cousin?" blurted Nic.

"Yup, in fact, I coach his in-line hockey team in town. We're two-time defending champs," bragged Tim.

Kevin snickered, "From what I hear, all you do is eat and snooze on the bench during Philip's hockey games, while Philip and the other players coach themselves."

Tim grabbed Kevin by his shoulders and said, "I think someone needs to be taught a lesson about respecting his elders," pulling Kevin onto the front yard grass.

Nic smiled and asked, "Doesn't he ever learn?"

"Afraid not," chuckled Jason, as they watched Kevin giggling in the middle of Tim's bear hug.

"Anyway, how did things go today, Nic?" asked Jason.

"Terrible! We got our butts kicked big time by Johnny's team," replied Nic.

Jason put his arm around Nic's shoulders and said consolingly, "Sorry to hear that. I've heard Johnny's team is pretty good this year."

"Is the Johnny you're talking about that brat, Johnny Parks?" asked Scott.

"That's the one," said Jason.

"Wish we could play against him. I'd teach him a thing or two about paintball, among other things," growled Scott. Nic smiled thinking it was too bad Scott couldn't fulfill his wish.

"I know Kevin has played paintball before, but has anyone else on your team played?" inquired Jason.

"No."

"Didn't anyone discuss strategies or techniques with you guys beforehand?" asked Jason.

Again, Nic's answer was, "No."

Jason shook his head in disbelief, "No wonder you guys were beaten so badly. None of you were prepared. Didn't any of you guys think about getting some advice or help?"

Nic shrugged his shoulders and felt his cheeks flush with embarrassment. Everything Jason was saying was so obvious, but no one had even thought about it. Nic then asked Jason if he would volunteer to help them.

"If I had the time, I'd work with you guys, but I don't," said Jason. Nic looked at the ground in disappointment. "There is someone who would be able to help you, though, if you asked him."

Nic's head jerked up quickly at this news.

"Who?"

"Captain Spencer," Jason answered.

"Captain Spencer?"

"Wait. I thought you knew who Captain Spencer was," said Jason.

Nic stuttered, "I do, but…"

Jason smiled, "You and Kevin aren't the only ones who Captain Spencer has befriended. Who do you think used to rake the Chamberlains' yard?" Nic shrugged. "It was me and my friends. But I'm getting off of the subject, aren't I?

"Captain Spencer was the one who first introduced my friends and me to paintball. He taught us all about the strategies and teamwork involved."

"I just can't imagine Captain Spencer playing paintball," mumbled Nic, trying to picture Captain Spencer in his black butler suit and shoes running around shooting a paintball gun.

"I know it's probably hard to imagine, but it's true. With his military background, he's pretty awesome," said Jason.

"You've played with him?" asked Nic.

"With him and against him. One time, after we were teasing him about getting too old to keep up, he took us all on and whipped us bad. That was the last time we did that," stated Jason.

Before Nic could say anything else, Tim plopped Kevin down on his back in front them. "Hope that little lesson taught you something, Kevin," Tim said laughing.

Kevin was blinking fast and looking up at everybody from the ground. His hair was even messier than before, and he had a dizzy look in his eyes from being spun around quite a few times.

"Oh, my head," moaned Kevin as he held it with both hands.

Scott, Rich, and Jason all laughed, clearly enjoying the moment at Kevin's expense. Jason snapped his fingers and said, "Would love to talk to you guys more, but we've gotta go. Remember what I said, Nic, about Captain Spencer."

"I will," replied Nic as he helped Kevin stand up.

Wobbling a bit next to Nic, Kevin said, "I could've taken Tim, but he surprised me too quickly."

Nic nodded in false agreement as he thought, sure you could've, Kevin.

"What did you and Jason talk about while I was letting Tim win?" asked Kevin.

"Jason was telling me about how we should go to Captain Spencer for paintball help."

"Captain Spencer? Why him?"

"According to Jason, Captain Spencer is really good at paintball and could teach us strategies," said Nic.

Kevin scratched his chin in thought before saying, "I guess it'd be okay. I suppose we don't have anything to lose, and we surely can't get any worse."

"Then it's settled. I'll ask him on my way home today," said Nic.

"Do you think he'll really help us?" asked Kevin.

Nic shrugged, "I don't know."

Nic and Kevin parted at Kevin's street. Nic was grateful for the silence and his thoughts. It would be so cool if Captain Spencer helps us, he thought. He was entertaining himself with thoughts of Johnny and the J Gang's demise, when he realized he was standing on the Chamberlains' front porch.

Nic swallowed hard as he rang the doorbell. Bong! Bong! Bong! That's one powerful doorbell, thought Nic, as he saw a familiar, friendly face opening the double doors.

"Good day, Master Nic. What may I ask is the pleasure of your visit?" asked Captain Spencer.

Nic replied nervously, while making motions with his hands, "I... um...I...um..."

"I'm afraid I'm not very good at charades, young master," said Captain Spencer with a slight smile.

"What I mean to say is, I was told by someone that you might know a little something about paintball."

Captain Spencer answered, "A little."

Nic swallowed hard before continuing, "I...we...my friends...we were wondering if you would be willing to help us out? We've entered a local paintball tournament, which is in three weeks, and none of us has any idea how to play."

Captain Spencer stood looking at Nic without answering. Nic fidgeted under his gaze.

"I'm sorry, I shouldn't have bothered you, Captain Spencer. I should have realized you're a very busy man. Thanks anyway." He began to back away from the front door.

"I would be honored to oblige your request, Master Nic," said Captain Spencer.

Nic exclaimed, "You will?"

"Yes, I will," declared Captain Spencer.

"Why? I mean, that's great; but why are you going to help us? We're just a bunch of kids you hardly know." Nic instantly regretted having said that.

Captain Spencer knelt down on one knee and placed his large hands on Nic's shoulders. Nic almost fell over from the weight of Captain Spencer's hands, which, given their size, seemed to swallow his shoulders whole.

"One of my illustrious countrymen, Sir Winston Churchill, once said, 'We make a living by what we get. We make a life by what we give,'" said Captain Spencer.

Nic responded, "I don't understand what that means."

"What Mr. Churchill was trying to say was the person who gives of himself to others will always be richer and happier than the person who only desires money and material things," explained Captain Spencer.

Nic nodded as Captain Spencer stood up. "I will be available from two until five tomorrow, if you and your friends still desire my services."

"Great! Thank you, Captain Spencer!"

Nic ran home. He couldn't wait to call the others with the good news about tomorrow. In his excitement, he'd forgotten how he looked. His mom listened sympathetically to his paintball story and, after dinner, treated him to homemade chocolate chip cookies to ease his bruised ego and painful muscles.

Nic's backyard was abuzz with excitement the next afternoon. The whole gang eagerly awaited Captain Spencer's arrival.

"Did he really tell you he was going to help us?" asked Dante.

"Yup," answered Nic proudly.

"We definitely need all of the help we can get. I'm still feeling my bruises every time I move," added Philip as he rubbed his shoulder.

"Here he comes now," said Cindy, pointing toward the Chamberlains' house.

The gang was shocked to see Captain Spencer wearing well-worn camouflage pants, a dingy white T-shirt and battered black boots.

Kevin, in typical fashion, saw the surprise on the others' faces and quipped, "What did you expect? That he'd play in a tuxedo?"

"Good afternoon, young masters. Ready to get started?" asked Captain Spencer. Nic and the others nodded and smiled. "Then let's begin," he continued.

"Master Nic, may I borrow your paintball gun?"

Nic handed it to Captain Spencer. Nic's thought was that it looked like a miniature toy in his hands. Captain Spencer turned the gun over his in hands inspecting it carefully.

"The Predator V paintball gun...it's a rather plain looking, but otherwise reliable, gun. I used one for years. I use my original as a backup. If wielded properly, it can be most effective for the user," he explained.

"It wasn't very effective for us yesterday," moaned Philip.

"I'm sure you believe that to be correct, Master Philip. Hopefully, I will be able to change your mind over the next three weeks," replied Captain Spencer. "Let us begin with learning how to hold and fire the gun correctly. Thank you, Master Nic, I see you've set up the target stand just as I had requested."

Nic beamed upon hearing this praise.

Over the next hour, Captain Spencer helped each of them learn how to aim and fire the paintball gun at the target. Everyone's accuracy was improving. Then, it was Herbert's turn.

"If you please, Master Herbert, it's your turn to fire," stated Captain Spencer.

Kevin nudged Nic and whispered, "I think this would be as good a time as any to go inside where it'll be safe."

Nic whispered back confidently, "He'll be fine with Captain Spencer. You'll see."

"That's good, Master Herbert. You are aiming it correctly. Now fire when ready," said Captain Spencer standing back.

The next moment, Herbert began firing the paintball gun; and when he was finished, everyone stared at the carnage. Not one of Herbert's paintballs had hit the target. He did, however, manage to repaint the surrounding trees behind the target with yellow splatter, while having caused quite a few birds to scatter for cover.

"Would you like to reconsider what you said?" whispered Kevin to Nic. Poor Herbert, maybe Kevin's right about him not being cut out for playing paintball, thought Nic.

"I'm sorry, Captain Spencer but I can't seem to fire very accurately no matter what. Maybe I should just give up," said a despondent Herbert.

Captain Spencer slowly approached Herbert and replied, "Before you decide on such a drastic course of action, might I be allowed to inform you of two humble observations, Master Herbert?"

Herbert looked up at Captain Spencer and said meekly, "Sure."

"One is: You never fail at anything until you fail to try. Two is: I have the utmost confidence in young master's ability to improve if he would attempt to fire with his eyes...open," stated Captain Spencer with a wink and smile.

Herbert grinned with embarrassment as the rest of the gang chuckled with delight. They yelled some encouraging words to Herbert as he took a second attempt at the target. Taking a deep breath, Herbert began firing. When he was finished, everyone gasped in astonishment. Almost all of Herbert's paintballs had hit near the center of the target.

"Gosh, Herbert, that's the best out of all of us!" said Dante.

Herbert was beaming with his newfound confidence as he turned to Captain Spencer and said, "Thanks! I didn't know I could do it!"

"You are quite welcome, young master," replied Captain Spencer with a slight bow.

The next two hours were spent learning military strategies and tactics as they relate to paintball. When the lesson was over, Nic was mentally and physically exhausted. Captain Spencer cheerfully waved good-bye and offered his services for the following Sunday, if needed. When Captain Spencer was out of sight, everyone collapsed on the ground in relief.

"I didn't know paintball could be so complex," muttered a worn out Philip.

"All we asked for was some help, not to go through basic training," joked Kevin.

"I'm not sure if I'll be able to do my piano lesson tonight. My arms are aching," said Cindy.

"I'm starving," said Herbert, rubbing his stomach.

"Me, too," added Dante. "I need to get going anyway," he added as he stood up. "Catch you guys later."

The others stood up, too, and followed Dante.

"Remember, everyone meet back here at Nic's house next Sunday afternoon for practice!" yelled Kevin.

"Sure wish I would have thought of saying that," said Nic jokingly to Kevin.

"No problem, Nic. I knew you really wanted to do that for all of us. Besides, your mom makes the best cookies in the neighborhood," laughed Kevin as he playfully patted Nic on his back.

"That's the only thing she can make that tastes any good. You should try my mom's other food. Blah!" said Nic making a face and sticking his tongue out.

"I better go, too, before my sisters eat all my dinner. See ya later, Nic!" Kevin waved as he hopped on his bike and took off down the street.

Later that evening, as Nic and his mom watched television, she asked, "Have you noticed any strange cars or people in the neighborhood lately?"

Nic immediately straightened up in his chair and replied nervously, "What do you mean, Mom?"

"Well, it's probably nothing, but the other day Mrs. O'Malley called and asked me that. It seems she's been noticing a certain car driving up and down our street with the same two men over and over at all hours of the day and night. I told her I hadn't noticed anything and that I would ask you. She sounded really concerned."

He squirmed under her knowing gaze. What should he do? If he told her what he and his friends knew, she might freak out or get mad for not trusting in her earlier. Or worse, she might laugh at him for thinking silly thoughts. Beads of sweat were forming on his forehead as he struggled with what he was going to say.

"I know what you're thinking, Nicolas," his mom said, continuing to gaze at him.

He gulped and squeaked, "You do?"

His mom nodded saying, "You don't think I know, but after being around you for ten years, I know how you operate."

"You do?"

"You're thinking that the only strange people in our neighborhood are the ones we live by. I know what you think of the Chamberlains, and I know how grumpy Mr. O'Malley usually is toward you and your friends. Am I right?"

"I guess so..."

He couldn't believe how close he had come to telling his mom about the Diamonds of Denmark. He knew he was eventually going to tell her, but he wanted to wait until after he had solid evidence to show her and the authorities.

She got up and said, "Regardless of whether or not what Mrs. O'Malley is seeing is true, I want you to be more careful from now on around here. Understand?"

"Yes, Mom, I will."

He wiped his forehead in relief. The shrill ring of the telephone broke the silence. Nic's mom scrambled around under the couch to find it.

"What's the phone doing under here?" she asked in frustration as she stared at Nic.

Oops, thought Nic, remembering he'd moved it there when he sat on the couch earlier.

"Hello? Hello? Yes, this is she...Who is this? What are you talking about? I have no idea what you're talking about! What's that supposed to mean? If this is some kind of sick joke, I don't find it very amusing! I think I'm going to notify the police! Hello? Aargh!" she said expressing her frustration as she hung up the phone and threw it onto the couch.

Her face was pale, and her hands were trembling. She looked up to see a worried look on Nic's face. She clutched her hands together to stop their shaking and said in a cracked voice, "Go to your room. Now, Nicolas!"

From his mom's tone of voice, Nic knew better than to try and ask her any questions regarding what the phone call was about as he marched up the stairs to his room. *I wonder what that was all about,* thought Nic, walking along the hallway toward his room. Whoever had been on the phone had really shaken her up. Nic couldn't remember ever seeing her that upset, except around snakes in the yard.

He shot a look into her bedroom as he walked by, noting that the message light on the answering machine was blinking. *I bet the answering machine was on during Mom's conversation,* he mused, remembering how many times the phone rang before she answered it. He stopped in her doorway as he wondered what he should do. Play back the answering machine to see what had been said and risk his mom catching him in the act? Or be an obedient son and keep heading toward his room like he was told? He paused a moment longer, then acted on his decision.

Nic first crept back to the top of the stairs to peek around for his mom. No sign of her. He then tiptoed quickly into her room, closing the door softly. The blinking light on the machine was mesmerizing, as if drawing him in closer. His stomach was knotting up over what he was about to do. He carefully moved his finger toward the play button until it was hovering just above it. He inhaled deeply and held his breath. "Here goes nothing." He pushed the "play" button.

"Hello?" asked Nic's mom. Nothing was heard but static. "Hello?" she asked again.

"Barbara Nelson?" asked a cold, robotic-like voice.

"Yes, this is she." Silence followed before Nic's mom asked, "Who is this?"

"That's not important. Do you still have your husband's notes?" asked the robotic voice.

"What are you talking about?" asked Nic's mom, with a hint of distress in her voice.

"I think you know, Mrs. Nelson," stated the voice.

"I have no idea what you're talking about," answered Nic's mom as her voice began to rise.

"It was a shame about your husband's accident. He was very knowledgeable in his field. Too knowledgeable," said the voice.

"What's that supposed to mean? If this is some kind of sick joke, I don't find it very amusing!" Nic's mom responded.

"Oh, this isn't a joke. I never joke," stated the voice.

"I think I'm going to notify the police," warned Nic's mom. The silence on the line was broken only by what sounded like a big bell ringing in the distance. With a loud "click," the line went dead.

"Hello?' Nic's mom said again before hanging up.

Nic exhaled and felt his heart pumping in his chest. Backing out of her room, his eyes were as wide as silver dollars, unable to take them off the answering machine. Opening the door so it wouldn't creak, he peeked out to be sure she wouldn't see him. He repositioned the door as it had been earlier, and made a beeline for his room. Thousands of thoughts were racing through his mind. He was shaking all over. Once in the safety of this room, he again buried his face in his pillow.

Nic was unable to stop the flood of emotions that call unleashed in him. He started to cry as he kept replaying in his mind the words said to his mom, 'It was a shame about your husband's…accident,' with emphasis on the word accident. Could someone have killed his dad on purpose, only to make it look like an accident? Why?

'He was very knowledgeable in his field. Too knowledgeable,' the voice had flatly stated.

Dad had been a history professor and nothing more as far as Nic knew. Why would anyone want to kill a college history teacher? And what was with the voice? It sounded as if the person was distorting his true voice to hide his identity. It didn't make any sense. It wasn't fair. It just couldn't be what he was thinking. It just couldn't.

"I miss you so much, Dad," whispered Nic as he cried himself to sleep.

CHAPTER FOURTEEN

Mr. Chen's Advice

Monday morning came too early. Nic had slept poorly and, judging by the way his mom looked, so had she. It was bad enough he had the phone call on his mind, but when he arrived at school, he found that he and his friends were the hottest topic with just about everyone.

Word had spread around about how badly Johnny's team had beaten Nic and the others on Saturday. Of course, Nic didn't need any guesses as to who was spreading this news. During class, some of Nic's classmates had made it a point of loudly discussing how some people (meaning Nic) had actually thought that Johnny's team with Commando 88s could be beaten, but were proven wrong. Nic tried to concentrate on schoolwork and did his best to ignore them. In the meantime, he found his mind wandering back to the phone call and what it meant.

Being with his close friends and teammates at lunchtime provided some relief from the teasing.

"Johnny is making me so mad. He has everybody in our classroom talking about what happened Saturday," declared Cindy, who looked upset and dejected.

"At least you guys aren't in the same homeroom as Johnny. He's being totally unbearable, isn't he Philip?" stated Kevin.

"Sure is. Wish he played hockey, 'cause I'd run into him on purpose and knock that chip off of his shoulder," said Philip.

"Not meaning to change the subject, but can anyone go to Chen's sports shop after school today? I was checking our paintball supply, and we need to pick up some more for our next training session with Captain Spencer on Sunday," said Kevin.

"Why can't you go? I thought you were such good friends with Mr. Chen?" asked Dante.

Kevin glanced over at Philip, then back to Dante, and said, "I can't, because I've got after school detention with Mrs. Payne today."

"What for?" asked Cindy.

Kevin took a deep breath and then explained, "I yelled out in class right before lunch to tell Johnny to shut up. He had been mouthing off at me all morning about Saturday."

Philip smiled and added, "Kevin was awesome. Everyone thought he and Johnny were going to fight right there, but Mrs. Payne stepped in too quickly."

"Did Johnny get into trouble as well?" asked Cindy.

"No, like always, he got off scot free," answered Kevin.

"Why don't you just go tomorrow or later in the week?" asked Dante.

"'Cause Mr. Chen has all of his paintballs half priced on Mondays, that's why," replied Kevin.

"I'll go today after I stop by home real quick to get some money," volunteered Nic. I could use the time riding on my bike to help clear my mind of everything that's happened, he thought.

"That's great, Nic. We'll pay you back our portion when we come to your house Sunday afternoon, okay?" asked Kevin.

"That's fine with me," answered Nic, as he and the others were getting up from their lunch table.

Unfortunately, Johnny and his *J Gang* stopped them from leaving.

"Well, well, well, look who we have here? It looks like Team Sokoor, or should it be Team Sucks!" snickered Johnny abrasively.

"Johnny, you sure are making a big deal over a practice session," countered Nic.

"Is that what that was supposed to be on Saturday? It didn't seem like it to me. I've had more of a challenge getting out of bed than with what you losers offered," said Johnny.

Kevin lurched forward angrily, while Dante and Philip held his arms. "Get over yourself already, Johnny," he replied

"Oooh, am I supposed to be scared? Oh, that's right. I forgot you got yourself detention after school today, Kevin. No wonder you're a little touchy. Hope you have fun with Mrs. Payne. See ya; wouldn't want to be ya," chuckled Johnny. Then he and his *J Gang* headed out of the cafeteria.

"I want us to win so badly that it's killing me," growled Nic to the others.

"We'll get 'em next time," said Dante.

"If we get the chance," said Philip.

Everyone looked at Philip in amazement.

"What's that supposed to mean?" questioned Cindy.

"Have you guys forgotten already? We might not get another chance at Johnny's team, because it's a tournament. We'll probably have to play other teams without losing before facing Johnny's team again," stated Philip.

No one said anything while this news sunk in.

"Well," Nic declared calmly, "I guess we'll just have to make sure we beat everybody else until we get to Johnny's team, now won't we?"

With the ring of the school bell, they scattered for class.

Later that day, Nic was peddling hard to Mr. Chen's, trying to outride his racing thoughts. 'It was a shame about your husband's…accident,' kept echoing in his head. No matter how hard and how fast he peddled, Nic couldn't shake it from his thoughts.

He hadn't mentioned what he had heard on his mom's answering machine to Kevin or the others, because he hadn't been sure what it all really meant. He hadn't said anything to his mom about the phone call at breakfast, because she was acting as if nothing had happened. He figured if he asked too many questions, she might become suspicious and find out he had listened to her call on the answering machine.

Nic knew how passionate his mom was about respecting the privacy of each other's rooms. She felt so strongly about it that she wouldn't even clean his room no matter how messy it was. Instead, she would threaten him with a grounding to get him to clean it up himself. Nic could only imagine how much trouble he would be in if his mom knew what he had done.

As he pulled up to Mr. Chen's shop, he decided he'd have to try to figure things out himself for now.

Walking into the shop, Nic was once again greeted by a thin layer of dust and dimly lit shelves. As he walked to the front of the store, Nic's feeling was that Mr. Chen really needed to dust the place and get some brighter lights.

Mom would die of a heart attack from the messiness, thought Nic. Doesn't anyone else ever shop here, he wondered, as he stopped directly in front of Mr. Chen's bell to ring for service.

He scanned the different paintball brands under the glass counter.

Today he was going to catch Mr. Chen as he appeared. He rang the bell three times and turned around to survey the store.

"What has caught the eye of young Nic Nelson?" asked a familiar voice. Nic spun around to find Mr. Chen gazing at him from behind the front counter with his arms folded across his chest.

"What?" Nic asked.

"I noticed you were looking at something in the store and was merely inquiring as to the object of your interest," stated Mr. Chen.

"Oh, nothing," lied Nic. He figured he would sound stupid if he tried to explain he was really trying to prevent Mr. Chen from sneaking up on him, which he had just done again, without making a sound. I sure wish I knew how he does that, thought Nic, trying to remember why he had come in the first place.

"Does young Nic Nelson require more paintballs?" asked Mr. Chen.

"Yes, that's right. How did you know?" asked Nic.

"By your eyes," stated Mr. Chen.

"Excuse me?" replied Nic.

"The eyes are like windows into the soul. I perceived your desire by what your eyes told me. They never lie," answered Mr. Chen.

"Oh," mumbled Nic. He wasn't quite sure what else to say.

"Might I recommend this brand? I feel it is the type most harmonious with the flow of nature," said Mr. Chen as he lifted out a 2000-count paintball box from below the glass counter.

Nic looked at the brand name on the box. "P-L-H," he read aloud. "What does PLH stand for?"

Mr. Chen paused. "It stands for peace, love and happiness." Nic's look of surprise amused Mr. Chen.

He explained, "The letter P represents peace. There is order to the universe when everything is at peace with one another. The letter L represents love. What greater power is there than the power of love? Finally, the letter H represents happiness. What could make a person happier in paintball than when their paintball strikes their intended target first?"

Nic smiled. He couldn't tell for sure, because of the dim lighting, but he thought he saw Mr. Chen wink from underneath his eyebrows.

"That sounds fine by me, Mr. Chen. I hope it brings me happiness by helping me get revenge against Johnny," said Nic.

"How so?" Mr. Chen asked.

"Johnny's a bully at school whose team beat mine at a practice paintball session last Saturday. He's really been rubbing it in, so that's why I want revenge so bad," explained Nic, who felt his anger building the more he thought about Johnny.

Nic noticed Mr. Chen looking at him with a sad expression. "Revenge is not a wise path to pursue," stated Mr. Chen.

"Why? Johnny deserves it. If you only knew who he was and how he treats people, you'd understand," pleaded Nic.

"I don't need to meet this Johnny to know what kind of person he is. If he can cause a gentle person like you to seek revenge, than I know who this Johnny is," said Mr. Chen without blinking.

"Revenge solves nothing, young Nic Nelson. To demonstrate, let me ask you a question. By achieving revenge on Johnny, what will you have accomplished?" quizzed Mr. Chen.

Nic thought for a moment before answering with a smug grin, "Satisfaction…knowing that I got Johnny back good for getting me. Then I could rub it in his face like he's done to me."

"This would make you feel good?" asked Mr. Chen.

"Yeah," declared Nic.

"How do you think Johnny would feel?" continued Mr. Chen.

"Terrible, because he couldn't stand losing to me," said Nic.

"What do you think Johnny would want to do next?" asked Mr. Chen.

"Get me back?" Nic asked meekly.

Mr. Chen slowly smiled and pausing a few seconds more, continued, "In other words young one, Johnny would want revenge on you for your getting revenge on him. This cycle would then repeat itself endlessly with no good to come of it."

"I…guess so," Nic muttered as he looked down at his feet. "But Johnny shouldn't be allowed to get away with his antics. Someone needs to stand up to him, don't you think?" he asked, looking for Mr. Chen's approval.

"Fear not, Nic Nelson, for there is a way to seek what you desire without using anger and hate as your guides," said Mr. Chen. "Retribution is what you seek, Nic Nelson. Through retribution, you can achieve your goal in a just way, seeking no more and no less. With retribution, you return to Johnny what he gave to you, but with compassion and restraint as your companions. Then, if this Johnny is wise, he will learn from your actions to become a better person."

"Retribution..." Nic searched his memory for a definition. "Retribution is correcting an unjust wrong? Right?" he asked.

"Yes, my young friend."

"What happens if he doesn't learn?" asked Nic, wondering if Johnny's vocabulary contained the words wise or compassion.

"Then his soul will eventually become consumed with hate and anger until he is a shell of emptiness," answered Mr. Chen.

Yikes, thought Nic.

"Thanks for the advice, Mr. Chen!" Nic put the paintballs into his backpack. "I'll probably be back at least one more time for supplies before the paintball tournament begins."

"Nic Nelson and his companions are always welcomed here. May good fortune smile upon you in your endeavors," smiled Mr. Chen as Nic left the store.

Mr. Smithton was right. Mr. Chen sure is a strange man, but he seems to be very wise about all kinds of things. I sure hope I can grow up one day to be as smart as Mr. Chen. I wonder if you have to talk in funny riddles in order to be like him, pondered Nic, while he rode his bike back home.

Over the next two weeks, Team Sokoor worked hard on improving their skills and teamwork under Captain Spencer's watchful eyes.

He was drilling them as if they were going to war. They all were doing their best to get ready. Even Herbert had agreed to cut back on his doughnuts in order to be in better shape. It seemed to Nic like everyone's confidence was growing by the hour as each one of them practiced and encouraged one another.

On the last Sunday before the tournament, Nic's mom treated the kids and Captain Spencer to fresh-from-the-oven cookies and cold lemonade to celebrate all their hard work.

"That was most kind of you, Lady Nelson, to provide refreshments for us. We are all most appreciative," stated Captain Spencer in his usual crisp tenor.

Nic's mom blushed, "Please, Captain Spencer, you make me sound like a princess or something. Just call me, Barbara."

"As you wish, Lady Barbara," replied Captain Spencer.

Nic knew his mom realized she wasn't going to make any headway with Captain Spencer concerning the way he addressed her, so she sighed and continued speaking.

"It's been awfully nice of you to help out the children like this for their paintball game. It's really meant a lot to them."

"I've enjoyed the challenge of working with them. They are all most attentive and well-mannered children," replied Captain Spencer.

Nic's mom's jaw dropped in playful astonishment.

"Are we talking about the same kids? I think you've been out in the sun too long, Captain Spencer," chuckled Nic's mom.

"Ha, ha, Mom. You're real funny," smiled Nic.

Kevin piped up, "Could I get you to say that to my mom, Captain Spencer? I don't think she's going to believe me when I tell her what you just said about all of us. She'll probably think it's a sign that the world is about to come to an end."

Even Captain Spencer smiled at Kevin's comment.

"Captain Spencer, can I ask you a serious question?" asked Philip.

"Why of course, Master Philip."

"Do you honestly think we have any chance at all of winning the paintball tournament next weekend?"

Nic and the others perked up eagerly to hear Captain Spencer's answer. Captain Spencer looked at each of them in turn.

"It doesn't matter what I think; it only matters what you think is possible. But if I might say so, Master Philip, I would be most confident with you and the other young masters at my side in any situation."

The day's lesson over, Captain Spencer took his leave, waving goodbye as he began his slow, short walk to the Chamberlains' house.

"He's one strange, yet okay dude," said Dante shaking his head.

"Hey, I'm not as sore as I've usually been. I must be getting used to all of this training. I must be getting bigger muscles," said Kevin proudly as he attempted to make a muscle with his right arm.

"The only thing getting bigger is your ego," declared Cindy while the boys laughed.

Kevin ignored Cindy and went on, "Nobody better forget to be ready by 8:00 A.M. Saturday morning. Philip's mom has offered to take all of us to the tournament in her van. And I'll buy more paintballs tomorrow from Mr. Chen. Any questions?"

"I think we'll all be ready, Kevin," Nic replied.

They all gathered up their equipment for their journeys home.

CHAPTER FIFTEEN

Framed

The day wound down, and Nic found himself in bed, wide-awake. Tossing and turning, he just couldn't get comfortable. It was so hot! He sat up in bed. "Whew!" His pillow and sheets were soaked from his sweat, and his hair was sticking to his forehead. *This must be what a sauna feels like. I bet mom must've forgotten to turn on the air conditioner again.*

While he cooled down, his mind wandered to the upcoming paintball tournament. *Even with all of our training over the past three weeks with Captain Spencer, are we truly ready to take on Johnny's* team? I mean, they've been playing paintball a lot longer than we have. Maybe everyone else is right. Maybe they really are too good for anyone to beat. They have the best paintball guns, and I'm sure Johnny's dad had something to do with that. And they beat us so bad in the practice session.

He began to feel hopeless and sighed while he dreamed up worst-case scenarios. His curtain fluttered slightly, and a puff of cooler air jarred him from his negative thoughts.

Wait a minute! What am I doing? I'm not going to roll over and admit defeat to Johnny and his team before we even play! That's exactly what Johnny would want me to do. I don't want to lose the game before we've even begun!

Nic walked into his bathroom to splash cold water on his face. He lifted his head and stared at his reflection. Mom's right. I do look a lot like Dad. He smiled at the thought and then… 'It's a shame about your husband's…accident' came into his thoughts uninvited. He felt the hairs on the back of his neck tingle. He shook his head to stop the drone of the cold voice.

'He was very knowledgeable in his field. Too knowledgeable.' Nic tried to focus on something else in order to turn off the nightmare playing in his mind. He closed his eyes and then heard a chilling laugh, 'I know you're listening, too, Nic. I'm glad, because you're next.'

Nic's eyes flew open, and he turned around with a jerk. Was someone here? He peered into his darkened bedroom, too frightened to move. One minute. Two minutes. Three minutes passed before he felt calm enough to turn off the bathroom light and venture into his bedroom. His hands were still shaking slightly as he sat down on the edge of his bed.

A brief flash of light in the distance caught his eye. Looking out his open window, he thought he saw movement in the Chamberlains' yard. He squinted as he quickly scanned over as much of the Chamberlains' yard as he could see in the moonlight. He was satisfied it must have been his imagination, fueled by his earlier thoughts.

"I really have to get some sleep before I start to lose my mind," mumbled Nic. He was about to turn around to go back to bed when a person stepped out of the shadows and disappeared again just as quickly. Nic strained to see or hear anything else. Nothing. Then the person reappeared. Again, Nic saw a quick flash of light. He couldn't tell who the mysterious person was or what the person was doing in the Chamberlains' yard.

Nic's heart was pounding as he backed away from the window. He closed his eyes and repeated, "This is just a dream. This is just a dream. I'm going to wake up, and it'll be time to go to school."

"Woof! Woof! Woof!" barked Wellington loudly from the kitchen. Nic opened his eyes and knew he wasn't dreaming, unless Wellington was having the same dream. What am I going to do now? He kept his eyes fixed on the window as he slowly sat down on his bed to consider his options.

I could go and wake up mom and tell her what I saw. Nah, she'd think I was seeing things in the dark and get mad at me for waking her up so late at night. She's also got enough on her mind since the phone call, and I wouldn't want to worry her anymore, decided Nic.

I could just call the police and let them handle it. Nah, they'd think I was a prank caller; and I'd probably end up in big trouble.

Nic rubbed his chin as he considered his last option -- checking it out himself. That seems to be the best option, he decided. If he could determine who the person was, he'd come back to his house and call the police immediately.

He put on some clothes and, as quietly as he could, crept along the upstairs hallway. He paused as he passed his mom's partially opened door and peeked inside. She was sleeping soundly. Just past his mom's room, he stepped on a creaky spot under the carpeting. He froze. Tense moments went by as he waited to hear his mom stir. She didn't.

"Whew, that was a close one," he whispered. He moved down the steps carefully, walking as lightly as possible to avoid squeaky spots. He started to head for the kitchen, but remembered that Wellington was there and might make noise that would wake his mom.

"Front door it is," he said under his breath.

He considered taking a flashlight but decided against it. After all, he wasn't going to confront whoever it was in the Chamberlains' yard;

and a flashlight would only bring attention to him and cost him the element of surprise.

Nic opened the front door, hoping that Wellington wouldn't bark. He crouched low on the porch and peered over the railing to see if anything was happening. *I must be crazy or stupid or both, coming out here at this time of night*, thought Nic. He stepped behind some bushes in his front yard.

How weird, he thought. *There's usually a light on at night over there. I wonder why it's not on?*

Nic stooped down to hide. He needed a plan! He could feel his heart pounding against his chest as he took a few deep breaths to try to calm down. He took another deep breath and held it, scurrying quickly to the edge of his yard behind yet another bush.

I've never been so happy to see bushes before, he mused.

A cloud covered the moon, just at the moment he raced across the road and hid behind a fence. He had taken that fateful step of no return by crossing into the Chamberlains' yard.

Nic slid into their yard with Ninja-worthy quietness. He dashed to the nearest tree for cover. Breathing heavily now, Nic forced himself to take a quick look around the tree. Nobody.

Nic ran down a list of suspects, as he took another peek around the tree. The primary suspect was Roger Marinovich. Ever since running into him and his partner last fall, Nic and his friends had suspected they were in the area searching for the diamonds without trying to attract any attention.

The next suspect was Captain Spencer. He might be out for a late night stroll or training run from his military days. The last suspect was Mr. Chamberlain. As everyone in town knew, Mr. Chamberlain enjoyed late night partying. So he could be hanging in the yard before he goes in to face Mrs. Chamberlain.

Nic still couldn't see anyone, but his ears picked up the sound of digging in a distant part of the backyard. Alternating hiding spots from bush to tree, then bush to bush, he slowly and quietly headed in the direction of the digging sounds.

He found himself behind a large oak tree. The digging sounds were so close now. He carefully peeked around the tree and saw two men, each holding something in their hands and whispering. Holding his breath, Nic strained to hear what they were saying.

"Look closer. Something's gotta be here. This is the spot where the detector made a noise."

"Are you sure, Boss? I don't see nothin'."

Nic's eyes widened as he gripped the tree. *Those voices...I know who these guys are! It's Roger Marinovich and his partner, Detective Walker, or whatever his real name is,* thought Nic. Fascinated, Nic was unable to move out of fear and curiosity.

"There, do you see it...something shiny, right there? Quick, pick it up," commanded Roger Marinovich as he pointed toward the ground.

A few seconds of frantic digging produced only an old quarter. Nic couldn't see Roger Marinovich's face, but he could tell the man was bitterly disappointed at finding only a quarter. His partner, on the other hand, was quite excited.

"This is the sixth quarter we've found tonight, boss. We must really be lucky!"

"Shut up, why don't ya? We're here for the diamonds, and we're going to find them this time, even if it takes us all night," hissed Roger Marinovich.

That was all Nic needed to hear. He decided that this was as good a time as any to call the police. He figured Roger Marinovich and his partner would probably be around for quite awhile.

Slowly backing away from the tree, Nic's plan was to turn around and move quietly back to his yard. As luck would have it, another cloud covered the moon, making it almost impossible to see. He was trying to move quickly and strained to see in the low light. Big things, like bushes, were easy. Small things, like holes big enough to fit a ten-year-old foot into, were not. As luck would have it, his foot found a small hole that tripped him up.

"Ow," yelped Nic, as he hit the ground hard, face first.

"Who's that? Who's there?" demanded Roger Marinovich.

Nic held his breath and froze, hoping they would think they imagined something.

"Go over there and look…quick!" commanded Roger Marinovich to his partner.

Nic knew he had no choice but to get up and make a run for it, before they knew what was happening. He pulled his foot from the hole and started running as fast as he could.

Ow, ow, ow, he thought. My ankle hurts! Making matters worse, the cloud that had hidden the moon moved away, bathing the yard in moonlight, making it extremely easy to see Nic limping away.

"Boss! It's one of those bratty kids we talked to last year!"

"Don't just stand there, get him before he gets away!" shouted Roger Marinovich. Apparently, both men had forgotten they were supposed to be quiet.

Nic was getting close to the edge of the yard. He slowed for a moment and looked behind him to see how far ahead he was. He misjudged his location; and when he looked forward again, he ran smack into a low tree branch. He hit it so hard, his feet left the ground. Nic's ears were ringing from the blow. Through the ringing, though, he could also hear Wellington barking in the distance.

"I got him now!" The man was mere feet away from where Nic was lying on the ground.

I'm done for now, thought Nic.

Just as he was about to be nabbed, Roger Marinovich's partner tripped over one of the holes he had dug earlier. He landed in a rose bush.

"Ow! Thorn bushes!" he yelled, as he struggled to free himself from the prickly bushes.

Nic was back on his feet, about to escape to freedom, when he felt a pair of strong hands grab his shoulders. A menacing voice said, "You're not going anywhere now, punk."

Nic knew he'd been caught by Roger Marinovich. I'm as good as dead now, he thought.

They were both blinded for a short time when the Chamberlains' house lights suddenly blazed into brightness. A police siren began wailing in the distance.

"Boss, the cops! We gotta get outta here!"

Roger Marinovich pushed Nic to the ground and pulled his partner out of the bush. The police siren was getting louder now, as the two men hovered over Nic.

Shaking a pointed finger at Nic, Roger Marinovich said coldly, "You may have stopped us this time, kid, but you won't stop us for long."

Without thinking, in a burst of bravado, Nic exclaimed, "I know all about you and the Diamonds of Denmark! You'll never find them!"

Bending down, Roger Marinovich grabbed Nic's shirt and demanded, "What do you know about the Diamonds of Denmark? Where are they hidden? Tell me now!"

"Boss, we've really got to go. The cops are about here!"

Roger Marinovich let go of Nic's shirt and threatened, "We're not through, you and me, not by a long shot. In the meantime, you'd better pretend you didn't see us tonight if the cops ask you any questions. Otherwise, something bad might happen to your dear old mom. Understand?"

Nic nodded his head, knowing Roger Marinovich seemed like the type of person who would carry out such a threat.

Turning to his partner, Marinovich commanded, "Let's go…leave the shovel and metal detector. Hurry up!"

Moments later, both men were gone. Nic heaved a sigh of relief. Somehow, he'd survived his encounter with those two.

Thinking the worst was over, Nic got up and slowly began walking toward his house. The lights of the police car flashed around the neighborhood, and the siren blared like a trumpet.

Too late to run off now, he thought; and even if he could, it would only make him look guilty of something. Nope, Nic decided, he was just going to tell the truth about seeing someone here, and that should be enough. Of course, he knew his mom wasn't going to be too happy about what he had done.

Two police officers were running toward him with their guns drawn. Without thinking, Nic put both hands into the air and prayed he'd be able to get out of this mess in one piece.

"Hold it right there, son!" yelled one of the officers.

Since Nic was afraid to move, it wasn't hard for him to obey the order. He tried to stay calm as the two officers approached him, searching him with their flashlight beams.

"What's your name, son?" asked one of the officers.

"Nic, Nic Nelson, sir."

"I know this kid, Sergeant Jones," said a familiar voice.

"Officer Williams, is that you?" asked Nic.

"Yes, Nic, it's me. You can put your hands down now," answered Officer Williams.

"Then I'll let you handle the questioning while I have a look around to secure the area," stated Sergeant Jones, as he walked off into the darkness.

"Okay Nic, I want the truth. What were you doing here at this time of night?" asked Officer Williams.

"I...I...I saw someone from my window; and next thing I know, I'm back here trying to find out who it was, and that's the truth," said Nic.

"Did you find out who it was you thought you saw from your window?" asked Officer Williams.

Nic shook his head no while looking down to avoid Officer Williams' face. He hated having to lie to him again, but he didn't have a choice this time.

Officer Williams placed a hand on Nic's shoulder and said, "I believe you, Nic, but you really should have called the police first, instead of coming out here by yourself. You never know who you might run into."

"You sure don't," whispered Nic to himself.

"Are you through questioning the suspect?" asked Sergeant Jones, emerging from the darkness.

Suspect? Why am I a suspect? I haven't done anything wrong, thought Nic anxiously. He felt his heart skip a beat.

Officer Williams must have thought the same thing as he asked, "Suspect?"

"That's what I said. There are a number of holes dug all over the backyard. I found a shovel, and you'll never guess what else I found." said Sergeant Jones.

"What?" asked Officer Williams and Nic at the same time.

"A metal detector." Sergeant Jones looked as smug as if he'd just found the Diamonds of Denmark. "It could be the one from Hornsby's," he added.

Officer Williams looked down at Nic and asked, "Did you dig the holes? Did you steal the metal detector?"

"No, sir, I didn't do any digging; and I haven't stolen anything," pleaded Nic, now worried that he would be taken away.

"I believe him, Sarge," said Officer Williams.

"Why? Look at his face and clothes. He's got dirt everywhere on him," pointed out Sergeant Jones.

"I...I...I fell down while running away," explained Nic.

"Running away from what? Who? Why?" countered Sergeant Jones.

"I...I panicked when I heard the sirens," answered Nic.

"Lay off, Sarge. He's just a kid who happened to be at the wrong place at the wrong time," defended Officer Williams.

"How can you be so sure? For all we know, he broke into Hornsby's Hardware Store and stole the metal detector so he could go and dig up other people's yards finding coins for fun. Darkness would have provided the perfect cover for him," stated Sergeant Jones accusingly.

"C'mon, Sarge, you're fishing. We both know a ten-year-old boy couldn't have kicked down the door at the hardware store. Plus, we still need to get fingerprints from the shovel and metal detector and see if they match Nic's. Remember, he's innocent until proven guilty," finished Officer Williams.

"Bah! All kids are criminals," said Sergeant Jones tersely.

Nic could see Mr. and Mrs. Chamberlain and Captain Spencer coming out of their house now and walking toward them.

"I'll talk with them and get their statements and see if they want to press any charges," said Sergeant Jones.

Charges? What charges? But I haven't done anything wrong, thought Nic.

"Nicolas! Oh Nicolas! What's happened? Are you all right?" his mom yelled out hysterically.

When she reached him, she engulfed him in a bear hug. Nic was never so happy to see her. He almost didn't mind her rambling, nonstop questions, hugs, and kisses.

"I'm all right, Mom. I thought I saw someone in the Chamberlains' yard, and I went to investigate."

"At this time of night? Nicolas Timothy Nelson, just you wait until I get you back home, young man," declared his mom, as she hugged him yet again.

Turning to Officer Williams, Nic's mom quickly composed herself and asked, "Did you catch whoever my son thought was back here?"

"No, Ma'am. We're looking into it right now, but I'm afraid my commanding officer believes your son is guilty of property destruction and stealing.

"Stealing! My son would never steal anything!"

"You don't have to argue with me about your son's innocence. I happen to believe him, but it's not up to me to decide on how we proceed next."

Just then, Sergeant Jones walked up.

"Mrs. Chamberlain sure is my kind of citizen. She wanted to press as many charges as possible and then some," smiled Sergeant Jones. Nic's heart sank as he considered what life would be like in jail.

"But her butler, a Captain Spencer from England, convinced her and her husband to hold off pressing any charges until we've investigated further. So for now, you're off of the hook," growled Sergeant Jones at Nic, stomping off toward the patrol car.

Thank you, Captain Spencer! Nic screamed in his head.

Officer Williams instructed Nic's mom not to have Nic leave town without notifying him first. He explained that he would need to see Nic at the police station sometime during the week to get his fingerprints to see if they matched any found on the shovel or metal detector. He also explained that Nic wasn't being charged with anything yet, but he was still considered the primary suspect until the investigation was completed. Officer Williams gave her his card and offered to answer any questions that she might have if she called.

She was remarkably calm, thought Nic, as she thanked Officer Williams and escorted Nic back to their house somewhat briskly.

For the next hour, his mom grilled Nic with a million questions. He tried to answer as best he could, but it was a no-win situation. It was like walking through a minefield with shoes ten feet long and ten feet wide. There was so much he wanted to tell her, but Roger Marinovich's words kept running through his head, 'You'd better pretend you didn't see us tonight if the cops ask you any questions. Otherwise, something bad might happen to your dear old mom.' He shuddered at the memory.

They were both exhausted by the time she sent him to bed. She ordered him to come straight home from school. Then he would hear her decision regarding his punishment.

Nic lay in bed staring at the ceiling. What a night. It's all Roger Marinovich's fault. If only I knew where those stupid diamonds were, I'd tell the police and be free from all of this mess, thought Nic, hitting the bed with his fists. He fell asleep, but dreamt of diamonds and bad guys.

The next morning, Nic learned how fast bad news could travel in a small town. He hadn't even had a chance to sit down in his seat at school before he was bombarded with questions from his classmates.

"Did you really trash the Chamberlains' yard?"

"Did anyone help you?"

"Why did you do it?"

"You da man!"

"What were you thinking?"

"Were you scared?"

"Are you going to jail?"

Nic denied having done anything wrong, but it seemed like that only fueled the other kids' imaginations more about what might have happened. He couldn't understand how so many people had found out about it so fast.

"That's an easy one to answer. New Bonn is the type of town where if something major happens, then everyone finds out rather quickly," summed up Cindy matter-of-factly at lunchtime.

"My mom found out from one of her friends who knows the police captain's wife," remarked Philip.

"My mom found out from a friend of a friend who lives on the same street as one of the police officers," said Dante.

Nic just shook his head in amazement. Kevin tapped his shoulder, leaned into his ear, and whispered, "Just like my dad always says, 'If you want any news spread around fast, you Telegraph, Telephone and Tell-a-Woman.'"

Nic chuckled as Cindy glared at Kevin and said, "I heard that!"

"I think you did the right thing by not telling the police who you ran into last night. They would've probably thought you were making it up to cover yourself," remarked Kevin.

"I'm not so sure anymore. With as much trouble as Nic's in, he might want to tell the police everything we know," recommended Cindy.

"Based on what? We don't have any hard evidence to prove anything yet. Don't you remember? We couldn't even convince Jason of what we know. Plus, if Nic told the police everything, he'd be putting his mom at risk for who knows what," argued Kevin.

All lunch long, the argument raged between Kevin and Cindy, with the others taking sides and poor Nic stuck quietly in the middle.

Just when things couldn't get any worse, thought Nic, they did.

Walking to his bike after school, he heard a familiar voice ring out, "Hey, Geek, I didn't think you had it in you, trashing the Chamberlains' house like you did."

Turning around, Nic saw Johnny walking up to him, but strangely without his usual crew of bullies.

"I've been meaning to trash that old cheapskate's place, but I just haven't gotten around to doing it. Looks like you beat me to the punch," said Johnny, patting Nic hard on the back. Nic pushed Johnny's arm away and took a step back.

"What happened to your buddies, Johnny? Did they finally get smart and leave you, or did your bad breath knock them all out?" asked Nic.

Johnny glared at Nic and replied, "Just wait. If you and your stupid friends are lucky enough to make it to the championship round on Saturday, we'll beat you even worse than before. In fact, it'll be so bad you won't know which way is up. So you'd better pray you guys lose before then or else."

"Talk is cheap, Johnny," replied Nic.

Johnny gave Nic a smirk, stomping off down the sidewalk.

Nic shook his head in disgust before hopping on his bike and leaving the school grounds. *What a day, and it isn't even over yet. I still have to face the wrath of Mom at home.* He wondered what his punishment was going to be, taking his time getting home. *I hope she doesn't make me drop out of the paintball tournament on Saturday. We've worked so hard getting ready; and without me, they won't have enough players to be able to participate.*

Nic's mom was waiting for him in the living room. With his head hung low, Nic trudged into the room like a prisoner about to be sentenced for life with no parole. As he sat down, he glanced up and caught his mom silently watching him. Nic looked back down at the ground, wishing his mom would hurry up. The suspense was killing him.

She surprised him by getting up and beginning to pace back and forth across the room. *Oh, great, she's really going to make me sweat it out,* thought Nic.

"Nicolas, Nicolas, what am I going to do with you?" stated his mom.

"Did I ever tell you that you're the best mom I've ever had?" asked Nic innocently, while giving her his best sad puppy face.

Nic's mom put her hands on her hips and said, "Nice try, but that isn't going to work on me this time, young man."

"I figured it was worth a shot. I don't think I had anything more to lose," admitted Nic as his mom sat down across from him.

She ignored his comments. "Okay, Nicolas, this is how it's going to be. I believe you, and I understand you were doing what you felt to be the right thing to do; but you should have known better. I have a feeling it's going to be quite awhile before everything is straightened out with the Chamberlains and the police concerning last night. Your misadventure has caused quite a stir in this town. Therefore, as punishment, you're grounded for the next two weeks from all activities. You'll go straight home from school with no stops at anyone's house. When you get home, you are to go straight to your room. No television."

"But, Mom…" stuttered Nic in desperation, as all hope vanished about playing on Saturday.

"Let me finish," she said, holding up her hand. "I realize that you have a prior commitment to your friends concerning the upcoming paintball tournament. I also realize they can't play without you, and I don't think it'd be fair to ruin their fun because of your lack of good judgment. I've decided to allow you to play with them on Saturday."

"All right! Thanks, Mom! You're the greatest!" shouted Nic, as he jumped up with glee and gave her a hug before dashing off into the kitchen.

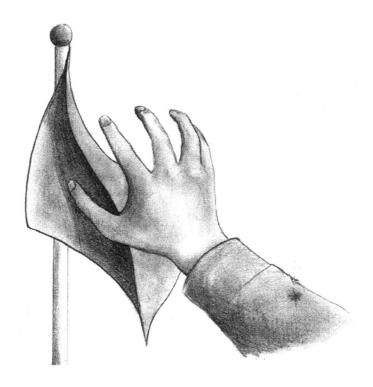

CHAPTER SIXTEEN

D-Day

Nic was surprised he survived the week. The talk around town hadn't eased up. In fact, the stories about what he 'did' were becoming more fantastic by the day. Having to give his fingerprints was cool and scary at the same time. For now, all he could do was wait for the results.

Thinking about the paintball tournament was a nice distraction. So when Saturday came, Nic was up early, eager to get moving. He was pacing in front of the living room window, while he waited for Philip's mom to pick him up.

"If you keep that up, at the rate you're going, you'll wear a hole into the carpet," joked Nic's mom.

Nic looked back sheepishly and offered, "Sorry, guess I'm really nervous about today. I just don't want to make a fool of myself again."

"You won't, dear. Just do your best, and everything else will take care of itself," encouraged his mom.

"I wish I could feel as confident about this as you are, Mom," replied Nic.

She walked over and kissed him on the forehead, whispering, "You'll do fine. Remember, you're a Nelson, and we Nelson's always find a way to persevere through tough times."

Nic smiled and kissed her on the cheek. "Thanks, Mom."

Honk! Honk! "That's the gang. Gotta go. Love ya, Mom!" smiled Nic, as he picked up his gear.

"Love you too, dear! Remember, you're still grounded!" she added.

"I know, I know!"

The van was strangely quiet as Nic got in.

"Thank you, Mrs. Browning."

She glanced at Nic with a disapproving look and simply grunted a response.

Philip whispered into Nic's ear, "I'm sorry for my mom's attitude, Nic. She thinks you're guilty. I've tried to convince her otherwise without telling her about the Diamonds of Denmark, but she won't listen. She didn't even want to pick you up today, but I reminded her that she had already made a promise."

"Thanks for trying, Philip," replied Nic, feeling a little less pumped up about today's contest.

"Cheer up, Nic. We believe you about what really happened last weekend," encouraged Cindy.

"Yeah, Nic, we're still on your side. Do you want a piece of my donut to make you feel better? I find eating something helps me to feel better when I'm sad," offered Herbert, holding out a half-eaten powdered donut.

"Thanks, but no thanks, Herbert," replied Nic with a meek smile.

"We'll get those crooks sooner or later, Nic, and then everyone will feel really bad for ever having doubted you," said Kevin confidently.

"That's right, Nic, you'll see," added Dante.

They spent some time going over the different strategies that Captain Spencer had taught them. This seemed to help distract Nic from worrying about what Philip's mom thought of him. The closer they got to the tournament location, the more tense everyone became. The van was silent when Mrs. Browning pulled up to the entrance.

"Here we are kids. Do be careful," said Philip's mom, as everyone piled out one at a time.

Nic thought Philip's mom gave him a dirty look, but he wasn't sure.

"We will, Mom," replied Philip, as he waved her on her way.

"Where to now, Kevin?" asked Dante.

"First, we have to register our team at the sign-in table over there, like last time," pointed Kevin, "Then we need to look at the information bulletin over there to find out what time we play."

"What are we waiting for? Let's go!" said Cindy.

After signing in, they ran over to a huge wooden bulletin board next to the refreshment stand. It was hard to miss the board as dozens of kids were hanging around it looking for their own teams' times. Herbert was the first one to find the bracket for their age group.

"Look, there we are!"

"Nice job, Herbert. Looks like Team Sokoor plays at 9:00 A.M., which gives us about one hour to kill," stated Kevin.

"Let's go find our old tree where we waited the last time," recommended Philip.

"I'll catch up to you guys in a minute. I'm going to use the restroom real quick," said Nic.

"Don't be too long," instructed Cindy.

"I don't think it's going to take me an hour to go to the bathroom," responded Nic.

The others trailed off, leaving Nic at the bulletin board by himself.

Nic didn't really need to use the restroom. He wanted to be by himself so he could take his time looking for Johnny's team and its playing times. It looked like they were on the opposite side of their age bracket.

"It looks like if we're going to play against each other again, Johnny, we'll both have to win all of our games, just like Philip said," mumbled Nic.

Turning around, Nic was stunned by the number of kids straining to read the board. It had to have doubled in size in the few minutes he had been standing there. As he made his way through the crowd, he bumped hard into someone.

"Excuse me, I didn't..." started Nic, stopping in mid-sentence, seeing that he was standing facing Jason.

"That's okay, Nic. It's a little tight around here," Jason replied with a small smile.

"Yeah, I guess it is," shrugged Nic in return. Jason's not acting mad. Maybe he's not angry with me. Maybe he's just being friendly to me, because there are so many other people around. Not knowing is eating me up. I just have to say something before it's too late, decided Nic. But what to say?

"Good luck today," said Jason, as he started to disappear into the crowd.

Afraid to lose his opportunity, Nic blurted out, "Jason, it wasn't me."

Jason looked at Nic curiously. "It wasn't you, what?"

Nic looked at the ground for a moment to collect his thoughts before responding, "I didn't have anything to do with the break-in to your dad's store."

A few awkward seconds of silence passed before Jason replied, "I really don't know what to make of everything that's happened, Nic. You seem like a good kid, but as I said a long time ago, looks can be deceiving."

"You've just got to believe me, Jason. I would never do anything against you or your family. You've been one of the few people who've been nice to me since I've moved here," pleaded Nic.

Jason put a hand on Nic's shoulder and said, "I think what I need is more time to let the facts speak for themselves before I make a final decision about you. No matter what the outcome, Nic, I'm not going to hate you. I may choose to not hang out with you for a while, if you're found guilty by the police, but I won't hate you."

Nic figured that was probably the best he was going to get from Jason for now.

"I understand...but I know the police will find me innocent. You'll see," stated Nic.

"I hope so, Nic. I really do. By the way, I hope you realize what a loyal friend you have in Kevin. He's been coming over to my house all week pleading your innocence to me, my parents, and anyone else with the last name of Hornsby."

Nic was surprised by this and smiled.

"Thank you for telling me, Jason."

"You're welcome. I gotta go, Nic. Good luck!"

"You, too," replied Nic, as he stepped out of the crowd.

Nic didn't realize how relieved he'd feel after talking with Jason. He felt like a ton of bricks had been lifted off his back. *I'm glad he hasn't passed judgment on me yet. like other people have. There's nothing else I can do or say to change how he feels, at least not until the police come out with their findings. Thankfully, since I never touched the shovel or metal detector, they won't find my fingerprints on either of them,* thought Nic. *That should go a long way toward proving my innocence.*

Fighting through crowds of kids, Nic finally managed to catch up with the rest of the gang at their meeting place.

"Wouldn't take you very long?" stated Cindy, looking at Nic and then at her watch.

Nic knew it would be useless to explain what had happened along the way so he just shrugged his shoulders and sat down between Philip and Herbert.

"Have I missed anything?" asked Nic casually.

"Nah, we've all just been sitting here," replied Philip.

"Are you sure you don't want a donut now, Nic? It'll help give you some energy," said Herbert, with his fingers and lips covered in white powder.

"Sure, Herbert, I'll take one," replied Nic, chuckling at the way Herbert looked.

Nic was hoping that eating a donut would get rid of the butterflies doing flip-flops in his stomach. It didn't work. The silence was broken when Kevin announced, "Time to go, guys."

Nic swallowed to get rid of the lump in his throat and slowly stood up with his gear. With Kevin leading the way, the gang arrived at the entrance to Field A for their first paintball outing of the day. Field A looked the same as it did when they had practiced on it three weeks earlier. Mr. Payne and their first opponents were already there.

"Move it! Move it! Move it, you sad-looking group of munchkins!" barked Mr. Payne, as Nic and the others broke into a run toward him.

Nic didn't recognize any of the kids on the opposing team. They're probably in different grades, thought Nic.

Mr. Payne began his presentation, while Nic, Kevin, and the others caught their breath.

"Are there any questions concerning the rules?" asked Mr. Payne, while rubbing his hands together.

Everyone on both teams silently shook their heads no.

"I can't hear you!" bellowed Mr. Payne.

"No, sir!" they yelled.

"That's better. Are there any questions about how a team wins?" asked Mr. Payne.

"No, sir!" responded everyone again.

"Then, what's everybody standing around for? Team Sokoor, go to that side," pointed Mr. Payne. "Team Tigershark, go to the other side, and wait for my air horn to officially begin the game."

Kevin led the way as everyone put their masks on and loaded up their hoppers with paintballs.

Nic wondered if everyone else's minds were racing like his. Thousands of thoughts were going through his mind. Can we win? What happens if we lose real badly again? How will we react? Nic shook his head vigorously to stop the negative thoughts and to concentrate on the situation at hand.

"Okay, guys, this is it. Remember what Captain Spencer taught us and we'll be fine," stated Kevin confidently. He removed his barrel plug and turned off the safety on his gun. The others did the same.

"Does everybody remember the plan we talked about in the car?" asked Kevin.

Everyone nodded; and without a word, they gathered in a circle placing their arms in the middle. Nic could see the nervous, but determined, looks of the others through his facemask, as they quietly stood there like statues waiting for Mr. Payne's air horn to blow.

It felt like an eternity for Nic. He and the others remained frozen in their tight circle. It was strange, but Nic never had felt as close with any other group of people as he did at this moment. For the first time in his life, Nic felt like people he cared about finally accepted him.

When the air horn sounded, Nic and the others yelled enthusiastically, "Team Sokoor!" and immediately began to sprint forward. Speed! That was the first tactic that Captain Spencer had drilled into them, thought Nic, rushing forward to get as far up front as he could.

Captain Spencer had instructed them to cover as much ground as possible initially, so they could be in a better and closer position to capture the flag.

After taking cover behind an overturned table, Kevin held up three fingers and pointed to Nic, Philip, and Cindy. Nic knew what to do and immediately took off, with Philip and Cindy trailing him to another overturned table across from Kevin.

Once positioned, Nic looked back at Kevin, Dante, and Herbert and pointed for them to move forward. As they began to press ahead, Nic, Philip, and Cindy popped up and gave them cover fire. This was the second lesson Captain Spencer had taught them. Never leave your teammates exposed without cover when they moved around.

Nic and Philip each were able to strike one of the opposing players with well-placed, blue-splattered paintballs across their masks. Nic could tell the other team hadn't been prepared for such an onslaught and saw them falling back.

"All right!" yelled Philip, as they ducked back down behind the table.

"Don't celebrate too much just yet, Philip. We still haven't captured the flag, and there are still four guys left on the other team," stated Nic calmly, not letting on that his stomach was doing somersaults.

A loud piercing whistle echoed across the field. This was Kevin's signal that his squad was safely in position. Now it was time for Nic and his crew to move forward again. Nic looked at the others and inhaled deeply. With a flick of his hand, they were off and running. They ended up behind two rusty oil barrels, just a few yards in front of the red flag they needed to win the game.

They heard Dante cry out, "Yeah! Gotcha!"

"Looks like I'm not the only one excited, Nic," joked Philip, as the three of them caught their breath.

"What now, Nic?" asked Cindy. Dozens of paintballs splattered against the oil barrels.

"Let me see what we can do," replied Nic. Careful to not expose too much of his helmet, he peeked around the barrels to assess their options.

Nic saw two opponents hiding behind an old mattress about fifteen yards to the left. Scanning to his right, Nic could see a player looking over an oil barrel like theirs about twenty yards away. Nic looked back toward Kevin, Dante, and Herbert. All three seemed unsure as to what to do next. They hadn't expected to do quite this well so quickly. Nic paused to consider various plans of action.

Nic came up with a plan that he thought might work. With Philip keeping an eye out for their opponents, Nic explained his idea.

"I don't know, Nic. It sounds pretty risky," said Cindy.

"Do you have a better plan?" retorted Nic.

Cindy didn't respond.

Philip said, "I think it's the best we're going to be able to do, Cindy. Let's go for it."

After a few seconds of silence, Cindy said, "Okay, Nic, let's try it your way; but I want it on the record that I disagree with it."

Nic and Philip gave each other startled looks with Philip saying, "Gosh, Cindy, I didn't know we were keeping records on what we do or say. Since when did all of this become a court proceeding?"

"Never mind! Let's just get this over with, shall we?" she demanded.

After waving frantically for a few seconds, Nic was able to get Kevin's attention. Then, using hand signals Captain Spencer had taught them, Nic tried his best to explain what he wanted them to do. After finishing, Kevin gave Nic a thumbs-up sign in return. Nic wasn't sure if Kevin had understood what he wanted, but he didn't have much choice. He was going to have to take the chance.

"On the count of three; one…two…three!" yelled Nic, as he scrambled around the oil barrel and dashed like a maniac toward the red flag.

Philip and Cindy popped up from behind the oil barrels and concentrated their fire on the opponent on their right. Kevin, Dante, and Herbert jumped up from their hiding place and directed all of their firepower at the two opponents on their left.

Nic didn't look at how things were going with the others. His focus was on getting the red flag and making it back to Philip and Cindy without being hit. He didn't attempt to twist or turn; he ran straight ahead. He figured the quickest and most direct path would be the best way to go about his business.

Grabbing the red flag, Nic began his mad dash back toward the oil barrels where Philip and Cindy were hiding. Noticing that no paintballs were flying by his face like earlier, Nic decided to take a chance and continued running past Philip and Cindy.

"Hey, where are you going?" asked a startled Philip, as Nic ran by.

"I'm going to try and end this game now! Keep me covered!" yelled Nic without looking back.

Nic clutched the red flag as hard as he could, continuing straight for their team's white starting circle.

"C'mon, Nic, you can do it," he said through gritted teeth.

A game referee was standing within the team circle just yards ahead. Seconds later, Mr. Payne's air horn blew as Nic held the red flag up high from Team Sokoor's base.

"Way t' go, Nic!" yelled Kevin, as he and the others tore off their masks and ran to Nic.

He was almost suffocated in a sea of hugs and high fives while everyone congratulated him for his daring. Walking off to the sidelines of Field A, Nic and the others shook hands with the members of Team Tigershark and Mr. Payne before heading back to the bulletin board to learn when their next match would be.

"That was awesome, Nic. Great job!" said Herbert.

"It was a team effort, Herbert. I couldn't have done it without you, Dante, and Kevin understanding what I had wanted you to do," remarked Nic.

"What was that?" asked Herbert.

Nic turned to face Herbert with a puzzled expression.

"What do you mean? You guys covered me perfectly against those two guys on our left, just as I made my dash for the flag."

Kevin, Dante, and Herbert all looked at each other and then at Nic with confused expressions.

"Didn't you understand my hand signals?" asked Nic.

"So that was what you were doing. We thought you had an itch or something," shrugged Kevin.

"An itch?" Nic asked in amazement. Everyone giggled as the gang arrived in front of the bulletin board.

"There we are!" shouted Cindy, pointing to where their team was posted on the bracket.

Their next opponent would be the Warriors at 11:00.

"Never heard of them before. Does anyone know who plays for the Warriors?" Kevin asked.

"I think Carlos Hernandez, the foreign exchange student, plays for them," said Dante.

"He's cool. It should be a friendly game," added Philip.

"Look, Philip, there's Chris from our homeroom. Let's go see how his team did," said Kevin. They all followed him over.

"Hey, Chris, how did you guys do in your match?" asked Kevin.

"Oh, hi, Kevin. Not so good. In fact, it was terrible. We got our butts kicked," Chris answered despondently.

"What happened?" asked Kevin.

"Johnny! That's what happened. They were too quick and overpowering for us to compete against. I feel sorry for anybody else who has to play against them. They won't have a chance." Chris said.

"We'll see," mumbled Nic, while Kevin gave Chris a pat on the back as consolation before catching up with the gang again.

CHAPTER SEVENTEEN

The Paintball Championship

T he next three matches went pretty much the same way for Team Sokoor. Using the techniques and strategies Captain Spencer had taught them to use as a team, they were able to overwhelm the opposition every time. With each victory, the gang's confidence in themselves and their abilities soared. After their win in the semifinals, they all began to think they just might have a chance to capture the championship as they approached the bulletin board to find out who their final opponents would be.

Without looking, Nic knew.

"It's Johnny's team, Bad to the Bone. They'll be playing against us for the championship," declared Dante grimly.

"We can take them. We've gotten this far, haven't we?" encouraged Kevin.

"Tough talk, Kevin. You guys have just been lucky so far, but your luck is about to run out," bragged Johnny from behind.

Nic and everyone else turned around to face Johnny and the rest of his team standing before them. Not one of them had any paintball splatter at all on their clothes. Everyone on Nic's team had been hit at least once or twice during the games.

"We were just playing around with you guys the first time. This time we're not holding back. After we're done with you, you'll wish you had never showed up today," declared Johnny.

Feeling the need to say something to rally his teammates, Nic was about to speak when Cindy said, "Johnny, if brains were dynamite, you wouldn't have enough to blow your nose."

Nic, Kevin, and the others looked at Cindy in disbelief before beginning to laugh. Even a few of Johnny's teammates were trying their best to stifle laughs.

Johnny took a step closer to Cindy and glared at her before speaking.

"Think you're funny, don't you? We'll see how funny you are when you're crying on the ground like last time. C'mon, guys, let's go get ready to cream these losers," said Johnny as he stormed off.

"That was a great put down, Cindy. One of your best," declared Philip.

"Way to go, Cindy!" agreed Herbert.

"You've never used that one on Kevin before. Were you saving it for a special occasion, like now?" joked Dante.

Kevin gave Dante a withering look while Cindy smiled and said, "That would be too mean even for Kevin, but it was just right for Johnny."

"I don't think anyone could have said what you did any better," commented Nic. He was glad Cindy had said what she did. It rejuvenated the gang and kick-started their determination to beat Johnny's team.

Too nervous to sit still, each member of the gang kept themselves preoccupied while waiting for the championship game. Dante hummed songs quietly. Cindy twirled her braided hair around her fingertips. Herbert munched slowly on a candy bar. Philip stared down at the ground, drawing pictures in the dirt with a small stick. Kevin flicked small rocks out of his palm with his thumb, and Nic paced back and forth in front of them like a general about to address his troops.

Kevin looked at his watch then said calmly, "Time to go, guys."

Everyone looked at him, nodded their heads, and proceeded to gather their stuff. Nothing was said as they strolled on over to Field A. Along the way, Nic saw some classmates looking at them as they walked on by. A few offered encouragements and good luck wishes, but the majority gave them silent stares of pity.

Mr. Payne and Johnny's team were waiting for them at Field A.

Kevin leaned over and whispered to Nic, "Watch out. Johnny has his daddy with him."

So that's Johnny's dad, thought Nic. He looks as angry as Johnny. No wonder he acts the way he does.

With everyone together, Mr. Payne spoke.

"Before I begin, I'd just like to say congratulations to both of your teams for reaching the championship game. It says a lot about the skill and determination involved in making it this far in what has been a very competitive age bracket."

At this, Johnny silently mouthed 'lucky' at Nic.

"No matter who wins or loses today, both teams should be very proud of their accomplishments," Mr. Payne added.

Thinking back to their ill-fated practice game of three weeks ago, Nic had to admit that they had come quite a long way since then. With Captain Spencer's help, they had learned how to gel as a team, which made their confidence grow. It's amazing how much one person can affect the attitude of so many others through their helpfulness. Nic brought his attention back to Mr. Payne as he repeated the same rules and stipulations for winning.

"If there are no questions, I suggest each team get their gear ready and head to opposite starting bases. Mr. Parks, you need to step back into the safety area as well," commanded Mr. Payne.

Both teams began to assemble their paintball guns. As Nic was attaching his CO2 cylinder to the back of his paintball gun, he heard a hissing sound. Suddenly, CO2 began leaking out like crazy. Nic was so surprised that he didn't move. He had never had this problem before. Everyone else had stopped what they were doing to watch Nic and his gun.

Nic tried to take the CO2 cylinder off but it was too cold to touch with all of the CO2 being sprayed on its surface. Nic tried, but couldn't loosen it. Mr. Payne, seeing Nic's problem, quickly snatched the gun from Nic's grip and easily detached the CO2 cylinder.

Nic let out a sigh of relief while Mr. Payne examined his gun more closely.

"Are you all right, Nic?" asked Cindy.

"I'm fine thanks to Mr. Payne," replied Nic.

"What's wrong with Nic's paintball gun, Mr. Payne?" Kevin asked.

"For starters, the O-ring from the CO2 cylinder is broken." He continued taking Nic's gun apart to assess the damage. "Secondly, I can't be sure, but it looks like the O-ring inside needs replacing and, possibly, the cocking mechanism is broken."

"Can it be fixed?" asked Nic anxiously.

Mr. Payne glanced at the gun and then at Nic, "Probably, but it would require too much time for what we have allotted today. I'm afraid the rules stipulate that if a player doesn't have a functioning paintball gun at the start of a match, then he or she is not allowed to participate, which automatically disqualifies whatever team the person was playing on."

Nic looked down at the ground in despair. He could feel his hopes of getting another chance at Johnny slipping away. And, he could hear snickering coming from Johnny's gang. His teammates tried to console him.

"It just wasn't meant to be," offered Philip.

"We'll get them next year," said Herbert trying to sound cheerful.

"Ignore Johnny, Nic. He's just happy he didn't have to face us or else he knew we'd win," added Kevin.

"Sorry, Team Sokoor, but I'm going to have to declare Team Bad to the Bone…" began Mr. Payne before stopping his sentence.

Nic looked up to see why and saw Mr. Payne watching someone approach in the distance. Murmurs went through Team Sokoor.

"It's Captain Spencer!"

Nic was surprised to see him, especially since he was still dressed in his butler's uniform. He walked toward them with a black duffle bag slung across one of his shoulders.

Upon reaching them, Captain Spencer said, "Hello, young masters. I do hope I haven't interfered with the beginning of your game. It wasn't until a few minutes ago that I was able to be released from any more obligations to the Chamberlains for today."

Nic and the others were too stunned by his arrival to respond.

"Sergeant Major Payne, I am truly sorry for any inconvenience I may have caused with my untimely arrival," apologized Captain Spencer.

"Think nothing of the sort, Captain Spencer. It's always an honor to have you grace us with your presence," replied Mr. Payne respectfully giving Captain Spencer a friendly salute.

"I'm sorry you made the trip out here, Captain Spencer. I was just about to disqualify Team Sokoor and declare Team Bad to the Bone the winners," stated Mr. Payne.

"May I inquire as to the reason, Sergeant Major Payne?" asked Captain Spencer calmly.

Mr. Payne explained, "Nic's paintball gun is broken, and there isn't enough time to fix it. So I'll have to disqualify him and his team."

Nic felt his heart sink again and wished Mr. Payne would get it over with so he could go home and get away from Johnny's smug smiling.

"I understand and concur completely, Sergeant Major Payne. But may I ask something before you declare a winner?" asked Captain Spencer politely.

"Of course," replied Mr. Payne.

"If he were given another paintball gun to use, would that be permissible?" asked Captain Spencer, as he winked at Nic.

Nic looked up at Captain Spencer in surprise and then at Mr. Payne, who rubbed his chin for a second before replying, "Yes, that would be acceptable under the rules."

Nic couldn't believe what he was hearing! What was Captain Spencer up to? Was this some joke? Captain Spencer knelt down next to Nic and opened his black duffle bag. Reaching in, he pulled out a Predator V paintball gun. It was painted black and green with a much longer barrel than what Nic's gun had.

"I trust you'll know what to do with this, young master," said Captain Spencer handing it to Nic.

Nic was still in shock but somehow forced a, "Thank you," from his paralyzed lips.

"That's not fair! He shouldn't be allowed to do that!" cried Johnny.

His dad came running back onto the field of play.

"I demand to know what's going on here!" barked Mr. Parks.

Before anyone could respond, Johnny whined and pointed, "They're cheating. Nic's gun is broken, and now he's getting a new one from some captain person."

"Is this true? What's the meaning of all of this?" demanded Mr. Parks.

"I don't like your son's tone or yours for that matter," stated Mr. Payne as he glared at Mr. Parks and Johnny.

Mr. Parks stared back at Mr. Payne for a few moments before straining to speak in a polite manner.

"Is what my son is saying true?"

"Not entirely. What's correct is the fact that Nic's gun is indeed broken and can't be fixed quickly. Also true is the fact that Captain Spencer has been kind enough to allow Nic to use his paintball gun instead. What's incorrect is that Nic is cheating by using this new gun. The tournament rules allow a player to use a replacement gun if the player's original gun is damaged during the course of the tournament. So you see, there is no problem," stated Mr. Payne.

"Maybe it's been modified. It hasn't been checked by anyone," protested Johnny.

"I assure everyone here, the gun in question has not been modified in any way other than what is permissible by the rules," replied Captain Spencer.

"Why should we believe you, a simple butler?" accused Mr. Parks.

"You'd better take that accusation back. I can personally vouch for Captain Spencer as a man of his word, which is more than I can say about other people standing here," spoke Mr. Payne.

"I would watch it if I were you, Mr. Payne. Remember whom you are addressing. As chairman of the school board, life could become very difficult for your school teacher wife," replied Mr. Parks coldly.

As Mr. Payne was about to take a step toward Mr. Parks, Captain Spencer stepped between them and calmly said, "Sergeant Major Payne, the legality of the gun in question can be answered quite simply. Attached to the barrel is a small yellow tag which certifies it has been inspected and approved by your assistants for use in today's tournament."

Looking at the gun again, Nic noticed a small yellow tag sticking to the end of the barrel, just as Captain Spencer had said. Nic handed the gun to Mr. Payne who inspected it closely for a few seconds.

Looking at Mr. Parks and Johnny, Mr. Payne smiled broadly before declaring confidently, "This gun has indeed been approved for use in tournament play. Now, if there aren't any more objections, let's get this game started."

Johnny continued to whine, but his dad whispered something in his ear. He then sent Johnny and his team off toward their base.

Walking past Captain Spencer, Mr. Parks remarked within earshot of Nic, "I'll have you know I'm on good terms with your employers, and I just may have to have a little chat with them concerning this incident of yours."

"That is perfectly within your right to do so, sir. May I be of assistance by giving you directions or a phone number to the Chamberlains' residence?"

Mr. Parks glared at Captain Spencer and then at Nic before stomping off into the distance.

"Captain Spencer..." began Nic, before he was cut off in mid-sentence.

"We'll talk later, young master. It's time for you to join your friends. Godspeed," he added with a wink and a small smile. Nic nodded his head, put on his mask, and ran to catch up with the others.

"Thanks to Captain Spencer, we're in business again," said Kevin. "Does everybody remember what to do?"

"No, Kevin, please tell us again. It's not like we haven't done the same plan over and over today," joked Cindy.

Everyone laughed, which seemed to break the tension. It was dawning on each of them that this was the final game; and when it was over, they could be the champions.

Like the previous games, the gang stood in a small circle with hands in the middle. They waited for Mr. Payne's air horn to blow.

Nic felt sweat slowly running down his forehead. His palms were sweaty, too, making his grip loose on his paintball gun. His stomach was butterfly free, but his heart was pounding hard against his chest. He had to blink his eyes several times to clear the stinging sweat from them.

Mr. Payne's air horn blared loudly in the afternoon air. They yelled, "Team Sokoor!" and then split into two groups. Running as fast as he could, Nic led Cindy and Philip forward while Dante and Herbert followed Kevin.

A hail of red- and yellow-colored paintballs convinced Nic to take cover behind an overturned table to his right about twenty yards away from the red flag.

"That was close," mumbled Philip. More paintball splatter echoed off the front of the table as Nic waited for Kevin, Dante, and Herbert to get into position on the other side of the field.

Nic was considering a number of plans as he, Philip, and Cindy gave cover fire for Kevin and the others while they moved ahead of Nic's group.

Johnny's team wasn't going to be as easily fooled as the others had been, thought Nic. While Johnny and his team probably had the most experience, knowing Johnny, they were likely the most overconfident team as well, surmised Nic. Hopefully, they could use that knowledge against Johnny and get the best of him.

During a lull in the action, Nic popped his head out for a quick peek to assess the situation. He could tell Johnny's team had progressed as far forward as his team had toward the red flag. It looked like Johnny's team had also split into two groups. Four members were on the same side opposing Kevin, Dante, and Herbert, while two members were facing himself, Philip, and Cindy.

"That's interesting," mumbled Nic, while keeping an eye out.

"What's interesting?" asked Cindy.

"Looks like Johnny is trying to overload one side of the field to try and outflank us," replied Nic.

"Outflank? What's that mean?" asked Philip.

"It's what they did to us last time," answered Nic.

"Are they going to be able to do it again?" asked Cindy.

"I don't know. But if they try, they're going to find it much harder to pull off. They probably weren't expecting us to split up like we've done," pointed out Nic.

Over the next fifteen minutes, neither team was able to get the upper hand. Eerily similar to the practice session, Herbert, Dante, and Philip were the first to be hit by paintballs. Unlike last time, Team Sokoor was able to return the favor by hitting three of Johnny's teammates.

With five minutes left, Nic and Cindy found themselves farther to the right of the red flag than Nic wanted to be. Every time they tried to move forward, they ran into a hail of red and yellow paintball fire. This forced them to duck behind the nearest object, which always seemed to be further and further to the right of the red flag.

They were currently huddled behind a small upright mattress about ten yards away from one of the two opponents that had begun the game opposite Nic and Cindy. Nic had hit the other player when he tried to go after the red flag.

Time was running out, and Nic knew it was going to be now or never to go after the flag. First, he knew they had to get rid of the opponent closest to them.

"Okay, Cindy, this is what we're going to do," said Nic, as he gave Cindy instructions on how they were going to go after him.

With Cindy on one side of the mattress and Nic on the other, he signaled to Cindy to initiate their plan. She took a small rock and was about to toss it near the other player, when she and Nic were startled by a loud yell to their left.

Charging toward the red flag was Johnny and his teammate, with guns blazing. Nic could tell it was Johnny from the unusual paint markings on his facemask he had noticed before the game. Nic popped up to shoot at Johnny, but his paintballs were off target. Johnny grabbed the flag and ducked for cover.

Figuring that Kevin was likely out of the game and sensing victory slipping away, Nic impulsively grabbed Cindy by her arm and began to run straight at the overturned table where the other member of Johnny's gang was hiding. He had heard Johnny's yell and had been so happy to see Johnny grabbing the flag, he forgot about Nic and Cindy. Too late, the opponent realized his mistake. When he turned to fire, Nic nailed him in the middle of his mask with a single purple paintball.

The game referee dutifully yelled, "Out!"

Nic didn't take any time to find out who he had hit as he continued to lead Cindy through the course running as fast as they could.

"Where are we going, Nic?" asked Cindy between gasps for air. They stopped behind two oil barrels deep within Johnny's side of the field.

Breathing hard, Nic responded, "We've got to get to Johnny's base before he does with the flag."

"But isn't the game over? They've captured the flag before we did," stated Cindy.

"They still have to get the flag back to their base; and as hard as Johnny was running to the side after grabbing the flag, I'll bet he's not sure how many, if any, of us are left," explained Nic.

"How can that help us, Nic?" asked Cindy.

Nic thought for a moment before replying, "We'll use the element of surprise to our advantage."

Cindy looked at Nic with uncertainty as he explained what he wanted her to do.

When he was finished, she whispered worriedly, "I don't like it. It's too risky. You're going to get hurt too bad. Let's just try and end the game in a tie and take our chances in the target shootout."

Nic shook his head vigorously and said, "This'll work. Besides, if it doesn't, there's a good chance the game will end in a tie like you want. There's no more time to argue. Just do what we planned, and we'll be all right."

Sensing Cindy's continued reluctance, Nic whispered, "Trust me," before dashing off to another hiding place.

"Boys," mumbled Cindy, as she headed to her assigned destination to wait for his signal.

Nic ducked behind a large pipe and readied himself. He heard voices coming his way. He wasn't sure if his plan would work, but he hadn't wanted Cindy to know that. He knew she was going to be anxious enough as it was, so he didn't want to add to her worries.

"Are you sure, Johnny?" asked a nervous voice much closer than before to Nic's position.

"Of course I am. I nailed that geek and his partner when I grabbed the flag," bragged Johnny.

"Then why hasn't Jerry joined us yet?" Nic recognized the voice as Mark's.

"I don't know. Maybe he's picking his nose. Who cares? We're about to win the championship just like I said we would." Johnny's voice was dripping with arrogance.

Nic felt his heart quicken as he prepared to ambush Johnny and Mark.

"I hope I can hit them both and end the game so Cindy won't have to do her part," whispered Nic.

Johnny and Mark's voices were beginning to trail off, which meant they were walking away. Nic decided it was now or never as he jumped up and took aim with his paintball gun. Johnny happened to be looking back in Nic's direction. He grabbed a stunned Mark and used him as a shield against Nic's paintballs. Nic nailed Mark squarely in the chest multiple times.

"Out!" yelled the game referee.

"Drats!" whispered Nic, as Johnny ducked behind a small wooden wall.

"Nice try, Geek, but you're going to have to do better than that to get me. Where's your partner?" mocked Johnny. Nic thought he heard a hint of anxiety in Johnny's voice.

"You hit Cindy when you grabbed the flag. I'm going to make sure I get you back real good for that," said Nic with mock anger.

I hope I sounded convincing, thought Nic, as seconds of silence went by.

Laughter erupted from Johnny before he responded, "I warned you guys about having a girl on your team. She probably couldn't hit the side of a barn if it was right in front of her."

"You're a load of laughs," replied Nic. He hoped Cindy wasn't getting too mad and too tempted to fire at Johnny before Nic was ready for her.

"You've lost the game already, so you might as well give up and let me pass by with the flag!" yelled Johnny brazenly.

"No way, Johnny! Last time I checked, a team didn't win until it brought the flag safely back to their starting base," replied Nic.

"Have it your way, Geek," said Johnny, as he ran off a spree of paintballs toward Nic in frustration.

Nic decided to dash toward another hiding spot directly in front of Johnny. As he rose up, he fired wildly in Johnny's direction, running toward an overturned table ten yards to the left of where he had been. Three yards from safety, Nic tripped over a rock. He fell hard, and his paintball gun went flying. Quickly recovering, he tried to reach for it, but a series of paintballs splattered between him and his gun. He pulled his hand back quickly.

"This isn't exactly what I had in mind," mumbled Nic, as he sat frozen on the ground. Looking up, he could see Johnny strutting toward him with his paintball gun pointed right at his head.

Stopping just inches from touching Nic's facemask with his gun barrel, Johnny said, "You lose, Geek."

Nic didn't say anything as Mr. Payne's voice came over the loudspeaker, "LAST MINUTE OF PLAY!"

"I'm not going to waste any time asking if you want to surrender, because I'm going to nail you right between the eyes," laughed Johnny menacingly, dangling the game flag in front of Nic's face.

"Wait, Johnny! Before you do that…I just have one last thing to say," said Nic with hands clutched tight.

"Now!" yelled Nic.

A split second later, Johnny howled in pain as he grabbed at his rear end. Johnny turned to see who had hit him, and Nic saw three paintball marks on the seat of Johnny's pants.

"You!" yelled Johnny in anger at Cindy as she came out from her hiding spot.

"Not bad shooting for a girl, huh, Johnny…unless your butt is bigger than the side of a barn?" mocked Cindy.

Realizing there wasn't a moment to lose, Nic got to his feet, grabbed the flag from Johnny's grasp, and took off running. He knew he had to make it back to Team Sokoor's base before time ran out or else the game would end in a tie. Running faster than he had ever done before, Nic saw his team's starting base just up ahead with a game referee standing next to it. Ignoring the pain in his legs and the burning in his lungs, Nic pressed forward until, at the last few feet, he flung himself forward, landing within the base circle as the game air horn blew.

Finally, it was over, he thought. He stayed lying on the ground, too exhausted to stand up.

CHAPTER EIGHTEEN

The Diamonds Revealed

Seconds later, his friends pulled Nic to his feet as they all jumped up and down in celebration of their hard-earned victory.

"We did it! We did it!" yelled Kevin.

"That was awesome, Nic! Nice shooting, Cindy!" yelled Philip, as he patted Nic on his back.

"You both da man!" said Dante excitedly pointing to both Nic and Cindy.

She frowned slightly before adding, "Don't you mean, da man and da woman?"

"Whatever you say," smiled Dante, while Nic and the others chuckled.

"Great job, Nic. I especially liked your dive at the end," said Herbert. Nic smiled back sheepishly, not knowing what else to say.

The celebration stopped as an angry looking Mr. Payne walked toward them. Captain Spencer was following closely behind. Uh oh, maybe I did something wrong? Maybe you're not supposed to dive in paintball, thought Nic. Mr. Payne stopped in front of him. With Mr. Payne's lips pursed tightly and eyes blazing down on him, Nic felt his knees turning into jelly as he glanced at the ground.

"Out of all my years of military service and of playing paintball, that was the most incredible finish I have ever witnessed!" bellowed Mr. Payne menacingly. He then broke into a smile. He gave Nic a hearty pat on the back that almost caused Nic to fall down. Nic looked up and smiled gratefully. Mr. Payne wasn't mad. One-by-one, starting with Nic, he shook everyone's hands as he showered them with praise and congratulations.

Nic walked over to Captain Spencer and said, "I…no…we couldn't have done any of this without you. Thank you." He impulsively gave Captain Spencer a hug. Nic could feel Captain Spencer's long arms engulfing him with a hug of his own.

Clearing his throat, Captain Spencer said, "I only taught young master a few strategies. That is all. It was your bravery and courage which allowed you to carry the day. These are qualities one cannot teach, but one must possess."

Nic blushed before adding, "We still couldn't have done it without you," as the rest of his friends thanked and hugged Captain Spencer, too.

"Team Sokoor, wait here. I'll return in a minute with your team's trophy and T-shirts for participating in the tournament," stated Mr. Payne as he walked away.

"Where's Johnny and his team? We should go and shake their hands for a good game," said Nic, looking around.

Dante looked at him with a funny expression and asked, "You still want to shake Johnny's hand after all he's said and done to you? Whatever happened to wanting revenge?"

"I don't want revenge anymore. It wouldn't solve anything anyhow. I'm happy with just being able to win this paintball tournament alongside the best friends a guy could have."

"Speak of the devil, here comes Johnny now," pointed out Cindy.

Walking past everyone else, Johnny got right up in Nic's face and said with a low angry voice, "Real clever stunt back there, Geek. Better enjoy your victory today, because next time I'm going to get you good."

"I'm sorry you feel that way, Johnny. I thought you and your team played well against us," said Nic with sincerity, as he held out his hand. Johnny ignored Nic's outstretched hand, smirked, and stomped off to where his dad was waiting.

Mr. Payne returned, handing the T-shirts out first. Then, with some flourish, he presented the tournament trophy to Team Sokoor for the 10- to 11-year-old division. The last thing to do was take a team picture for the New Bonn Gazette.

Mr. Payne was about to take it when Nic stopped him.

"What do you mean, 'Hold up'?" barked Mr. Payne at Nic.

"We couldn't have done it without Captain Spencer's help. He needs to be in the team picture with us. He's as much a part of our team as anyone else," proclaimed Nic.

Kevin chimed in, "Yeah, Nic's right. C'mon, Captain Spencer. We need you to stand with us."

Captain Spencer smiled slightly and replied, "I appreciate the compliment, young masters, but this is your moment of glory, not mine. I do not wish to take it away from you."

Too stubborn to give up, Nic responded, "If you won't move over here then we'll just have to move over there where you are."

The gang surrounded Captain Spencer.

"I think we're ready now," Nic said to Mr. Payne.

The photo of the group had Captain Spencer in the middle.

"You all are much too kind," said Captain Spencer.

"Party at my place!" yelled Kevin, as the gang picked up their equipment.

While walking to their pickup point, Kevin touched Captain Spencer's arm and said, "You're welcome to join us, Captain Spencer."

"I'm afraid I must decline your most gracious offer, Master Kevin. I'm obligated to return to the Chamberlains' residence, but I do wish you all a happy victory celebration."

Nic thought he heard a hint of regret in Captain Spencer's response.

Captain Spencer started walking toward his car after saying his goodbyes to the group. Nic ran after him and asked quietly, "You're not going to get into any trouble with the Chamberlains, are you?"

"What do you mean, Master Nic?"

"Well, you know, about what Mr. Parks said to you earlier?"

Captain Spencer smiled, "I wouldn't worry about Mr. Parks' threats, young master. I do not put much weight in what he says. Besides, without me around, I am quite sure the Chamberlains' house would quickly smell of undone laundry."

Nic, relieved at hearing this, smiled and said goodbye again to Captain Spencer. He jogged to rejoin his friends.

Philip's mom was already waiting for them.

"How did you guys do?"

Everyone shouted at once, "We won!"

After scrambling into the van, they spent the ride to Kevin's house comparing the best and worst highlights of the day's events.

Easily voted as the best highlight was Nic's game-winning dive in the championship game. Voted the funniest event was when Herbert and Philip ran into each other, falling down while looking for cover in the third game. Amazingly, neither was hit with paintballs. The worst highlight for the group was when Nic's gun broke, and they were almost disqualified from playing in the championship game.

"That was way too scary," said Kevin, as they pulled up to his house.

Kevin's mom was sitting in the dining room when they made their noisy entrance. She looked up, startled at the onslaught of kids.

"Kevin, what's all of this about?"

"We won, Mom! We won!" yelled Kevin as he hugged her.

"That's wonderful! I knew you could, but why is everyone here?" she asked.

"I invited them over to celebrate our victory," declared Kevin.

His mom looked at him and the others in turn before joking, "I'm sure glad you asked me first before inviting them."

"Wouldn't think of doing it any other way, Mom," replied Kevin with his big flashy smile.

The next couple of hours were spent laughing and goofing around in Kevin's basement and outside patio. Nic figured Mrs. Becker must be used to Kevin's last-minute parties, because she had plenty of food and snacks prepared to go around. If Nic had done the same thing without giving his mom advance notice, she would've been pulling her hair out while scrambling to find something for everyone to eat.

"Oh, no," Nic groaned. "My mom! She's going to kill me."

"What did you say?" Cindy asked.

"I never called to tell my mom where I am. On top of that, I'm supposed to be grounded, and I'm sure being at this party is no exception," said Nic.

"Why don't you just call her now and explain what happened?" suggested Cindy.

Nic shook his head and replied, "I don't think that's going to do any good at this point. I'd better leave now," as he dashed to the front door.

"Wait, Nic! Why don't you at least let Kevin's mom take you home? It's dark outside," said Cindy.

"I don't want to wait for her; and besides, I only live a few blocks from here." He grabbed his gear and ran outside. The front door slammed behind him.

Kevin ran up to Cindy, "Where's Nic going?"

"He's going home. He's afraid he'll be in a lot of trouble for not telling his mom where he's been," replied Cindy.

Kevin slapped his forehead, "Gosh, darn it. I forgot to tell him that my mom called his mom earlier tonight. His mom said it was okay for him to stay."

Nic ran along the brightly lit town sidewalks as fast as he could. His legs were sore and tired from the tournament, but he pushed on, knowing that time was of the essence. How could I have been so stupid? All I had to do was pick up the phone and call mom, but nooooo, I had to be enjoying the party too much.

When he came within sight of his house, Nic slowed down his pace, rehearsing what he was going to say to his mom. Distracted by his thoughts, Nic didn't see the movement in the shadows nearby. He had just walked past the Chamberlains' house and was about to cross the street when he was grabbed from behind. Before he could scream, a rough hand covered his mouth.

He struggled to escape. Whoever had him was much bigger and stronger. Fighting was useless. He was dragged into the shadows of a large bush in the Chamberlains' yard where it was pitch black. Tonight there was no full moon to light the landscape.

Nic's heart skipped a beat as a frighteningly familiar voice growled, "I warned you I'd be back to settle our score, kid."

Though Nic's eyes were slowly becoming accustomed to the dark, he didn't need them to tell him who had spoken. It was Roger Marinovich's voice, and he was standing right in front of Nic. His partner was holding Nic firmly.

Roger Marinovich stepped closer and grabbed Nic's jaw. "Let's start where we left off before we were so rudely interrupted," he whispered.

Nic tried again to wriggle free from his captor's bear hug; but the more he struggled, the harder it became to move or breathe.

Squeezing Nic's jaw harder, Roger Marinovich commanded, "Stop squirming around and cooperate. All I want from you is a few answers. If you give them to me, I'll let you go. However, I warn you, if you make one sound, I'll cut your throat. Of course, screaming won't do you any good anyway because nobody's home."

Nic stopped moving, not because he wanted to, but because he realized he was getting nowhere by continuing it. He would have to bide his time until an opening presented itself.

"That's better. See, it doesn't hurt as much when you're not struggling against us," pointed out Roger Marinovich as he patted Nic's head.

"What do you want?" asked Nic defiantly.

"I think you know already, boy. Where are the Diamonds of Denmark hidden?"

"Shouldn't you know? After all, wasn't it your brother who had stolen them in the first place?" asked Nic.

Getting right up into Nic's face, Roger Marinovich sneered, "My dear brother wouldn't tell me where he hid the diamonds. All he gave me was this lousy address."

"Why? Didn't he trust you?" Nic was trying to keep Roger Marinovich talking for as long as possible until help could arrive.

"He thought our employer and I might double cross him out of his cut of the profits while he was in jail. Funny thing was, he was right. We would have left him out of his share without blinking an eye." The laugh that followed chilled Nic to the bone.

"Wouldn't you have been worried about him exposing you and your employer if you had taken the diamonds and left him nothing?" asked Nic with genuine curiosity.

Roger Marinovich laughed again. "Not for a moment. Nobody would've believed him if he had fingered our employer as part of the heist. Our employer is too well respected and admired to be thought of as being a criminal. As for me, I would've disappeared, never to be found again."

"Who is your employer?" asked Nic.

Roger Marinovich smirked and said, "Sorry, kid, can't tell you everything."

"Whatever happened to your brother?" asked Nic, desperate to keep the conversation going and his kidnappers distracted.

"He died of a heart attack while in prison, just days before he was to be released. It was a cruel irony, as he would've retrieved the diamonds for my employer and me if he had survived prison. Of course, I would've killed him afterwards."

"Enough with the questions, kid. Wasting time isn't going to do you any good. Where are the diamonds hidden?" Roger Marinovich demanded.

"I don't know. My friends and I never found them," explained Nic.

"I don't believe you. I'll only ask you one more time before I'll have you join my dear departed brother. Where are the diamonds hidden?"

To emphasize the seriousness of Nic's situation, Roger Marinovich whipped out a knife from his pocket and twirled it in front of Nic's eyes.

Nic felt sick. Roger Marinovich could, and most likely would, carry out his threat if Nic didn't say something quick.

"Time's running out, kid," sneered Roger Marinovich, as he twirled the blade ever closer to Nic's face.

Suddenly, an idea came to Nic, and he said, "Okay, you win. I'll show you where the diamonds are, if you promise to let me go afterwards."

Roger Marinovich stopped twirling his blade just before reaching Nic's neck and replied, "Sure, whatever makes you happy. Lead the way." He signaled his partner to let Nic go.

"I warn you, if you attempt to escape, you won't get very far; and you'll suffer in a most painful way," he threatened.

Nic knew Roger Marinovich was probably going to kill him anyway, regardless of whether he helped them or not.

"I sure hope my plan works," whispered Nic, as he led them to the tool shed in the Chamberlains' backyard.

"What are we stopping here for kid?" asked Roger Marinovich suspiciously.

"The Diamonds of Denmark are in the shed. They're underneath an old stool in the corner by the door," explained Nic with a straight face.

"I don't believe him, boss. It sounds too simple," remarked Roger Marinovich's partner.

"Quit playing games, kid. Where are the diamonds?" demanded Roger Marinovich.

"They're in this shed, in one of its corners…honest," pleaded Nic, as he saw them hesitating.

Taking a big gamble, Nic said, "To prove it, I'll go in first and get them for you."

He took a step toward the shed door.

Roger Marinovich grabbed his arm and jerked him back from the door. "Not so fast, kid. Nice try."

"What do you mean?" asked Nic.

"I know what you were going to do. Once inside, you were going to lock us out so we couldn't get to you and the diamonds."

Nic kept a straight face while thinking…not exactly what I had in mind, but that would've been a good idea, too.

"Stand back, kid. I'll go in, and I want you to watch him," commanded Roger Marinovich to his partner.

Way to go, rusty lock, thought Nic, as Roger Marinovich struggled with it. His partner, curious as to what was going on, stepped close to look over his boss's shoulder. Nic, meanwhile, was slowly moving backward from the scene.

Nic was about to find out if his plan was going to work as Roger Marinovich swung the shed door open. For a second, nothing happened. Then, an avalanche of leaves came pouring out of the shed, surprising and covering Roger Marinovich and knocking his partner to the ground.

"It worked!" yelled Nic with joy, lost for a moment in admiration of his plan's success.

A furious Roger Marinovich screamed, "You'll pay dearly for that! Get him!"

Nic began running toward the front yard. He heard heavy breathing right behind him, as he crossed the street into his front yard.

Somebody grabbed his ankles, which caused him to trip. He hit his head hard on the ground.

"Ugh!" he groaned. Everything was blurry, and he felt woozy and dazed. He struggled to get back to his feet, but his arms and legs wouldn't cooperate.

"Gotcha!" yelled Roger Marinovich's partner, roughly pulling Nic to his feet.

Nic was still trying to clear his head when he saw Roger Marinovich coming toward him, knife drawn. He steeled himself for the end. He knew begging probably wouldn't do any good at this point. He decided he would die with dignity and his pride intact.

Stopping his blade an inch away from Nic's throat, Roger Marinovich sneered, "No begging or pleading for your life? Either you're very brave or very stupid. I've never killed a kid before, but somehow I think I'm going to enjoy doing away with you. Your father was just as troublesome for me and my employer as you are. Oh well, like father, like son."

He swung his blade back to finish Nic off.

Strangely, Nic wasn't thinking about the blade coming at him, because he was focused on what Roger Marinovich had said about his dad.

"What do you know about my father?" screamed Nic angrily, with tears welling up in his eyes.

The knife stopped in midair. For a moment, Nic thought Roger Marinovich was going to spare him. Then he saw why the knife wasn't moving.

"What the ...?" mumbled Roger Marinovich as he turned around, coming face-to-face with Captain Spencer, who was holding his arm.

"There's going to be no blood spilt by your hand tonight, sir," stated Captain Spencer.

"Says who...some old has-been English butler? What was the problem back home? King or Queen kicked you out for messing up the palace?" mocked Roger Marinovich, yanking his arm free. His full attention was directed at Captain Spencer.

The two men circled each other like predators ready to pounce. Police sirens pierced the air. Nic heard Roger Marinovich curse under his breath.

Then...

"Boss, it's the cops. We've got to go."

Nic was relieved at Captain Spencer's timely arrival, but desperately wanted to help him. Roger Marinovich was armed, and Nic didn't know if Captain Spencer was going to be able to hold out long enough against him or his partner until the police arrived. Thinking quickly, Nic swung his leg back and kicked Roger Marinovich's partner in his shin.

Nic was released as the partner bent down to rub his shin saying, "Ow!"

Nic started to run past Captain Spencer and Roger Marinovich toward the Chamberlains' house. Nic wanted to get Mr. Chamberlain's help.

Before getting far, Nic was grabbed by Roger Marinovich, "No you don't, kid. I'm not finished with you."

Nic froze as Roger Marinovich swung the blade toward him. Then, like a bolt of lightning, Captain Spencer punched Roger Marinovich in the jaw with his huge right hand, knocking him backwards. The impact of the blow was so great that Nic fell to the ground, too. Looking up, Nic saw Captain Spencer backhand Roger Marinovich's charging partner across his face, knocking him out cold.

Out of the corner of his eye, Nic saw Roger Marinovich charging at Captain Spencer from behind.

"Watch out!" yelled Nic, as he got to his feet.

It was too late, as Nic saw Roger Marinovich's blade plunge into the butler's lower back. Captain Spencer grunted and grabbed at his back, falling to his knees. Inhaling noisily, Captain Spencer fell face first onto the ground.

"No!" Nic screamed as he charged toward Roger Marinovich to stop him from stabbing Captain Spencer again.

"Hold it right there!" yelled a voice from the street. Officer Williams was pointing his gun at Roger Marinovich from the side of his squad car.

"You don't have the guts," mocked Roger Marinovich, as his blade swung toward a fallen Captain Spencer.

Bang! The unfamiliar noise echoed across the neighborhood. Roger Marinovich slumped to the side. Officer Williams pulled Nic away from the fallen men, but Nic pulled free to kneel beside Captain Spencer.

Tears were streaming down Nic's face as he begged, "Captain Spencer! Captain Spencer! Are you all right? Please tell me you're okay!"

No response. In his mind, Nic saw his dad being struck by the hit and run car. Nic had been powerless to stop that, too.

"Not again. Please, God, not again," cried Nic. Suddenly, Captain Spencer opened his eyes and with great effort sat up.

"Captain Spencer, you're all right!" cried Nic happily, as he hugged him.

"Of course I'm all right, Master Nic. How else should I be?" replied Captain Spencer calmly, giving a reassuring pat on Nic's back.

After another police car arrived, three ambulances pulled up, sirens blaring to announce their arrival. An injured man was put into each, and they wailed off to the local hospital, police in tow.

A couple of days later, the gang was sitting in Nic's backyard after school.

"So tell me again, Nic, what's going on with Captain Spencer?" asked Cindy.

"I talked to him yesterday when he came home from the hospital. Luckily, the knife missed any vital organs or nerves. He should be up and running like normal in a week or two. I also apologized to him for not telling him the truth about what we knew about the Diamonds of Denmark. He said he understood," explained Nic.

"What happened to Roger Marinovich and his partner?" asked Herbert.

"Don't you read the paper?" snorted Cindy. .Herbert shrugged his shoulders.

"Let me handle this one, Cindy," said Kevin. "Evidently, Roger Marinovich is in a coma, and nobody knows when or if he'll ever recover. As for his partner, otherwise known as Carl Hoffman, he suffered a broken jaw and facial cuts," explained Kevin.

"Good thing Captain Spencer is on our side. I'd hate to have him mad at me," said Dante.

"Anyway, Carl Hoffman spilled the beans to the cops about everything. From the break-in of Hornsby's Hardware Store to tricking the Chamberlains to leave their house on the night they grabbed Nic to hooking back up with Roger Marinovich last summer to renew their search for the Diamonds of Denmark," stated Kevin.

"Did he say who had hired them to steal the Diamonds of Denmark in the first place?" asked Herbert.

"He said he never knew their mysterious employer's name and that only Roger Marinovich ever communicated with him."

"I guess we'll never know his identity as long as Roger Marinovich is in a coma," stated Philip matter-of-factly.

"Who called the police, Nic, when Roger Marinovich had captured you in front of the Chamberlains' yard?" Dante asked him.

"Captain Spencer did. When the Chamberlains left for the night, he remained behind and luckily saw what was going on from a window. After calling the police, he figured out what I was up to by leading the crooks to the shed and decided to wait before coming to help," explained Nic.

"That pretty much sums everything up, Herbert," Kevin added.

Not quite, thought Nic. He hadn't mentioned to anyone about what Roger Marinovich had implied about his dad. He still wasn't sure what Roger Marinovich had meant about his dad being troublesome to him and his employer and his quote, 'Like father, like son,' but it seemed to indicate he somehow had something to do with his dad's death. With Roger Marinovich in a coma, he might never know. Nic also wondered if Roger Marinovich had anything to do with the mysterious phone call to his mom.

"Nic?" called Cindy.

Nic shook his head from his thoughts and asked, "What did you say?"

"I asked you where you think the diamonds are hidden, if they really are hidden in the Chamberlains' backyard. After all, the police seem to think that Carl Hoffman may be leading them on a wild goose chase concerning the true location of the diamonds," said Cindy.

"I don't know, but that reminds me…I forgot to give Captain Spencer his picture back that he loaned us last fall," said Nic as he ran inside to find it.

"He emerged with the picture in hand. I'll be right back," he said as he headed toward the Chamberlains' house.

"We're coming, too," Kevin said, as everyone followed Nic.

Captain Spencer answered the door, as usual. "Good afternoon, young masters. To what do I owe the pleasure of your visit?"

"Nice to see you're okay, Captain Spencer," said Cindy.

"Thank you, Lady Cindy, for your interest in me. As I informed Master Nic earlier, I should be fully recovered within a week or two."

"I came by to return the picture you loaned us last fall," Nic said, holding it up.

"I had forgotten about that. I'm usually pretty good at remembering things," mused Captain Spencer.

As Nic looked at the picture one last time, Philip mentioned with frustration, "Too bad we'll never know where the Diamonds of Denmark are hidden."

"It would've been cool to find them and have seen what they look like," added Kevin.

"Some mysteries are never meant to be solved, young masters," stated Captain Spencer, as he held out his hand to take the picture from Nic.

Glancing one last time at the picture, the answer hit Nic.

"I know where the diamonds are hidden!"

Everyone's jaw dropped right before Kevin asked, "What? Are you sure?"

"I've never been more sure about anything in my life," replied Nic.

"Go on, tell us. Where are they?" Cindy quizzed.

"It was right in front of our noses all along. The diamonds are in the shed or, more precisely, buried under the shed," said Nic.

"You're crazy," said Dante.

"No, I'm not. Look at the picture. Michael Marinovich is looking at the newly poured concrete shed floor as he's being led away by the police. No one would think of looking there. By the time the concrete had set, everyone would assume it had been that way always," explained Nic with excitement.

After a few moments of passing the picture around, everyone began to get excited. Even Captain Spencer became convinced of the possibility and immediately informed the Chamberlains and the local authorities.

Needless to say, Mrs. Chamberlain was not happy with all kinds of people roaming her backyard and shed searching for the Diamonds of Denmark, but she had come around when it was mentioned how grateful the art and history world would be if they were found on her property.

Sure enough, just as Nic had guessed, the Diamonds of Denmark were buried within the concrete base of the old tool shed. Reporters from all over the world flocked to New Bonn to interview Nic and his friends about what had happened to them over the past year. They each received a letter of congratulations from the United States and Russian governments, as well as medals.

Even Mrs. Chamberlain gave them a compliment, sort of. She said that she would be glad to hire them again next fall to rake her leaves, if they wanted to. Nic had to smile at this, as he and the others knew it was probably the best they were going to get from her in the way of a compliment.

An ocean away, in a large, dimly lit room, a man sat staring at the embers of a dying fire. A younger man, wearing a well-tailored suit, entered the room, carrying a silver tray with a note on it. He bent down and obediently placed the silver tray on a table next to the man. The older man read the note quickly, crumpled it up, and tossed it into the coals where it briefly burst into flames.

His deep voice was filled with disgust. "This is most disappointing and unacceptable. Failure will not be tolerated. See to it the fat one is eliminated immediately. As for the other, let's wait and see. He might prove useful if he recovers," he commanded.

The younger man bowed and left the room without a sound. Turning his attention back to the fire, the man whispered menacingly, "Looks like I'm not finished with the Nelsons yet."

THE END?

Nic Nelson will return

About the Author

errik Richard was raised in Edwardsville, IL , a town just across the river from St. Louis, Missouri. After majoring in Biology at SIU-E, he went on to obtain a D.M.D. degree at SIU Dental School. When he's not volunteering time in his church's youth programs, he is participating in various sports, playing paintball and reading books about history.

Derrik states, "For the past 20 years I've contributed countless hours of volunteer work to young people and youth groups. Through these experiences, I observed a growing interest among kids for good, wholesome, adventure/mystery books about characters and environments familiar to themselves. I feel my novel, *Nic Nelson and The Diamonds of Denmark*, adequately meets this need. My book would be the first in a series of stories covering Nic Nelson's adventures from boyhood to early adolescence. Young readers would grow with Nic and see how he deals with the loss of his father and overcomes life's obstacles through the love of his mother, a neighborly father figure and the loyalty of his friends.

Readers will also be able to learn and share in some of Nic's favorite pastimes such as paintball. These stories are also intended to stimulate young readers' interest in history as each Nic Nelson adventure will have some aspect of history tied into the mystery. Another aspect of the book is how it reflects the diverse makeup of America with the main characters being White, African-American and Asian. Lastly, my book touches on a few of the issues of being a fatherless child. Unfortunately, this seems to be a growing problem but Nic Nelson could give other fatherless kids hope by being someone they could relate and look up to."

33821033R00143

Made in the USA
Lexington, KY
11 July 2014